Bell Harry

A CANTERBURY NOVEL

BELL HARRY

NICHOLAS BEST

LUME BOOKS

LUME BOOKS

First published in 2020 by Lume Books
30 Great Guildford Street,
Borough, SE1 0HS

ISBN 978-1-83901-241-9

Typeset using Atomik ePublisher from Easypress Technologies

www.lumebooks.co.uk

Contents

Chapter One: *The Luftwaffe's Canterbury Raid*...1

Chapter Two: *The Yank's Tale*..6

Chapter Three: *Thomas Becket and the French King's Ruby*......................27

Chapter Four: *The Scrivener of Magna Carta*..34

Chapter Five: *Bell Harry and the Black Prince*..41

Chapter Six: *Wat Tyler and the Beheaded Archbishop*................................47

Chapter Seven: *Geoffrey Chaucer and the Harlot of Mercery Lane*.............54

Chapter Eight: *Henry V Gives Thanks for Agincourt*................................62

Chapter Nine: *Edward IV and the Wars of the Roses*.................................69

Chapter Ten: *Henry VIII and the Boleyn Girl*..73

Chapter Eleven: *The Looting of Thomas Becket's Shrine*............................80

Chapter Twelve: *Christopher Marlowe and Queen Elizabeth's*

                              Birthday Party...88

Chapter Thirteen: *A Pilgrim Father Charters the Mayflower*......................96

Chapter Fourteen: *King Charles I Consummates his Marriage*..................101

Chapter Fifteen: *Roundheads Storm the Cathedral* 107

Chapter Sixteen: *The Restoration of Charles II*...113

Chapter Seventeen: *Wolfgang Mozart and the Infant Prodigy*.................120

Chapter Eighteen: *John Adams, Future U.S. President*...........................127

Chapter Nineteen: *Napoleon's Troops in the Precincts*............................133

Chapter Twenty: *Jane Austen and Lady Hamilton's*

                   Enormous Behind...139

Chapter Twenty-One: *Sir Thomas Picton Returns from Waterloo*............146

Chapter Twenty-Two: *George Stephenson's New Steam*

                   Engine on Wheels..152

Chapter Twenty-Three: *Charles Dickens and David Copperfield*...........158

Chapter Twenty-Four: *The Skeleton in the Crypt*...................................164

Chapter Twenty-Five: *The Unknown Warrior*...171

Chapter Twenty-Six: *The Yank's Tale Continued* 177

Chapter Twenty-Seven: *The Search for the King's Ruby*...........................184

Chapter Twenty-Eight: *The Bomb Disposal Squad*.................................189

To have seen the place where a great event happened is the next best thing to being present at the event in person. In this respect, few spots in England are more highly favoured than Canterbury.

Dean Stanley

Chapter One

The Luftwaffe's Canterbury Raid

Just before one a.m. on the first of June 1942, a German chandelier flare exploded over the old town of Canterbury. It hung motionless for a moment, filling the sky with a bright yellow light. Then it began to drift downwards, dropping silently towards the cathedral far below.

The flare lit up the tower of Bell Harry as it fell, and the sandbagged buildings around the cathedral, and the frightened faces of the people in the streets. It lit up twenty thousand people, all running for cover, desperate to find shelter before the bombs began to fall.

The flare was followed by another flare, and then another — sixteen in all. They fell in rapid succession all over the sky, lighting up the whole town, making it bright as day.

The flares were followed by the ominous drone of German aero engines, the familiar thump thump of Junkers 88 bombers on their approach run. The bombers' target was Canterbury cathedral. The tower of Bell Harry lay right in front of them, brilliantly outlined against the flares exploding all around.

There were seventy bombers on the raid. They had flown at wave height over the English Channel, crossing the coast north of Dungeness, picking up the railway line from Ashford to Canterbury and chasing it along in the moonlight until they came to the cathedral at the end.

Canterbury was not a military target. There were no factories in the town. It was the cathedral the bombers were after, the Mother Church of all England. They had orders to destroy it from Reichsmarschall Goering himself.

The bombers attacked in several waves, coming in so low over the rooftops that the black crosses on their wings were clearly visible as they unloaded their bombs.

Most of the bombs were incendiaries, thousands of them, designed to start

1

fires in hundreds of different places. But some were high explosive, capable of bringing Bell Harry crashing to the ground if they scored a direct hit.

Others were land mines, delayed action monsters that lay ticking for days where they fell, fraying the nerves of the sappers trying to defuse them, who never knew when they would blow.

The first bombs fell at eight minutes to one. They landed just south of the cathedral, in the medieval heart of the city. The tightly packed wooden houses along Burgate Street had been there since Shakespeare's time.

By one o'clock they were blazing from end to end, the roof timbers collapsing, the walls crashing outwards, filling the streets with smouldering heaps of rubble.

The Longmarket was burning too, and Butchery Lane, all the shops to Watling Street. The flames rose a hundred feet into the air — so high that the cathedral itself was obscured by a giant pall of smoke.

The explosions sucked debris up and flung it so far into the sky that papers and documents from Canterbury were found next day in villages seven or eight miles away, hurled there by the blast.

In the streets there was panic as the fires took hold. People ran everywhere with no idea of where they were going — easy targets for the Germans machine-gunning them from above. The Archbishop of Canterbury was doing his best to restore calm, striding among the wounded in a steel helmet and a coat over his pajamas. His wife was with him, both of them white with shock at what was happening.

Above them the bombs kept coming, but Bell Harry still stood. The cathedral had been showered with incendiaries, but the fire watchers on the roof were dealing with them, working frantically to seize the bombs by the tailfins and manhandle them over the parapet to burn out harmlessly on the grass below.

There was little else they could do, because there was no water for the fire hoses. The mains had been cut at the beginning of the raid. There were no fire engines either, because the streets to the cathedral were blocked with rubble. Nothing could get past.

Yet Bell Harry still stood — the tallest tower of the greatest cathedral in England. Thomas Becket had been murdered in Canterbury cathedral. King John had worshipped there. Henry V had given thanks on his knees for the victory at Agincourt.

Bell Harry still stood — but for how much longer no one knew, as the next wave of bombers arrived over the town and winged downwards to begin their assault on the ancient tower.

2

Bert Marden was a fire watcher at the cathedral. He wore overalls and a steel helmet and carried a gas mask slung over his shoulder. His job was to identify the incendiaries on the north side of the building and make sure they were extinguished before they could do any damage.

It was dangerous work, with all the explosive coming down. Marden was scared out of his mind.

'Bastards!' What kind of people were they, who machine-gunned civilians in the street? Marden had fought the Germans in the First World War. He had served with the Royal West Kents in France and Belgium. He had thought that was the end of it, when the Armistice came, but now here they all were again.

Marden was a greengrocer by trade. He had a wife and grown-up daughter and he was too old for any of this. He just wanted to be out of it, safe from the bombing. He didn't want to get killed at his time of life.

His post was at the Sellingegate, near the cathedral library. He could cover most of his side of the cathedral from there. There was supposed to be another fire watcher to help him, but the man hadn't shown up for duty.

Few of them had, when the bombing began. They had stayed home, or run for the shelters, or joined the rush for the open fields outside Canterbury. Anything to avoid the attack on the centre.

'Bastards!' Marden threw himself to the ground as more bombs fell, a rapid succession of deafening blasts that ripped into the earth and tore it violently apart.

Shrinking down, he counted the blasts one by one. High explosive usually fell in sticks of eight. If you heard eight bangs, you knew you were all right. There wouldn't be any more after that.

'Six, seven, eight...' Marden lay still after the last one, hugging the ground for another few seconds before cautiously picking himself up again. But there were no more bombs, after the eighth. He was going to live, this time.

Shaking the dust out of his eyes, he looked around to assess the damage. The cathedral library had gone, for a start. The whole building had vanished, as if it had never been there at all.

One wall was still intact, with pictures still hanging on it. The rest had fallen into a huge crater which had suddenly appeared. The walls had gone first, taking thousands of books with them.

The roof had followed, in a great shower of dust and rubble that swept everything before it. The whole cathedral library had been blown to pieces, by a single German bomb.

3

Next to the library, another crater had appeared, about twelve feet across. Marden walked unsteadily to the edge and shone his flashlamp into it.

He saw water at the bottom, flowing into an underground tunnel that led towards the cathedral. The tunnel was ten feet down, built of Kentish stone. It was the conduit for a subterranean spring, channelling the water under the foundations of the cathedral and out again the other side.

Another bomber began its dive. Instinctively, Marden leapt into the crater and ran for the tunnel. It was the safest place, with ten feet of earth over his head.

He ducked into the opening and took cover again as the bombs hit. They were further off this time, too far away to be a danger.

Marden slumped thankfully against the wall. His hands were shaking beyond control. He badly needed a cigarette to steady his nerves.

He shone his lamp down the tunnel. It led straight under the cathedral. In days gone by, the stream at his feet had supplied the monks of the monastery with fresh drinking water.

The monks had been gone for centuries, but the water still flowed, forgotten in its own private tunnel until the Luftwaffe blew a hole in the roof for everyone to see.

The water came up to Marden's knees. Playing his light along the tunnel, he saw a set of stone steps further along, leading out of the stream to a recess in the wall.

Wading towards it, he saw that the recess was a narrow alcove ten feet long by five wide, built into the foundations of the cathedral. The entrance had been bricked in at some point, because a few of the bricks were still in place. The rest had just collapsed, hit by shock waves from the bombing.

Marden shone his light into the alcove. He saw the dead men at once. There were three of them, slumped unnaturally across the stone floor.

For a moment, he assumed they had been killed by the bombing. But then he looked closer and saw that the men had been dead much longer than that.

Boots, spurs, broadswords. Lobster tail helmets. Buff riding coats made out of cowhide. They were soldiers of Cromwell's Parliamentary army. They had been dead for three hundred years.

The men were skeletons now, with a few wisps of hair still attached to their skulls. Two lay on their backs, the third on his side, with one arm flung outwards. A broken sword lay by his hand; beyond it an upturned copper casket with the contents scattered all around.

Marden caught a glimpse of gold and silver as he lifted his light to the wall at the far end of the alcove. There was a shrine on the wall, with a man praying on his knees in front of it. A man in the sovereign robes of a Tudor king. He was as large as life, human in every detail, but made entirely of silver gilt.

Above the king, there was a golden angel on the wall, and an enormous ruby as big as a plum. There were other jewels as well, and a human skull mounted between two candlesticks in a casing of solid silver.

The skull had a large piece missing from the top of the crown — gouged out, Marden guessed, by a blow from a Plantagenet sword almost 800 years ago. The skull of St Thomas Becket.

Marden turned to run. In two strides he was out of the passage and heading for the exit, splashing along the tunnel as fast as he could go. Another stick of bombs was coming down, but Marden didn't care. He just wanted out as quick as he could.

'One... two... three...' The bombs were right in front of him, coming his way. 'Four... five...' Marden felt the impact as they thudded into the ground ahead.

He heard the sixth as it landed almost on top of him, in a shower of flying debris, but he didn't ever see it. The blast twisted him round and sucked the eyeballs out of his head before he had a chance to turn away, leaving him blind for ever.

His last memory was of being hurled high into the air, then thrown down again under a vast pile of rubble. He remembered the shock of his fall, the weight of the masonry pressing down, the sudden darkness all around. He remembered the dust clogging his nostrils as he struggled to breathe — and that was all Bert Marden ever remembered of the Luftwaffe's little visit to Canterbury, on the first day of June, in the year of grace nineteen hundred and forty-two.

Chapter Two

The Yank's Tale

Hi. I'm dying. I only have a few weeks to live, so it's now or never if I'm going to say what I want to say. If I don't get it off my chest now, I never will, and that's a fact.

My name is Ezra Tyler. I'm from Colorado, Larimer County. I was born in 1923 and raised in the Depression. A farm boy. There were six of us altogether, two older brothers, two sisters, and one who died.

We were poor, like everyone else we knew. So poor we didn't eat, sometimes. That's how it was, back then. Nobody's fault. Just the way it was.

What I have to say is about World War II, and what I did in it. I don't know if anybody will be interested, but if I don't film myself now and get the story down on tape, no one will ever know what happened.

So I'm going to do it now, while I still have the chance, and hope somebody else can make some sense out of it some time. There must be someone out there who knows more about it than I do. Maybe what I say now will help them track it down and find the answer after I'm gone.

Here goes, anyhow.

I was eighteen when the war came, working on the farm. I remember it like it was only yesterday. Pearl Harbor on the radio, President Roosevelt, the whole bit. I couldn't believe it, what the Japs had done. Bombing the US Navy! What the hell did they think they were playing at?

We went into town soon as we heard the news, took the truck to Fort Collins and went to see what was happening. Everyone else was there too, all the folks we knew. They'd all come in, from all over. They were all fighting mad, just itching to drop everything and get back at the Japs. I never saw so many angry people in my life.

6

Of course we all enlisted, first chance we got. Soon as the doors opened we were in there, signing up for Uncle Sam. I guess we'd known a war was coming, with the fighting in Europe and all of that. It was time to do our bit.

It was exciting too — I won't pretend it wasn't. Better than working the farm. I was eighteen, as I say, only a kid. I'd never been anywhere or done anything, never in my whole life. The chance wouldn't come again. I grabbed it with both hands, joined the military as soon as I could. Nothing would have stopped me, if you want the honest truth.

I guess I owe the Army, one way and another. They gave us three meals a day, for a start. You didn't ever have to worry about your next bite to eat. It was always right there, as much as you wanted.

Medical care too, and dentists, all right there. They looked after us real good, I'll say that for them. Didn't cost us a nickel.

Boot camp was in North Carolina, Fort Bragg. It was the first time I'd ever been out of state. I thought I'd be going with my buddies from back home, seeing as how we'd all enlisted together, but it didn't work out like that. We all went every which way, got separated from the first.

Some joined the Rangers, some went in the Navy. And some we never saw again, after the war was over.

I joined the infantry like most everyone I knew. There were guys from all over at boot camp — Oklahoma, Kansas, New York, Seattle, you name it. Nebraska. There were Jews, Catholics, Lutherans, Episcopalians, all kinds of people thrown together who'd never seen each other before.

The only thing we had in common is we were all Americans, just waiting for a crack at the Japs. Sooner we got at the Japs, the happier we would be. That's how we felt, after what they'd done at Pearl Harbor.

But I can't say I enjoyed boot camp, and I doubt any of the others did either. It wasn't meant to be fun. It was meant to turn us into soldiers, and it did that, right enough. I didn't enjoy it though — not even with all the food, and money in my pocket. I just didn't like it, never met anybody who did.

Anyhow, I got through it okay and came out the other end — Private Ezra B. Tyler, United States Army. We all saluted the general at the big parade and threw our hats in the air and then went to join our outfits.

I was sent to the 1051st in Maryland. They were front line infantry, or so I was told, but actually none of us had ever been in a real fight before, not even the ones who were regular army — and there weren't many of those.

We were all just rookies who didn't know one end of a bazooka from the

7

other before we joined the military. Not like the Japanese, who'd been fighting in China for years.

That was the summer of 1942, but it wasn't until the fall of 1943 that we shipped out to join the war. So much fighting going on — Guam, Bataan, Guadalcanal — and we weren't even in it, for a whole year. And when we did finally ship out, it wasn't to the Pacific, like we were expecting. It was to England, to fight the Germans. We never got to fight the Japs at all.

Well, I don't mind saying, it was a shock to some of the boys, going to Europe. We'd enlisted to fight the Japanese, no one else. Way we saw it, the war in Europe was nothing to do with us, not our business in the least.

If the British and the Germans wanted to slug it out, then let them. It was nothing for us to get involved in.

Why should we, when the Germans done nothing to us? The British had run like rabbits at Dunkirk and now they were prepared to fight to the last American, is how we saw it. Why should any of us die for them?

But there wasn't a whole lot we could do about it, even if we'd wanted to. Not even the guys with German names who still had family over there. We just had to do what we were told in the army, and if that meant shipping out to Europe, then that's what it meant. You had to obey orders, in the military.

We shipped from Baltimore, first time most of us had seen the ocean. The ship was an old rust bucket, some kind of tramp steamer that had known better days. It had room for eighty passengers, but now it was carrying three hundred GIs, eight or nine to a cabin, all crammed in there like sardines.

That's what it felt like, sardines. We were in this old tin can, no room to turn around, just waiting for the Germans to take a shot at us as we came by. They had packs of U-boats on the ocean, sitting out in the middle just waiting for us.

That's all they had to do, wait till we came by. Must have been a real turkey shoot, from where they were sitting.

First day at sea we had lifeboat drill, everyone on deck in their life preservers, mustering at the lifeboats. The way the officers explained it, we were in enemy territory the minute we left harbor and we had to know what to do if we were torpedoed.

Actually there wasn't much we could do, because even if we did manage to get away in the lifeboats, nobody would stop to pick us up. Other ships couldn't afford to, in case they got hit too. They had orders to keep right on going, leave us to our fate. Like I said, a turkey shoot.

The rest of the time the deck was off limits and we had to stay down below, keeping out the way. I don't remember how long that crossing took — maybe nine or ten days, maybe more — but it seemed like forever. I hated every minute of it. I'm no sailor, and I never pretended to be. The ship pitched and rolled like you'd never believe, never stopped moving for a moment.

I was sick as a mule from day one right up until we reached Liverpool — never stopped puking even when I didn't have anything left to puke. The other guys were the same.

We all just lay in our bunks, barfing into our helmets and waiting for a torpedo to come through the wall and put us out of our misery. It wasn't a happy time.

Anyhow, we reached Liverpool in the end, got there all in one piece. The Germans must have missed us, or maybe the Navy kept them busy. Whatever the reason, we made it to the other side, came in safe and sound with no U-boats bothering us and saw land out the porthole, the first we'd seen since leaving home.

Liverpool was a big town, but it didn't look like much, from the porthole. Half of it was in ruins, far as we could tell. There were buildings everywhere just lying in heaps, rubble every which way.

We learned later they'd been bombed eight nights in a row. The German air force kept coming back night after night, hitting them again and again, trying to put the docks out of business, knock the whole town down once and for all. That's how the Germans operated, knocking everything down.

There was a band on the dockside when we arrived, playing Sousa marches and *Over There*, all those kinds of tunes. We were glad to get ashore after being cooped up so long. But it was a shock too, because we'd never seen anything like Liverpool before.

The people all looked deadbeat, for one thing. Their clothes were patched and most of them were pale and hungry. Food was rationed in England, they couldn't just eat what they wanted. They had to have a ration book, and even then they only got powdered egg and a hunk of bacon every other week.

We'd only been there a few days when we heard our first air raid siren. We were out of Liverpool by then, in a place called Catterick in Yorkshire. We were in our bunks, about midnight, when the siren began to sound, which meant German bombers were coming over.

It took us a while to figure out what the noise meant, and then we panicked, every one of us. We thought the bombers were coming for us, personally, like they even knew we were there. Why else would the siren sound, if they weren't coming for us?

Turned out though the bombers were just passing through, on their way somewhere else. It was routine for the sirens to sound, but we didn't know that at the time. We thought our last moment had come, which just shows how much we had to learn.

The British were very polite about it, but you could tell they didn't think much to us, shitting our pants the first time we heard the siren go. We wised up real quick, didn't let it happen again.

I had two friends by then, buddies from my platoon. One was Billy Williams, an orange picker from California. He was a farm boy like me, and we both came from big families. We'd been together since boot camp.

The other was Dutch Branigan, from Illinois. He was a city boy, older than us, and he'd been around. I don't know what he did back home, because he never said, but I guess maybe it wasn't legal.

Dutch was a hard-looking guy, the kind who either makes sergeant or winds up in the stockade. He knew about girls too, which neither of us did, so we both looked up to him, a man who knew the score.

He was good in a fight as well. I saw him in a pub once, when some British soldiers came over and asked when the Yanks were going to do any fighting. Dutch showed them, right there. And when the snowdrops came and broke it up, Dutch was nowhere to be found.

He was out the back and over the wall, too smart to stay there with the others and get caught. That's the kind of guy he was.

We all lived in a tent together in Catterick, and later in a Nissen hut, which was a kind of tin shack that you could build in a hurry. The British were putting them up in thousands, with so many troops coming through.

The huts had a stove in the middle, which was okay for anyone who could get near it. Everyone else froze to death.

We stayed there right through the winter of 1943 and the early months of 1944. We knew it couldn't last much longer than that, because there was bound to be a second front in 1944. We'd be invading Europe soon enough to fight the Nazis and take pressure off of the Russians.

The word was we'd go into combat in the spring maybe, or the summer at the latest. It's what we were there for.

Sure enough, in the spring of 1944, we got the order to move out, pack up the camp and go. We didn't know where, just 'someplace in England'. We went by truck some of the way, then by train, sitting up all night in one of those strange little trains they have in England.

We still didn't know where we were, because they'd taken all the station signs down, and the road signs as well, to confuse the enemy. We only knew it was south, a long way south from Yorkshire. And a lot nearer France.

Next day, we were put in trucks again and driven across country for a couple of hours. It was different country to Yorkshire, different kinds of houses and villages, very pretty in the spring sunshine. This was early March, when things were starting to look good again after the wintertime.

We knew where we were as well, because a British kid had told us when we threw him some gum. We were in Kent, near the English Channel.

Well, I was interested in that, because Kent is where my folks came from, way back. We got a family Bible that says so. A place called Maidstone some-place, I don't know where. It's where the Tylers were from, before we came to Colorado.

You can check it out on a website nowadays, if you know how those things work. The Mormons got it all written down, where every American family comes from. The Tylers were from Maidstone, Kent.

But it wasn't Maidstone we were going, or anyplace near. We couldn't see much from the back of the truck, but we weren't in country anymore, we were coming to some kind of town. The trucks were slowing down, the whole convoy bunching up through the streets.

It wasn't long before we turned in through a pair of gates and found ourselves in an army camp, a real one, with real buildings, not just a bunch of tents and Nissen huts. It belonged to the British army, but now it was ours. It was where we were going to stay, until we moved over to France.

We were glad to get out of the trucks, after the long ride. Billy and me found our beds first, bunking together and keeping one for Dutch, like we always did.

We found out where we were too, because our officer told us. We were in Canterbury, a little old town in the middle of Kent that had been there since Roman times. It's where Christians got started, in England.

They kept us busy for the first couple of days, cleaning the camp up and getting it properly fixed. It took a while to make it look like the US Army lived there. It wasn't until the third day that we were given time out to go into Canterbury.

We were issued a pass until midnight and told the liberty truck would leave from Canterbury bus station at eleven to bring us back to camp. We could walk if we missed it, because it wasn't far. About a mile, at most.

So we went in to Canterbury that afternoon, soon as we were done for the day — hitched a ride in a jeep and went to see what a town looked like, that had been there since Roman times. A lot like Liverpool, is the answer,

11

because the Germans had bombed Canterbury too, bombed a lot of it flat. Most of downtown was flatter than a pancake, with rubble piled up and weeds growing all around.

There'd been a Woolworth's there once, the same Woolworth's as back home, right on the main street. But there wasn't a Woolworth's now. There wasn't anything at all, except an open space for hundreds of yards and old bits of junk scattered all around that had belonged to someone once. They had little wooden signs up in front of every shop, saying what used to be there.

The rest of the town didn't look so bad, the bits the Germans missed. It was real old, like a Hollywood movie. Some of the streets were so narrow the houses were almost touching overhead.

It was pretty too, the bits that were still there. There was a cathedral in the middle, the only tall building in the place. It had a big central tower and two little twin towers at one end. Up above, way above the central tower, they'd fixed a barrage balloon on a steel wire. It was there for the Germans to run into, if they ever came over again.

We went to look at the cathedral, in through a little door with sandbags all around. It was quite a place, the biggest old building I ever seen.

They'd taken all the windows out, so they wouldn't get broken in the bombing, and done a lot of other stuff as well. I guess they knew what they were doing, because the old cathedral was still standing, while everything else had fallen down. The British have experience of that kind of thing.

It was getting dark by the time we'd finished looking at the cathedral, so we found a pub that was still standing and went in for a drink. It was a nice old place down by the river that had missed the bombing.

There were other guys from the 1051st in there before us, hanging around the dartboard. There were a few British as well, old men mostly, so we bought them a drink and made sure they didn't feel left out.

We were under orders to make sure the British weren't left out. They didn't like Yanks, most of them, and there was trouble sometimes. Our orders were to not rile them if we could avoid it — keep out of trouble and see nobody got upset.

We'd only been in Canterbury a week when we had a dance at the camp, all the British girls from the neighborhood and anyone else who wanted to come. A couple of hundred did, all tripping along the road to the camp in their best dresses.

They didn't have any stockings, so they browned up their legs with gravy and let that do instead. They didn't have much soap either, which meant they stank a

12

bit, some of them. Not their fault, when they couldn't get anything in the shops.

We were all in our best uniforms too, nice and smart for the girls. Billy and me were nervous, because we weren't much good with dames.

The Yanks were all supposed to be sex maniacs, according to the British, but actually we were just a couple of nice boys who didn't know much about women. We didn't keep nylons in our pockets and trade them for sex, like some guys are supposed to have done. We wouldn't have known how.

Actually, I liked British girls. They weren't so grabby as Americans and they had softer faces, something to do with the climate. They paid their share on a date, always insisted on paying half, even if they were short of money. That's what I was told, anyway.

It was a good dance. The girls were as shy as we were, but they warmed up quick enough. There weren't any men for them around Canterbury, because the British boys were all away at the war.

The girls had gotten tired of waiting, some of them. The war'd been going on a long time and they never knew whether they might be killed or not. So they lived for the moment and worried about the rest later.

Some of the older British men didn't like it, seeing them go with GIs. One old Brit used to pour glue in their hair, to show what he thought. Must have been crazy in the head, if you want to know what I think.

We didn't get laid at the dance, like some of the guys claimed they done, but we did meet a girl who invited us back to her house, next time we had a pass.

She was called Ivy, and she lived near the cathedral in a little row house that hadn't been bombed. She gave us her address and said we'd be welcome to come by, if we wanted. We could have tea with her parents.

We did, a few days later. Dutch, Billy and me, we went round to Ivy's house one afternoon and had tea, British-style. We brought some chocolate with us, and cans of fruit, so we didn't arrive empty-handed. The British appreciated that kind of thing, when food was so hard to come by.

Her mom was real pleased with us, fussing round and making sure we were comfortable. She was glad to have us in the house.

But it was her dad we noticed most, Ivy's old man. The house was a store as well, a greengrocer's store that sold vegetables and stuff. The front part of it was the store, looking onto the street, and then you went through to the back, where the family lived.

Ivy's dad stayed in the front, running the store. He was a little old man of about fifty, completely blind in both eyes. Couldn't see a thing. He didn't even have any eyes, just a pair of empty sockets, where they'd been once. He looked like a skull.

Ivy told us he'd been hit in the bombing. The blast tore his eyes out before he knew what was happening, sucked them right out of his head. They dug him out of the rubble a few hours later, but it was too late for his eyes, even though the rest of him was okay. That was that. Nothing anyone could do.

Well, that just about brought it home to us, what the war was all about. Guy loses his eyes for no reason. What did he ever do to the Germans, that they did that to him?

But he didn't let it bother him, I'll say that much for him. He was a gutsy old guy, Ivy's dad. Me, I'd have never stopped hollering about it, but old Bert Marden just got on with his life, did the best he could and never complained.

He still ran the store every day, handling the merchandise and weighing it up on a pair of scales, with brass weights. You never would have guessed he was blind, if you didn't know.

He did everything by touch, that old man, didn't miss a trick. He just carried on as normal, because anything less would have meant the Germans had won.

He never got cheated either, because nobody would have dared. I can see him now, handling those weights, running his fingers over everything to feel what it was. He was scary in a way, that old guy with no eyes. I've never been able to forget him.

Before long we were stopping by two or three times a week, whenever we could get a pass. We liked it at Ivy's because it was a real home, not an army camp. We'd been in the military more than two years by then, sleeping in bunks all the time, nothing but soldiers all around.

It was good to get away from that for a while, spend time in this little old English house, pretending there wasn't a war on for a few hours. I was homesick by then and so were the others. We all just wanted the war to be over, so we could go back home and get on with our lives.

We got to know Bert Marden real well, sitting on an upturned crate in the back of the store, helping him out with sacks of carrots and potatoes. He'd had a bad time in the bombing, even though he didn't complain about it. He came out with things sometimes, showed his mind was still dwelling on what had happened. He couldn't let it go.

He seemed half-crazy, some of the things he said. Kept babbling on about a tunnel, and a river under the cathedral. He said there were skeletons in there,

14

and a skull belonged to a guy named Becket. There was a silver king and jewels on the floor, and golden treasure in a casket, like in a movie.

It had all been there for hundreds of years, according to Ivy's dad, all just lying there, buried under the cathedral.

We didn't believe him at first. Like everyone else, we just thought he was some mad old guy who'd lost his mind. Easy to do, after what he'd been through. There were plenty of people like him in England, after four and a half years of the Germans dropping bombs on them.

But then we got to thinking. He didn't seem mad, Ivy's dad. Anything else you talked about, he was sane as anybody. He wasn't a nut. He didn't have eyes, but that didn't make him a nut. He was as sane as the rest of us.

So we wondered if what he had to say was true. That maybe there was buried treasure there, right under the cathedral. Maybe he was right all along.

'Let's go see,' said Dutch.

We strolled round there one afternoon, looking like tourists in the sunshine. The whole of that side of the cathedral was a bombsite, craters everywhere and rubble every which way. There wasn't any opening into a tunnel, like old Bert had said, but then maybe it had all got rearranged with more bombs coming down.

It was easy to see where a tunnel would be, if one was there. The crater nearest the cathedral was full of rubble. Half an hour of digging and we'd know if Bert Marden was telling the truth or not.

Back in camp, we figured out how to do it. We'd have to go at night, when no one could see us. Take a flashlamp and a couple of spades, dig down and see what we found. We'd be AWOL, but what the hell? We'd be back in camp by dawn. No one would even know we'd been off base.

'Let's do it,' said Dutch.

'What if we're caught?' asked Billy.

'We won't get caught. Nobody will see us. And we ain't committing no crime. Digging on a bombsite ain't a crime.'

Billy wasn't sure about that. Neither was I. It might not be a crime, but it didn't seem quite legal either. Digging in the cathedral, in the middle of the night.

'No one will see us,' said Dutch. 'There's no one there in the middle of the night. The place is a graveyard.'

It was full of bodies, sure enough. Old man Marden had told us there was death in the tunnel. Three dead soldiers and the skull of this Becket guy.

'Let's do it,' said Dutch.

Billy didn't want to know. Me neither. It had been a joke at first, but now it was something else. We couldn't quite believe what we were hearing.

But Dutch insisted. 'I'll get the flashlamp and the spades,' he told us. 'We'll go tomorrow night. We'll be in and out before anyone even knows we were there. Leave it all to me.'

The next day passed slowly, like the evening would never come. We were off duty at five, but it wasn't until after midnight that we slipped out of bed and followed Dutch to the back wall of the camp, where GIs used to meet their girls for R&R against the brickwork. Dutch was first over, then Billy dropping the spades to him in a couple of backpacks, then me in rear.

It was dark as we hit the ground. There were no lights, because of the blackout. No people either. But the moon was out and we could see the cathedral, with the barrage balloon hanging over it to keep the Germans away.

Dutch handed out the spades. We started out in single file, him leading the way. Twenty minutes later, we reached the cathedral and snuck in through the ruins to begin digging for buried treasure.

It took much longer than we thought, but we found it in the end. There was an old tunnel in front of us, stretching out toward the cathedral, just as Marden had said.

'You keep watch,' Dutch told Billy. 'Ezra and me will go down there and see what we can find.'

We took our flashlamps and dropped down into the tunnel. We splashed along until we came to the skeletons at the end. There they were, just like Marden told us, the bodies, the ruby, the skull, the gold and silver all over the floor. Everything he had told us was true.

'We're rich!' Dutch couldn't believe his eyes as he flashed his lamp over the jewels. 'Rich, Ezra. Yes we are. We're gonna be rich men for the rest of our lives.'

We took our backpacks off and filled them at once, cramming in all the gold and jewels we could see. We didn't bother with the skull or any of the big stuff that we couldn't carry. We just scooped up the ruby and anything else that would fit in the packs. We were so excited we hardly knew what we were doing as we crammed our pockets as well. Then we turned back down the tunnel and lit out of there as fast as we could go.

It was getting on for dawn by the time we got back to camp. Dutch was first up the wall, then me, then the two of us leaning down and giving Billy a hand. We made it back in and headed for our bunks before anyone noticed we'd been gone.

16

Dutch took all the gold and jewels. He shoved them into his locker and kept the key around his neck. We stripped off and got into our bunks. We were all tucked up just in time for the sergeant to find us when he came in a while later to turn the lights on and get the squad up for the day. We'd never even been asleep.

It bothered me for the rest of the day, the thought of all that loot burning a hole in Dutch's locker. What if anybody found it? What if somebody came in during the day and held a snap inspection?

There'd be nothing Dutch could say, if they found him with a bunch of jewels and a big red ruby in his possession. He'd be for the stockade, five years at least, and maybe the rest of us as well.

We got together that afternoon to discuss what to do. We had to get the jewels out of Dutch's locker, that was for sure, but then what?

Billy and me were for giving them back, handing them over to the cathedral or maybe just dumping them someplace for someone else to find. We'd never expected to find anything when we dug into the tunnel. We'd just done it for the hell of it.

We wanted to give the jewels back and forget we'd ever seen them. But Dutch wouldn't hear of it.

'Who we going to give them back to? The British don't even know they're lost. We give them back, the British will say "thanks, boys" and that'll be that, nothing in it for us. And whose are they, anyway? Who do they belong to? Who says they belong to the British?'

'They don't belong to us, Dutch.'

'They do now. Possession is nine tenths of the law. We found 'em, we keep 'em.'

Billy wasn't so sure, and neither was I. Jewels would be hard to explain, if the lieutenant spotted them in our kitbags. We couldn't just say we found them someplace and couldn't remember where.

'We give them back, the British will want to know where we got them,' Dutch pointed out. 'You want to tell them we broke into the cathedral in the middle of the night? AWOL from camp. You want to tell them that?'

No, we didn't.

'The British won't miss what they never knew they had. They don't have legal title. They can't say the jewels are theirs, any more than we can. The jewels belong to whoever found them.'

Billy and me still weren't sure about that. But we didn't have any other ideas either. It was all too difficult for us. More than we could handle.

'So what are we going to do, Dutch?'

'We hide them.' Dutch didn't want the jewels in his locker either. 'We bury them someplace and come back for them later. After the war, maybe.'

'After the war?'

'You got any better ideas? You got something else you want to do?'

Neither of us did. Burying them seemed as good an idea as any. Once the jewels were out of Dutch's locker we'd all of us breathe a lot easier. That's all we wanted, to get rid of the jewels so no one could tie them to us. The sooner the better.

There was a training ground back of the camp, a wilderness area that belonged to the British army. It was where we did our maneuvers, digging foxholes and practising our attacks, honing our battle skills for the invasion of Europe.

We knew it well because we'd spent a lot of time there, sleeping out sometimes and learning to fight in the dark. It was a good place to dig a hole and hide something you didn't want found. There was nowhere better that we could think of.

We went out there right away. Dutch took the jewels out of his locker and we got a look at them again, the first time we'd seen them in daylight.

They were quite something, I can tell you. They were... I don't know, I never saw anything like it in my life. There were diamonds there, and emeralds, and that big red ruby. All stuff given to this Becket guy, I suppose. I don't know.

Anyhow, Dutch took it all out of the locker and wrapped it up tight in a waterproof cape. He put the cape into an old ammunition box and then we marched out of camp with it, looking like we were on fatigue duty.

We took a pair of spades with us, and an army compass, and headed up into the training ground. We kept going until we were out of sight of the camp, about three or four hundred yards away. Then we put the box down and looked around for somewhere to bury it.

There was a little hollow in the bushes, a place easy to remember. We took a good look around, making sure the location was imprinted on our minds. Then we got busy with the spades, digging deep down until we had a hole in the ground almost big enough for a man to stand in.

Dutch and Billy dropped the ammo box in the bottom and began to cover it up again. We filled the hole in and stamped the earth down all around.

We stood back when we'd finished while Dutch opened up the compass and hooked his thumb through the holding ring.

'We'll take bearings,' he told us. 'That way we'll always know exactly where to come back to, even if we don't recognise it on the ground.'

We'd been taught how by the army. You lined up the compass on some distant object and made a note of the bearing. You did this on three different objects in different directions and then you could figure out where you were. I think it's called triangulation, or some such.

The first marker was the cathedral tower. We were on high ground and the cathedral was in the valley below, but Bell Harry tower was still higher than us.

Dutch took a bead on it with one eye closed and called out the numbers, while Billy wrote them down. Dutch made sure to check what he'd written after he'd finished, because Billy didn't write too good, even for an orange picker.

The second marker was an old windmill on the skyline, east of the cathedral. The third was in back of us to the northwest. Tyler Hill. I've never forgotten that name, for as long as I've lived. Tyler Hill. Same name as mine.

Dutch took the bearings on all three and Billy wrote them down, one by one. Then Dutch copied them out so we each had a set of our own, in case we got separated in the future.

Dutch went even further, himself. He got the numbers tattooed on the back of his hand a few days later, where they could never get lost. The way he figured it, a bit of paper could easily disappear, but a tattoo on his hand was there forever. He'd always know where to look, if he couldn't remember what the bearings were.

It was the end of May by then. We didn't know it, but we didn't have much time left in Canterbury. The invasion came on June 6, the Allies storming ashore in Normandy, of all places.

We'd expected Calais, because that was the shortest way across the Channel, so it took us all by surprise when we woke up that morning and heard the news. Normandy! Wasn't a guy in our whole outfit who even knew where Normandy was.

Of course, we forgot all about buried treasure as soon as we knew what was happening. The invasion was the only game in town. We couldn't think of nothing else. There wasn't nothing else to think about.

We got orders to move at once, the orders we'd been expecting so long. We packed our equipment and loaded it onto the trucks, everything we were going to need in France.

There wasn't time to say goodbye to Ivy, or Bert Marden, so we left a note for her on the camp gate, telling her we were going and it had been nice knowing her. Then we climbed aboard the truck and headed out the camp, on our way to join the invasion in France.

Or so we thought. In fact, it was several weeks before we got anywhere near

19

France. We went to Dover that day, and to someplace else the next. Kept moving from one place to another, driving in convoy all across Kent.

We were here, there and everywhere, marching, counter-marching, stopping for a while, then hitting the road again until we thought it would never end.

We got real mad about it, moving all around while the real action was happening the other side of the Channel. We couldn't figure it out at all. We thought the war was going to be over before we got a chance to see any combat.

In fact there was a reason for what was going on. We were part of a deception plan, which we didn't know at the time. The Germans thought Normandy was just a trick and the real invasion was going to come at Calais. It's what you'd have expected to happen.

Our job was to keep them thinking that way, marching up and down and keeping real visible so their spies would report a lot of troop movements in Kent.

The longer the Germans thought the real attack was coming at Calais, the longer they'd keep their troops there, instead of sending reinforcements to Normandy. And the quicker we'd win, in the end. It was smart of us, when you think about it.

Anyhow, we got to France soon enough — the fourth of July, as it happened. Two days later, we were in combat for the first time, on the road to St Lo.

There was a farmhouse outside a village, full of Germans. We were sent forward to clear it, first time any of us had ever even seen a German, let alone tried to kill one.

We done fire and movement, like we'd been taught, one squad advancing while another stayed put and gave them covering fire. It didn't work like it had in training. The Germans hadn't read the script. They had a machine gun someplace, we couldn't see where.

Every time we tried to move, it opened up and sent us running for cover again. There wasn't a darn thing we could do about it, because we didn't even know where it was.

We called up mortar fire in the end, bombing the farmhouse to pieces until the Germans were forced to withdraw. They took the machine gun with them, which was okay with us. We'd had enough of war by then, every one of us. We'd seen as much combat as we ever wanted to. Three of the boys in our squad had been killed in the attack. One of them was Billy.

I didn't find out about it until afterwards. I was too worried about my own skin to think about anyone else. It wasn't until after we'd cleared the farmhouse and were taking muster by the barn that we noticed Billy was gone.

No one had seen him die. We went back across the field and there he was, lying face down in the brush. He'd taken a bullet between the shoulder blades and the shot had come out all over his chest.

It was an awful sight. I went down on my knees when I saw him and cried like a baby. I still do, sometimes. Can't get it out of my mind.

But there was no time to worry about Billy. We were in combat again next day, and a couple of days after that as well. We were all too busy staying alive to worry about the dead. There were too many other things to think about, far more important than Billy.

It was a week before I killed me my first German. We were in bocage country, lots of little fields with hedgerows and sunken roads, all crawling with Germans. We were moving up toward a crossroad, with orders to recon the position and check it out for the enemy.

They were there, sure enough — the other side of the hedgerow. I know, because I looked through a gap in the hedge and came face to face with one, about three feet away.

He was just a kid under the helmet, younger than me. A little blond kid, couldn't have been more than sixteen or seventeen. He should have been in school at his age, not staring bug-eyed at me through a hole in the hedge.

We brought our guns up together, but I fired first. Took him out with a head shot, right through the lip. I couldn't have missed, at that range.

I killed other Germans too, after that. So many in the next few weeks that I lost track after a while. They were just shapes in the distance, most of them. The first is the only one I remember, because he had a face. The rest were just shapes, like targets on the range.

I nearly got killed myself, plenty of times. The worst was near Soissons, on the way to Belgium. We were in another fire fight when I made a stupid move and ran right into Dutch's line of fire, darn near got killed by somebody from my own side.

A couple of bullets whistled past me before I knew what was happening, closer than anything the Germans had ever managed. It happens a lot in war, casualties from friendly fire. Something you can't avoid.

Dutch himself got hit about a month later, on the road to Aachen. The Germans were counter-attacking with Panzer tanks, trying to close the gap in the line. I can tell you now, there's nothing worse than watching Panzers coming straight at you, nothing between you and them and no way of stopping them coming.

We had an anti-tank gun, but there were too many of them for that. The tanks just kept on coming, their turrets swivelling from side to side as they searched for targets.

We did stop them in the end, but not before Dutch took a shell splinter in the leg, right through the fleshy part of the thigh. It was the end of the war for him. Nearly the end of his life as well.

The wound wasn't as bad as it looked, but we didn't know that at first. It looked real bad, is all I can say. Blood everywhere, and Dutch screaming with pain because we'd run out of morphine and had nothing to give him.

He looked like he was going to die and there wasn't nothing any of us could do except stand there and watch him.

We got him back to the dressing station soon as we had a chance. I helped with the stretcher, although it wasn't my job. Dutch was still screaming, clinging to my arm and begging me not to leave him.

'Stay with me, Ezra,' he begged. 'For Christ's sake stay with me, make sure I'm okay. Don't let them dump me. They'll just dump me if you don't stay with me. You stick with me, Ezra, make sure I'm okay.'

'I will, Dutch, of course I will.' I squeezed his hand. 'It's all right, old buddy. I'm with you. It'll be okay.'

I did stay with him, making sure he got seen by the surgeon. They cut the pants off of his leg and assessed the damage, decided he was going to live. The nurse gave him morphine to calm him down and told me they'd fix him up real good, no chance of gangrene setting in.

He might have died if we hadn't gotten him back to the dressing station. But he was safe now, they'd make sure of that. He was going to be okay.

So I left him there and went back to the war. It was the last I saw of Dutch for a while, because he never came back to the 1051st. He was sent to England and hospitalized in Portsmouth. By the time his wound had healed, the war was over, so he never had to rejoin his outfit.

It was September 1945 before I got back to England myself. I was on my way home by then, one of the first to get my discharge from the army. I'd been in the war right from the start, so I had more points on my card than most. First in, first out was the deal, when it came to GIs going home. Seemed fair enough to me.

I had a week in England before the ship sailed, so I went down to Canterbury first to see Ivy Marden and find out how she was. I guessed she'd want to know about Billy and Dutch, and I ought to be the one to tell her what happened to them. Better that than her finding out from someone else.

Ivy was in bad shape when I saw her. Her fiancé was in the British army, and he'd been killed in Burma. He'd been dead for years, but she'd only just found out with the Japanese surrender.

All those years of waiting, hoping she'd get a letter, hoping he might be a prisoner, and he'd been dead all along. Ivy'd taken it real bad. She didn't have any grief left over for Billy.

I said goodbye after a while and took a walk, heading out toward our old camp outside town. It was a sunny day as I went, just a few clouds drifting along in a lovely blue sky. The town was lying there all quiet and peaceful, hard to believe the war was really over at last.

They'd pulled the barrage balloon down, over the cathedral, but there was still plenty of bomb damage around. It took them years to clear it all away and rebuild everything like it was before.

I walked past our old camp and up into the training area, aiming for where we'd buried the ammo box. I didn't need any bearings to tell me where it was. I found the place straight away.

You couldn't miss it when I got there. A great big hole in the ground. Nothing at the bottom where the jewels used to be.

I couldn't believe it at first. Dutch must have been there. He'd dug up the box. It must have been him. No one else knew where to look.

Dutch had taken the treasure. Taken it and cut me out. He wasn't going to share it with me. He'd taken it all for himself, every last penny of it.

I couldn't understand it, at first. Dutch wouldn't do this, I kept telling myself. Not Dutch. We were buddies. I saved his life.

But then I got to thinking. About Billy, and how he died. A bullet in the middle of the back. How come Billy got shot in the back when he was facing toward the enemy, where the fire was coming from? How come no one saw him die?

And me, outside of Soissons. I didn't run into Dutch's line of fire. It was me he was trying to kill. I just didn't keep still long enough for him to succeed.

I felt like I'd been jackknifed in the stomach. Dutch had done this. Dutch! After all we'd been through together.

I didn't want to believe it, even with the evidence of my own eyes. Even looking at the hole in the ground and knowing Dutch had been there and taken everything and never said nothing about it, I still didn't want to believe it. I just didn't want to.

But he'd done it. There was no getting away from it. Dutch had killed Billy, and tried to kill me, just so he could keep everything for himself. That's what he'd done.

I was mad as hell about it, is all I can say. So mad I couldn't speak. So mad I'd have killed Dutch right there if I'd only known where to find him.

I was still mad when I got back to the States. All the way across the ocean I lay sprawled in my bunk, figuring out what to do about it when I got home.

We came in to New York, all the GIs cheering the Statue of Liberty and letting off condoms blown up like balloons, but I didn't take part in any of that. All I could think of was Dutch, and what I was going to do to him when I caught up with him.

I didn't even know where he was, or how I would find him. I just knew that I would, somehow, and when I did, the lousy sonofabitch was going to regret the day his mother ever gave birth to him.

I'm coming to the end of my story now, just a little bit more to tell. It's the bit I don't want to talk about, but I got to do it. I have to get it off of my conscience before I die. I need a clean slate if I'm going to meet my Maker in a few weeks' time.

I did catch up with Dutch, much sooner than I expected. He was still in the 1051st when I got back to the States. He was waiting for his discharge, same as me.

I was sent to the depot in Maryland, soon as the ship docked. Dutch was one of the first people I saw when I arrived. There he was, large as life. The guy who had killed Billy Williams and then taken the gold and jewels all for himself.

He saw me the same time I saw him. His face fell at once, but he quickly recovered. He came straight over, all smiles as he held out his hand.

'Ezra! How are you, buddy? It's good to see you.'

'Don't give me that, Dutch. I went back to Canterbury.'

'Yeah?'

'The treasure was gone. You dug it up. You took it all for yourself.'

'No, I didn't.' Dutch was all innocence. 'I don't know what you're talking about.'

'Yes, you do. You killed Billy and you tried to kill me. You wanted everything for yourself.'

'No, I didn't. You've got me wrong, Ezra.'

Dutch kept denying it for a while, but we both knew he was lying. He'd done it, all right. He'd thought he would never see me again. And now here I was, standing right in front of him.

'I didn't kill Billy,' he claimed, after a bit. 'Honest to God, Ezra, I never did. But I did dig up the treasure. You're right about that.'

'Where is it now?'

'I buried it again, somewhere close by. It's still there, old buddy, not far from where it was before. We can go back and get it when everything has settled down.'

'You think I'm going to believe that?'

'It's there, all right. I didn't want to bring it back to the States right away in case I got caught. A lot of guys have been caught, looting stuff in Europe. I just left it where it was until the heat's off.'

'You're going to go back for it?'

'You can come with me, Ezra. We'll go together.'

Yeah, right. I'd have killed Dutch there and then if I could have gotten away with it. I wouldn't have killed him for the money, though. It was never about the money. I never thought the treasure belonged to us anyway.

It was about what Dutch did to Billy. All those years of life Billy missed, because Dutch shot him for a bunch of jewels. What kind of a guy was Dutch, that he could do something like that? I've never figured it out, for as long as I've lived.

All I know for sure is they never done us any good, those jewels. Not Billy, with a bullet in his back. Not Dutch, after I'd finished with him. And not me, either. All I ever got out of it was a bad conscience by the time it was over. I just wish we'd never found them, is what I wish.

I don't want to talk about what happened next. Not about the details, anyway. I'll just say what I have to and leave it at that.

I caught Dutch alone a few days later, in the dark, when no one else was around. I was planning to beat the hell out of him, but I got carried away. I ended up stamping on his head so hard that I killed him by mistake. Then I dumped his body by the roadside for someone else to find.

I got away with it too. There were cops all over the place next day, but they never came looking for me. Why would they, when there was nothing to link me to the crime? They never found out who killed Dutch or why. I guess he's still on a list of unsolved murders in Maryland.

Time was, I would never have dreamed of killing anyone like that. I'm not that kind of guy. But the war changed everything for me. Killing didn't seem so hard, after I shot that German kid in France. Quite easy to do, in fact.

Anyhow, that's all I want to say. About Dutch Branigan, and the big ruby, and the rest of the stuff we found down that tunnel. I guess it's still there, most of it; the silver statue and the skeletons and Becket's skull with a hole in the top where somebody took a chunk out of his brains. The jewels are in a field somewhere, buried outside of Canterbury.

Everything's still there, one place or another, unless anyone knows any different. I'm the only person alive who's seen any of it, and I'll be gone soon. Then all that'll be left is this tape.

So that's what I'm doing here, putting it on record for somebody else to figure out. I'm not going to show this tape to my family. I don't want my grandkids to know what I did in Europe. I don't know what I'm going to do with it instead. I guess probably I'll send it to some experts somewhere, England maybe, people who know what the treasure was all about. Must be someone, somewhere who knows what it was about.

Not me, though. I'm done now. Time for my medication. I'll turn the tape off now and then I'm going to the bathroom.

Chapter Three

Thomas Becket and the French King's Ruby

Ezra Tyler was right about a big ruby in the cathedral. A jewel answering that description had been kept on public display in Canterbury cathedral for many hundreds of years. It had had pride of place at the tomb of Thomas Becket before vanishing mysteriously in Tudor times. What had happened to it since then was anybody's guess.

Thomas Becket had been Archbishop of Canterbury before being murdered in the cathedral in 1170. He had been King Henry II's closest friend and ally until his appointment as Archbishop. The two men had become bitter enemies thereafter.

Henry had made Becket Archbishop because he wanted royal control of the Church. He wanted the clergy to be under the same laws as everyone else in the land. The King's laws, not the Church's.

Henry had expected his friend to carry out his wishes. Becket had stubbornly refused, insisting that the Church had the right to be governed by its own laws. Relations between the two men had sunk so low by December 1170 that Henry had resolved to get rid of his tiresome Archbishop, one way or another.

Henry was Duke of Normandy, as well as King of England. He had moved the royal court to his castle at Bures for that Christmas. He was at Bures, in Normandy, when the Archbishop of York and two other bishops came to complain that Becket had just excommunicated them from the Church. Becket had done so without good cause, in their opinion. They wanted absolution.

It was the last straw for Henry. He was outraged as the three men poured out their grievances.

'As long as Thomas is alive, you will never have a good day, or a peaceful kingdom, or a quiet life,' one of them told him.

Henry agreed. He was spitting with rage by the time the men had finished speaking.

'Becket has eaten my bread,' he complained to the assembled court. 'The man has lifted his heel against me. I showered him with gifts and he dares to insult the King and the whole royal family. He came to court on a lame pack animal and now he thinks he sits on the throne itself.'

The courtiers all nodded agreement as Henry continued.

'What wretches there are at court. What cowards, who care nothing for their allegiance to their master. Not one of them will deliver me from this low-born priest!'

That was a challenge that couldn't be ignored. The courtiers looked at each other after Henry had stormed out of the room. He clearly expected something to be done about Thomas Becket. It was up to them to decide what.

'Where is Becket now?' somebody asked.

'Canterbury. He went there for Christmas.'

There were several knights among the gentlemen of the King's bedchamber. Four of them got together to discuss what to do.

'We'll have to stop Becket somehow,' one of them said. 'The King wishes it. He'll reward us if we do.'

The others agreed. Calling for their horses, they set out that same day, heading by different roads for the French coast. Three other courtiers were sent in haste to stop them, but the courtiers were too late. The four knights crossed to England next morning and made their way to Saltwood Castle on the Kent coast, a few miles south of Canterbury.

The castle was occupied by an old enemy of Becket's. He welcomed the knights and helped them to carry out their plan. A few local men were levied as troops in the King's name. On the morning of 29 December, the men assembled behind the knights and followed them to Canterbury. They arrived that afternoon at St Augustine's, the abbey just outside the city walls.

At the abbey, the knights issued another proclamation in the King's name, forbidding anyone to offer any help to the Archbishop. Taking a dozen men with them, they then made their way around the side of the cathedral precincts to the gate in Palace Street.

It was beginning to get dark as the knights stationed their men at the house inside the gate. From there, it was only a few yards to the Archbishop's residence, where Becket and the cathedral clergy had just had a late lunch in the great hall. After Becket had left, the floor of the hall had been strewn with fresh straw before his servants and a crowd of Canterbury's poor sat down to enjoy their own meal.

The four knights left their weapons at the door and strode in. They were greeted by the Archbishop's seneschal, who led them upstairs to Becket's room.

'Here are four knights from King Henry,' he told the Archbishop. 'They want to talk to you.'

Becket had been warned that the knights were coming. He had been drinking heavily during lunch, telling anyone who wanted to escape the impending violence that they should do so immediately, while they still had the chance. He himself had no intention of going anywhere.

He was talking to a monk as the knights came in. Becket knew three of the knights from his time as Lord Chancellor, but he ignored them all as they joined the other people sitting at his feet. He finished his conversation before turning at length to Sir William de Tracy and greeting him by name.

Tracy didn't reply. It was Sir Reginald Fitzurse who broke the silence after a while.

'We have a message for you from the King over the water,' he told Becket. 'Do you want to hear it in private, or in front of everybody?'

'Whichever you wish.'

The monks got up tactfully and prepared to withdraw. Becket stopped them. He didn't want to be left alone with the knights if they were going to murder him.

'The King over the water commands you to do your duty to the King on this side of the water, instead of trying to steal his crown,' Fitzurse told Becket. 'You've caused a lot of trouble in the kingdom. The King orders you to come to court to answer for it.'

Becket shook his head. He had only recently returned to England from many years of foreign exile. He wasn't about to leave once more. 'I won't let the sea come between me and my Church again,' he replied. 'Not unless I'm dragged there by my feet.'

It wasn't what the knights wanted to hear. Becket complained in turn that he had suffered too. The King wasn't the only one with a grievance, in his opinion.

The knights took great exception to that. Jumping up, they crowded around Becket, yelling abuse at him, nose to nose. His own people sprang to his defence. Fitzurse ordered them to seize the Archbishop and arrest him in the name of the King. The monks took no notice. They clustered defiantly around Becket instead, daring the knights to do their worst.

The knights decided to withdraw. They went to collect their weapons, calling for their own men at the same time. Throwing off the cloaks that had concealed their armour, they headed back to the hall with reinforcements, only to find that the door had been barred against them.

There was another way into the building from behind the kitchen. The knights used a carpenter's axe to break in. Most of Becket's attendants fled at the sound, fearing what was coming. Becket was determined to stand his ground until it was pointed out to him that it was now five o'clock in the afternoon, time for vespers in the choir. He reluctantly allowed his few remaining followers to hustle him through the cloisters into the cathedral, where he would be safe.

The knights followed. They caught up with Becket's party just inside the cathedral door, by the entrance to the crypt. It was hard to tell who was who in the gathering gloom.

'Where is Thomas Becket, traitor to the King?' demanded one of the knights.

'I'm here,' Becket answered. 'I'm not a traitor. What do you want?'

Fitzurse shoved the carpenter's axe against Becket's chest. 'You're going to die,' he told him. 'I'll tear your heart out.'

Another knight hit Becket across the shoulders with the flat of his sword.

'Run,' he advised. 'You'll be killed if you stay.'

More people were arriving every minute. The townspeople had heard what was happening and were rushing into the cathedral, crowding headlong up the nave. There were too many witnesses around for comfort. Rather than be seen abusing the sanctity of the cathedral, the knights grabbed hold of Becket and tried to drag him outside.

Becket refused to go. He was a big man. He seized Tracy by his coat of mail and threw him to the ground. Fitzurse drew his sword in reply and took a swing at Becket's head.

He succeeded only in knocking Becket's cap off. Tracy too swung his sword and wounded the only remaining monk in the arm before grazing Becket's head and cutting into his shoulder.

Blood trickled down Becket's face. He wiped it off with his sleeve. He could see that there was no hope now.

'Into thy hands, O Lord, I commend my spirit,' he declared.

Becket fell to his knees as Tracy hit him again. He was face down on the floor when another sword stroke severed the top of his head from his skull. He was hit so hard that the sword point broke on the flagstones.

To finish the job, another of the killers poked the end of his sword into Becket's brains and scattered them all over the floor. Then they all fled, whooping in triumph as they headed back to the Archbishop's house through the cloisters.

It was some time before the monks could bring themselves to return. Approaching very cautiously, they held up a light. Becket was lying face down where he fell, his scalp hanging by a single piece of skin. Blood was oozing slowly all over the floor.

The monks turned the body over and bound Becket's wounds with a torn shirt. They collected the broken sword pieces and scooped up Becket's blood and brains, precious relics of the martyr. The townspeople were pressing forward by then, determined to see the corpse for themselves. They wanted to dip their clothing in the blood in case it had miraculous properties.

Benches were placed across the floor to keep them away. Opinion about the murder was strongly divided in the town. Plenty of people thought that Becket had got what he deserved, openly defying the King. What they all agreed on was that his comeuppance should never have happened in the cathedral. Murder in the house of God was sacrilege.

Becket's body was placed on a bier and carried up the stairs into the choir. It was left in front of the high altar for the remainder of the night. Vessels were positioned underneath it to catch any further blood. Then the weeping monks took it in turns to stand guard over the corpse until daybreak.

They received bad news next morning. A messenger came to them from the King's men.

'Becket is not to have an Archbishop's funeral,' he told them. 'He was a traitor to his King.'

'But it's the custom. He must be buried among former Archbishops.'

'He was a traitor. He is to be treated as such.'

'And if we refuse?'

'His body will be dug up and hanged on a gibbet. Then it will be torn apart by horses. The pieces will be fed to pigs or thrown onto a dung heap for the dogs to feed on.'

'What should we do with it, then?'

'Bury it anonymously somewhere, so it can't be found.'

The monks decided on a compromise. Closing the cathedral to the public, they gave Becket a low-key burial in the crypt. His body was carried down the stairs and laid to rest in a marble sarcophagus. His blood and brains were placed in a casket next to the sarcophagus. Then the door to the crypt was sealed and all entry forbidden to the public for the immediate future.

It was another three months before the monks judged it safe to open the crypt again. After tempers had cooled, ordinary people were allowed in at last to view Becket's resting place. They came in droves, curious to see the spot where Becket had been murdered, before kneeling down and saying their prayers at his graveside

The miracles began soon afterwards. There were astonishing stories of cures for the old and sick, cripples arising from beside the martyr's tomb with their prayers answered and their bodies made whole again. The tales of Becket's miraculous powers were so many and so persuasive that the Pope sent two sceptical officials to Canterbury in 1172 to investigate their accuracy. The men returned to Rome convinced of Becket's powers. He was made a saint in 1173.

King Henry visited his tomb a year later. Terrified of excommunication, the King had sworn from the first that he had never meant St Thomas to be killed. It had all been a dreadful misunderstanding. Henry was suitably penitent as his ship arrived at Southampton and he rode from there to Canterbury to express his remorse at Becket's graveside.

The King dismounted at St Dunstan's, a church in the fields outside the town walls. It was half a mile from St Dunstan's to the cathedral. Changing out of his royal clothes, Henry dressed as a pilgrim for the rest of the journey. He was barefoot, wearing only a rough woollen shirt and a cloak to keep off the rain as he crossed the river at the West Gate and made his way on foot to the cathedral.

His feet were muddy and bleeding by the time he arrived at the gate. Henry went straight to the scene of the murder. He fell to his knees at the spot and kissed the stone where Becket had fallen. Then he went into the crypt and knelt in obvious distress at the tomb of the martyr.

He was in tears as he prayed. Shrugging off his cloak, he bowed his head over the grave and nodded to the Bishop of London. The Bishop stepped forward and gave him five lashes with a monastic rod, penance for his carelessness in bringing about the death of St Thomas Becket.

The other senior clergy followed suit. Then the cathedral's eighty monks took it in turns to give the King three lashes each, enough to tear his back to ribbons. Henry was a broken man as he slumped against a pillar, ready to spend the whole night in fasting and prayer at Thomas Becket's graveside.

He attended mass next morning before leaving Canterbury at length and setting off for London. The monks gave him a phial of the martyr's blood as a souvenir. It contained only a few drops, liberally mixed with water. The monks were doing a good trade in Becket's blood, selling it off drop by drop in return for a substantial contribution to the cathedral's funds.

Henry went away, his penitence done. In his footsteps came other pilgrims bearing gifts and offerings for the shrine of St Thomas. Among them, in the summer of 1179, was King Louis VII of France.

Louis was the first French king to set foot on English soil. His only son lay sick and close to death as he arrived in Kent for a five-day pilgrimage to Canterbury. It was unanimously agreed that only a miracle from St Thomas could save the child's life as Louis strode through the cathedral gate to make his mark at the shrine and beg the saint for help.

Henry II was with him as they went down to the crypt. Both kings had known Becket in life. The monks stood back respectfully as King Louis crossed himself at the tomb and got down on his knees in front of it. It had been arranged that he would stay there all night in fasting and prayer.

Louis had brought several valuable gifts with him to present to St Thomas. They were advance payments for the miracle that he hoped was about to be performed on his son. One was a solid gold cup. Another, the most precious offering of all, was an enormous, blood-red ruby.

Chapter Four

The Scrivener of Magna Carta

Henry II's son John became king in 1199, but his reign was not a success. Exasperated by years of autocratic rule, England's most powerful barons rose against him in May 1215. They raised an army at Northampton and marched on London. King John was forced to retreat to Windsor and sue for peace.

The negotiations were handled by the Archbishop of Canterbury. Stephen Langton was tasked with drawing up a treaty for the future government of the country acceptable to both sides. The work in progress had yet to be given a name. If it grew any longer though, it would surely have to be called Magna Carta before it was finished.

Langton did some of the work for it in the cathedral library. There were people in there, educated monks, who could assist him with the wording of the agreement. They were learned men, schooled in the law, who knew how to draw up a legal document and make it watertight. Langton was relying on them to help make the treaty a success.

It was no easy task. The barons couldn't even agree among themselves about what should go into the great charter, let alone the King and his counsellors. Langton's job was to advise both sides and bring them to the conference table with an agenda that they could all accept, even if they didn't like it much. He was finding it uphill work.

'The King refuses to listen,' he complained to his scrivener. 'He resents any challenge to his authority. He's only agreed to talk at all because the barons have captured London. It'll be a nightmare getting him to accept anything he doesn't want to.'

'And the barons?'

'Their demands get worse every day. The list goes on and on. Inheritance, marriage portions, money owed to Jews. One of them even wants all the fish weirs removed from the Thames and the Medway. I mean, I ask you.'

'I believe it's a good idea, Archbishop. The weirs are a terrible nuisance to traffic.'

'It's irrelevant. That's the point. The man wouldn't stop talking about it at the last committee meeting. Went on and on about fish while the rest of us were trying to discuss great affairs of state.'

'I'm afraid there's always somebody like that.'

'Yes, there is. Every meeting, there's always some idiot droning on interminably about something irrelevant while everyone else has to sit and listen. Never sit on a committee, Scrivener. It isn't worth it.'

The scrivener nodded. He had no intention of doing so. He was happy with his lot in the cathedral scriptorium.

'You don't think much of the barons, Archbishop?'

'Gangsters, most of them. Fighting is the only thing they know about.'

'And the King?'

'He can't even read or write.' The Archbishop, a university man, spoke with contempt. 'Or if he can, I've never seen any evidence of it. He's just as bad as the barons.'

Worse, in fact. King John had roundly abused his powers as monarch. He had slept with other men's wives, cheated them out of their money and confiscated their estates. He had even had his own nephew murdered, his brother Richard's son. King John had been a despot from the very beginning of his reign.

The most abominable crime in a long list had been the murder of Maud de Briouze, the Lady of Bramber. Maud had had the courage to speak out against the killing of John's nephew, where everyone else had held their tongues. John had had her thrown into a dungeon for her presumption. She had been left to die of starvation in Corfe Castle, alongside one of her sons.

The son had died first. Maud Bramber had been so mad with hunger by the end that she had tried to bite her own child's face off before dying too. The story had shocked the nation when it emerged. The barons were not the only ones who wanted to see their errant monarch called to account for his actions. The rest of the country did as well.

'There has to be a law,' the Archbishop insisted. 'The King can't just be allowed to do what he likes. Not if he's going to make his subjects eat their own children.'

'But you say he won't listen.'

'He will if the barons force him to. He'll have to, if he wants to keep his throne.'

'What kind of law?'

'I don't know. Something that prevents him from throwing people into prison without good cause. We must put it into the charter that he can never do that.'

'It would have to be carefully worded.'

The Archbishop agreed. 'The King will certainly try to wriggle out of it if we don't get the wording right.'

They thought for a while. It was the scrivener who broke the silence at length.

'Are we including the serfs in this?'

'Not for the moment. Maybe later.'

They thought again. Then the scrivener came up with a suggestion.

'No free man shall be cast into a dungeon without just cause. Would that do, Archbishop?'

'Too vague. The King could easily find a way around it. He could lock them up somewhere else or insist that his cause was just. It can't be left to him to decide. He's not to be trusted.'

'What about this, then? No free man shall suffer imprisonment of any kind without just cause, the merits of the case to be decided by someone other than the King?'

'Getting there.' The Archbishop was cautious. 'Something along those lines. It needs to be better worded, though. Give it some thought, Scrivener. See what you can come up with.'

'I will, my Lord.'

'And property. There ought to be something in there about not taking other people's property without compensation. We need to protect the rights of property.'

It took a week and many long discussions with colleagues before the scrivener found the appropriate wording at last. The Archbishop was packing his bags for the conference as the man hurried in, proffering a sheet of parchment. He handed it to Langton.

'I think I've got it right, this time. What d'you think?'

The Archbishop read it. *No free man shall be seized or imprisoned, or stripped of his rights or possessions, or outlawed or exiled, or deprived of his standing in any way, nor will we proceed with force against him, or send others to do so, except by the lawful judgment of his peers or by the law of the land.*

'Yes.' Langton was pleased. 'That's it, Scrivener. That's exactly what we need. Good work.'

'Thank you, my Lord.'

'I'll take it to the meeting with me. It'll be interesting to see the King's face when we read it to him.'

'Will it get into the charter?'

'All depends. The King's advisers will certainly try to water it down. We shall have to stand our ground and see what happens.'

'I hope it does.'

'I hope so too. We need something like this in England.'

The conference was to be held under an agreement of safe conduct. King John had suggested Windsor Castle for the meeting place, but the barons weren't having that. He could easily murder the lot of them once they were inside the castle walls. They had opted for a patch of neutral ground instead, a riverbank midway between Windsor and the little village of Staines.

The Archbishop went to pray at the shrine of St Thomas before setting out. It was a good idea to get the saint's backing for the formidable task that lay ahead. Whatever else happened during the negotiations, Stephen Langton was determined to make sure that the Church came out of it all right.

St Thomas's body still lay in the crypt, although not for much longer. Plans were afoot to move it to a much grander setting upstairs, where the flow of pilgrims would be easier to manage. The eastern end of the cathedral was being enlarged for the purpose.

For the moment though, Becket lay in the crypt, where he had first been buried. To keep his body safe, the sarcophagus had long since been walled in and covered with a heavy marble slab. Small apertures in the side walls enabled the pilgrims to put their arms through and touch the coffin containing the sacred relics.

Pride of place at the shrine had been given to the Régale de France, the beautiful ruby donated by King Louis VII of France in 1179. The ruby was said to be the most fabulous jewel in all of Christendom. It had certainly worked its magic for the King. His son had recovered from near death within two days of Louis presenting the jewel to the shrine.

Stephen Langton wondered if it would do something similar for him as he completed his respects to St Thomas. When he had finished, he headed off for Windsor to mediate between King John and the rebellious barons gathering under flag of truce in a meadow nearby.

The King was in his castle high above the river when the Archbishop arrived. Langton went to see the royal advisers first, the men negotiating the peace treaty on the King's behalf. He delivered the barons' latest demands, neatly written out by the monks at Canterbury. Then he went to meet King John.

He found the monarch in a foul mood. John was outraged at the prospect of a humiliating peace treaty with his enemies.

'I suppose I do have to do this?' he asked.

'I fear so, Your Majesty. The barons are determined on change.'

'They're trying to tell me what to do.'

The Archbishop could not deny it.

'They're saying that the people should command the King, instead of the other way about. How can that be right?'

'We live in difficult times.' Langton's sympathies lay with the barons, but he wasn't going to say so to the King.

'The barons shouldn't be dictating terms to me. I'm the one who's King.'

'Nevertheless, Your Majesty, it would be wise to listen to them. They can make a lot of trouble if you don't.'

King John knew it. He had been hoping that the Archbishop might suggest a way out for him, but the man wasn't being helpful. His loyalties were to the Church before anything else.

'You're saying I must talk to the barons?'

'Yes, you must, Your Majesty. It will bring peace, if nothing else.'

'All right, then. If it can't be avoided. We'll meet them tomorrow. In a field, I believe?'

Langton nodded. Runnymede had been chosen because it was an open space, easy to defend. The meadow was almost an island, protected by the river Thames and long stretches of marshland that were difficult to cross in a hurry. There was no chance of the King ambushing the barons there or taking them by surprise.

The two sides met next morning. It was a blazing June day as the King arrived from Windsor. The barons were already at Runnymede. They had pitched their tents at the far end of the field and were watching in stony silence as the King and his entourage rode towards them across the grass.

There were fewer than forty barons in all, only a minority of the country's nobles. The bulk of the nobility either supported the King or were guardedly neutral, careful not to get involved. But the barons who had come to Runnymede were all of them powerful men, impossible for the King to ignore.

They each had their own private army, for a start. They had brought their retainers with them, armed to the teeth and ready for trouble. Between them, the barons at Runnymede had more than enough men-at-arms to overwhelm the King's people and take him prisoner if he declined to listen to the barons' grievances or discuss their terms for a treaty.

John saw at once that he was beaten. He would have to concede to some of the barons' demands at least if he wanted to retain his throne. There were too many big names ranged against him, too many powerful warlords sitting menacingly at the head of their troops for him to do anything else.

A throne had been provided for King John at one end of the conference table in the pavilion. Taking his seat, he looked around unhappily and gave the signal for the talking to begin.

The horse trading began at once. The King's advisers sat on one side of the table, the leading barons on the other. The remainder stood behind them, listening intently as a clerk read out the terms of the treaty in full, sentence by sentence.

A few of the terms were nodded through immediately without debate. Most were set aside for further discussion. The negotiations continued for the rest of the day and for the next three days as well. The barons retired exhausted to their tents at the end of the proceedings every night. The King went home to his castle.

The final details weren't hammered out until 19 June. The terms were still not to the King's liking, but there was nothing he could do about it. The barons had all stood firm against him. He did his best to put a brave face on the situation as a draft of the final agreement was drawn up on the last day for everyone's approval.

'My chancery clerks will make fair copies,' he promised the barons. 'I'll have them distributed around the shires so that everyone can see them. They'll be placed in cathedrals for safekeeping.'

'Will the copies have your seal attached?'

'They will. Every copy will carry the royal seal. You have my assurance on that.'

The barons were sceptical. The King's assurance wasn't worth much. But at least agreement had been reached. It would mean the end of civil war if King John kept to his word.

There was no signing ceremony. The documents weren't ready and few people could write anyway. The agreement was sealed by a communal oath instead. Archbishop Stephen Langton presided as everyone vowed before God to respect the Runnymede agreement and uphold its many provisions. A vow taken in the eyes of God bound them much more tightly to the charter than any ragged X scrawled on a piece of parchment. After they had all made the vow, the barons swore an oath of loyalty to King John as well.

He nodded curtly to his enemies when the ceremony was over and returned to Windsor Castle without further ado. The barons waited until he had gone before dispersing in their turn. Camp was struck and tentage loaded onto wagons. The men-at-arms shouldered their weapons and fell into line behind their leaders. Within a few hours of Magna Carta being sworn, the long columns of men had all left the place and were on their way out of there, heading back to London. Runnymede had become a rural meadow once again.

It was several weeks later before Stephen Langton returned to Canterbury. He brought good news when at last he came.

'I have our copy of the charter,' he told the assembled monks. 'Here it is. All written out by the chancery clerks.'

The Archbishop laid it on the table. The sixty-three provisions of Magna Carta had been translated into Latin and carefully copied onto a single piece of parchment. The King's seal at the bottom signified royal assent. The monks crowded around to have a look.

'It's all there,' the Archbishop told them proudly. 'Everything we asked for. Freedom of the Church, trading rules, repayment of fines. The King had to agree to everything in the end.'

'Excellent news, Archbishop.'

'He wasn't happy about it, but there was nothing he could do. The barons refused to let him off the hook.'

'That's very good to hear.'

'Inquests, lawsuits, forestry. It's all been written down in Magna Carta. There's going to be a law for everything from now on.'

'Does that include my bit?' the scrivener asked shyly.

'Which bit was that?' The Archbishop had forgotten.

'No free man shall be seized or imprisoned except by the lawful judgment of his peers.'

'Absolutely. The King didn't like it, but the barons refused to back down. They added a bit as well.'

'Yes?'

'To no one will we sell, to no one deny or delay right or justice. That'll stop the King charging people a fortune just to have their case heard.'

'That's wonderful, Archbishop. A splendid result.'

'Yes, it is,' Langton agreed. 'And congratulations where they're due, Scrivener. You did a remarkable job there.'

Chapter Five

Bell Harry and the Black Prince

The Black Prince was coming. Edward, Prince of Wales, was back in England after his magnificent victory at Poitiers. He had landed at Plymouth early in May 1357, bringing with him a very important prisoner. Jean the Good, King of France, had been forced to surrender to him after the battle.

The two men were on their way to London, where a great welcome awaited them. The victory parade was taking a while to organise, so the Black Prince had decided to delay his arrival for a few days. Instead of going straight on to London after Winchester, he was travelling across country to Canterbury to visit the shrine of St Thomas in the cathedral.

It was wonderful news for Canterbury. The inhabitants could hardly wait for him to arrive. The Black Prince was a war criminal to the French, the leader of an army that murdered and looted wherever it went. To the English, he was a fine military commander and a remarkable young man. It was widely agreed that he would make a splendid king one day, after his father, Edward III, had died.

The streets were thronged with sightseers as he rode in. The King of France rode beside him as his honoured guest. The two of them were cheered by enthusiastic crowds all the way to the cathedral gate. The applause continued even louder as they went through and came to a stop at the entrance to the cathedral.

To add to the excitement, Prior Henry's bell was ringing frantically above their heads as they appeared. Old Prior Henry of Eastry had had the bell cast at enormous expense and hung in the cathedral's northwest tower. It could be heard all over the city when it rang out in joyous celebration, as it did now. The monks had named it Bell Harry in the Prior's honour.

'Greetings, my Lord. Welcome to Canterbury.' The Archbishop stepped forward to meet the Prince as he and his guest dismounted. 'You had a pleasant journey from Winchester?'

'Very pleasant. I'm glad we've got here, though.'

The crowds watched respectfully as the two royals were escorted into the cathedral. They were taken to the Martyrdom first, to see the spot where St Thomas had been murdered. The Martyrdom was always the first place people wanted to see when they visited the cathedral.

An altar marked the spot now, with a statue of the saint in front of it. A gold ring of St Thomas's lay on the altar, next to a piece of his brain preserved in rock crystal and a case containing the sword point that had broken off on the flagstones when he was killed. They were all objects of veneration to the thousands of pilgrims who flocked to the site every month.

The Archbishop stood back as the two men paid their respects at the altar. When they had finished, the Prince rose again and told King Jean a bit about the Martyrdom.

'This is where my great-grandfather got married.' He waved a hand at the altar. 'Edward I.'

'The Hammer of the Scots?'

'And the Jews. He married his second wife here. Margaret of France.'

'Here?' King Jean looked around in surprise. The Martyrdom seemed rather cramped for a royal wedding.

'It was only a small affair, second time around. My great-grandfather wanted St Thomas's blessing for the enterprise. King Richard was here too, before he went to the Crusades.'

They left the Martyrdom after they had seen everything and were escorted up a flight of steps towards the choir. St Thomas's new shrine lay at the far end of the choir, beyond the high altar. Priests showed them the way.

The shrine had been moved from the crypt in Stephen Langton's time, not long after the death of King John. The translation had been an occasion of great pomp, attended by dignitaries from all over Europe. The Pope's personal representative had travelled to Canterbury for the ceremony. So had King Henry III of England and many great bishops and nobles. They had all wanted to see the extraordinary spectacle for themselves.

Ordinary people had wanted to see it as well. So many people had come to Canterbury for the event that every bed in the city had been taken. Tents had had to be erected in the surrounding fields to accommodate the overflow. The Archbishop had generously provided barrels of wine at each of the city's gates so that everyone could have a free drink before making their way to the cathedral to watch the proceedings.

St Thomas's body had been removed from its sarcophagus beforehand and transferred to a lighter wood and iron chest for the move. The corpse had crumbled into dust as soon as it was exposed to the air. Only the saint's bones had remained to be collected up and placed in the decorated chest. The Archbishop had selected a few choice ones first for distribution to favoured churches after the ceremony.

The chest had then been conveyed with much ritual to its grand new home beyond the choir. It had been reinterred in a magnificent setting specially designed for it amid the high stone columns and dramatic Gothic arches of the cathedral.

The spot was packed with pilgrims as a rule, but it had been closed to the public for the Black Prince's visit. He and King Jean had the shrine to themselves as the Archbishop led them forward to admire the craftsmanship and say their prayers to St Thomas.

'This way, my Lords.' The Archbishop waved a hand. 'This is where St Thomas lies now.'

He showed them to the shrine. An imposing marble plinth lay in the middle of a wide-open space, approached from all sides by flights of stone steps. The chest containing the saint's bones lay on top of the plinth, hidden from view beneath a decorated wooden canopy.

The Archbishop gave a signal. As if by magic, the canopy rose from the shrine, hauled upwards by a rope pulley. It revealed the iron chest on the plinth, lavishly adorned with gold trellis-work and decorated all over with an astonishing array of pearls, sapphires, diamonds and emeralds.

The two visitors were spellbound. There were more jewels at the shrine than they had ever seen in one place before. More jewels than they had ever seen anywhere.

The most brilliant jewel of all was still the Régale de France, King Louis VII's great ruby. It was attached to the chest in a prominent position and surrounded by a display of agates, cornelians and precious onyx. There was no more arresting sight in all of Christendom.

'We're very proud of it,' the Archbishop told the visitors, as they gaped. 'I don't think there's ever been a ruby quite like it before. Certainly not in Canterbury.'

The Archbishop withdrew discreetly as the Black Prince and King Jean approached the shrine. Together they mounted the steps to the plinth and sank to their knees at the top. The plinth was recessed so that worshippers could get close to St Thomas as they prayed.

Closing his eyes, the Black Prince gave thanks to the saint for his great victory at Poitiers, a victory undoubtedly ordained by God. Beside him, the King of France accepted God's decision on this occasion but prayed for better luck next time. The two men remained at prayer for ten minutes while courtiers and church officials watched from a distance. Then they rose again, their devotions done, and thanked the Archbishop as they withdrew from the shrine.

'I'm going to have myself buried here,' the Black Prince told King Jean as they continued their tour of the cathedral. 'When the time comes, I'll put it in my will that I'm to be interred in the cathedral, somewhere close to St Thomas.'

'Yes?'

'In the undercroft probably, where he was first buried. Somewhere like that.'

King Jean's mind was still on his ancestor's ruby at the shrine. What a wonderful sight it had been. Perhaps France would have better luck on the battlefield if he could produce a similar gift for St Thomas.

'I'd like to make an offering at the shrine when I get the chance,' he told the Black Prince.

'Good idea. You should.'

'Something like the ruby. It's time France made another gift.'

'Another jewel?'

'In due course. When the time is right.'

They both knew it wasn't right at the moment. King Jean was a prisoner of the English, as were many of his most prominent nobles. An enormous ransom for their release would have to be agreed before they could all go home. This was no time for further expense.

'One day,' Jean promised. 'As soon as it can be arranged.'

The two men stayed the night in Canterbury before setting off for London next morning. They received a rapturous reception when they arrived in the capital. The victory at Poitiers was tremendous news, if it meant an end to the war and lots of ransom money as well. Londoners were as delighted to welcome the Black Prince and his illustrious prisoner to their city as Canterbury had been.

They were out in force as the two men arrived. The mayor and aldermen were waiting at the gates to greet them. So were the officials of the city's guilds. All of them were on horseback, wearing new clothes for the occasion. They quickly formed a procession and led the returning hero in triumph through the narrow streets towards St Paul's cathedral and Ludgate beyond.

It was pandemonium all the way. The Black Prince had won the cup and was bringing it home. Everyone turned out to cheer him as he passed. Houses had been elaborately decorated for the event. Free wine was on tap all along the route. Pretty girls hanging from elevated ropeways had been hired by the goldsmiths to sprinkle gold and silver leaf on the heads of all the notables as they rode along in the procession below.

The crowds applauded the Black Prince all the way past St Paul's and on towards the bridge over the Fleet river. They were still cheering when his entourage arrived at the Palace of Westminster. His father King Edward III was waiting there to greet his eldest son after his great victory and bid welcome to his distinguished cousin, King Jean of France.

'Fortunes of war,' Edward consoled the Frenchman, as he showed him into the palace. 'I'm sorry that you have to be our guest for a while. We'll get you back to France as soon as the ransom money can be raised.'

'I hope it won't be too long.'

'You can stay with one of my other sons, while you're in London. The Savoy Palace on the Strand.'

In the event, it took three years to negotiate the French king's return to France. The Black Prince escorted him to Dover when at last an agreement had been reached. They stopped at Canterbury again on the way. King Jean retraced his steps to St Thomas's shrine and presented it with a beautiful jewel worth at least two hundred marks, according to the monk who priced such things. Then he thanked God for his deliverance and went home.

The Black Prince was not so fortunate. He was only 45 when he died of a mysterious illness in 1376. All of England was horrified that so illustrious a life had been cut short in its prime. The Prince hadn't even lived long enough to succeed his father as king.

He was buried in the cathedral, as he had wished. Two knights bearing the Prince's armour and carrying his royal insignia were waiting on horseback as his body arrived at the West Gate after the long journey from London. The hearse was surrounded by black banners and drawn by twelve black horses as it wound slowly through the streets towards the cathedral. A great crowd was there to watch in silence as it passed.

The knights halted at the cathedral gate, as was the custom for armed men since the time of Thomas Becket. The hearse continued through towards the door of the cathedral. There the coffin was unloaded and carried slowly through the choir to the high altar beyond.

Above, Bell Harry rang again, tolling sombrely for the Black Prince in the northwest tower. The bell was in mourning for a great leader. Its clapper had been half-muffled by the monks to soften the backstroke and produce an echo that rang out sonorously across the city. The sound reverberated through the cathedral as his body was conveyed through the choir and laid solemnly before the altar for the funeral service.

The Prince wasn't buried in the crypt, as he had requested. It had been decided that a national hero should have a far more distinguished resting place in the main body of the cathedral, very close to St Thomas himself. A tomb had been built for him just a few yards from the shrine of the martyr.

It was a masterpiece of construction. The base containing his body was of Purbeck marble. On top lay a life-size effigy of the Prince at prayer. The effigy was in full body armour, made of brass and gilt, its helmet adorned with precious stones. Above the effigy hung a carved wooden tester, a canopy, with a painting of the Holy Trinity on the underside.

After the funeral service, the Black Prince's shield, gauntlets and surcoat embroidered with the arms of England and France were placed on permanent display above the tester. So was his helm, the huge iron helmet with a lion crest on top that he had worn for jousting. They were all hung above the tester, high in the cathedral close to St Thomas, for everyone to see and admire. And there they have remained ever since.

Chapter Six

Wat Tyler and the Beheaded Archbishop

Their enemies called them peasants, but the men heading for Canterbury on 10 June 1381 were far more than that. There were skilled carpenters among them, weavers, bakers, cobblers, masons and tailors, even a few gentry sympathetic to their cause. They weren't just ignorant serfs working in the fields.

There were several thousand of them by the time they reached the city gates. They were led by Wat Tyler, a plain-speaking man from Maidstone. The peasants were looking for Simon of Sudbury, the Archbishop of Canterbury. They were going to kill him if they found him in the cathedral precincts.

Sudbury was Chancellor of England, as well as Archbishop. The peasants held him responsible for the savage increase in poll tax that was causing so much distress across the land. Neither the Church nor the King's officials had taken any notice of their plight, so the peasants had decided to take matters into their own hands.

They were welcomed with open arms in Canterbury. The city too had been hit by the poll tax. To add insult to injury, the people were also being made to pay for the rebuilding of the West Gate and the repair of Canterbury's walls. They were all in favour of stringing up whoever was responsible for squeezing them so hard.

'The Archbishop's palace first,' Tyler yelled, as the peasants streamed towards the cathedral. 'If he's in there, we'll drag him out at once. Make him suffer for what he's done.'

The palace lay only a few yards from the west door of the cathedral. The peasants stormed in. They raced from room to room, looking for Simon of Sudbury. They searched the place from top to bottom, but he was nowhere to be found. A servant told them why.

'He's in London. Gone to see the King.'

Disappointed, the peasants decided to ransack the Archbishop's possessions instead. They were outraged at what they found. So much finery in every room, so many beautiful things and lovely furniture and expensive clothes. England's Chancellor lived very well at the taxpayer's expense. The common people struggled to feed their children.

'Take everything,' Tyler ordered. 'Smash it. Destroy it all.'

It was almost noon by the time the peasants had finished with the palace. The monks were gathering nervously for midday mass in the cathedral next door. To their dismay, several thousand angry peasants decided to join them.

Tyler headed the mob. The monks watched aghast as he pushed through everybody and mounted the steps to the pulpit to interrupt the mass. He looked down at the holy men from on high.

'You're going to have to find yourselves a new Archbishop when this is over,' he told them bluntly. 'Simon of Sudbury is a traitor. We're going to cut his head off when we find him.'

'We certainly are,' someone else yelled. 'Sudbury's the man to blame.'

The monks weren't happy about that. They watched uncomfortably as Tyler's followers wandered around the cathedral. The peasants went to see the Martyrdom first, then crossed themselves piously in front of the ruby at St Thomas's shrine. They all admired the Black Prince's tomb nearby. It had become a major tourist attraction since his death, second only to the shrine itself. Everyone in England wanted to see where the Black Prince was buried.

Wat Tyler joined the group clustered around his tomb. The Prince's helm, shield and royal surcoat all looked splendid above the tester. Tyler wasn't the only one who regretted it that the great man had died so young. The Black Prince would have been King now, if he had lived, instead of his teenage son.

The peasants didn't linger long in the cathedral, after seeing the tomb. There was too much to do elsewhere. If the Archbishop wasn't in Canterbury, they could still ransack the town hall and destroy the tax records. They could also burn the tenant rolls containing the names of all the serfs in Kent.

It was essential to burn the rolls. If they destroyed all the legal documents, the serfs would be set free from their bondage. No one would be able to say that they were serfs anymore, without the paperwork to prove it.

The peasants wasted no time. Spreading out through the cathedral gate, they quickly made a bonfire of all the legal documents they could find in Canterbury. They forced open the Norman castle, now the county gaol, and set the prisoners free. They also seized three alleged traitors denounced by local people and beheaded them publicly in the street.

When they had done that, they rounded up the mayor, the city bailiffs and Canterbury's most prominent citizens and forced them on pain of death to swear a new oath. The men were required to pledge loyalty not only to King Richard II but to the Commons of England as well. It was the ordinary people of England that the mayor and his officials were supposed to serve.

The townspeople were happy to help the peasants administer the new oath. They were delighted that something was being done at last. They were so enthusiastic that five hundred of them left Canterbury next morning and joined the peasants on their march to London. The remainder stayed behind to continue the good work and spread the revolution to other towns and villages.

The peasants were going to London because the King was there. They had arranged to gather at Blackheath, just south of the river Thames, while their comrades from Essex approached the capital from the north. Together, the two peasant armies would be a formidable presence when they arrived in London at the same time and combined their forces.

'We're looking for the Archbishop,' Tyler told the Kentish peasants, when they reached Blackheath. 'He's in London somewhere. We'll find him, wherever he is. He'll get what's coming to him when we do.'

'And then what?'

'Then we'll talk to the King. Our quarrel is with his officials, not with him. King Richard doesn't know what is being done in his name. We'll talk to the King and tell him exactly what's been happening in his kingdom.'

'Will he listen?'

'Of course he will. There's no reason why he shouldn't.'

The peasants continued to London. It was three days before they managed to track the Archbishop down. Simon of Sudbury had taken refuge in the Tower of London at the first sign of trouble. The Tower's thick walls were famously impenetrable. He knew he would be quite safe behind them until the revolt was over and the peasants had been dispersed.

Unfortunately for him, the Tower's gatekeepers disliked the poll tax just as much as the peasants did. They saw no reason to protect the Archbishop from his enemies. On the morning of 14 June, one of them opened the gates for the peasants and let them all in.

Wat Tyler was one of the first across the moat. The peasants found Simon of Sudbury hiding in the chapel at the White Tower. He was reciting a prayer for the dying, as they burst in. Seizing him at once, they took him outside and dragged him up Tower Hill for execution.

Sudbury didn't go quietly. He tried to talk his way out of it as the peasants hauled him to his death.

'You can't possibly do this,' he told them. 'I'm the Archbishop of Canterbury. You can't murder the Archbishop of Canterbury. It would be sacrilege.'

'We're not going to murder the Archbishop,' one of them assured him. 'We've got nothing against the Archbishop of Canterbury.'

'What are you going to do, then?'

'We're going to kill the Chancellor of England. The man responsible for the poll tax.'

A huge crowd gathered to watch. There was no official executioner, so a peasant with a sword volunteered for the task. Stepping forward, he raised the weapon as Sudbury's neck was bared. Then he swung it hard.

Only those in the front rank saw how many strokes it took to do the job. In the split second that remained to him after he had finally been decapitated, Simon of Sudbury caught a brief glimpse of the sky spinning round and round and the Tower of London apparently standing on its head. Then everything faded to black.

'So perish all tax gatherers,' said an onlooker, when it was done. Everyone nodded in agreement. It was the cry of the Englishman through the ages.

The Archbishop's body was left where it lay for the moment, but his head was scooped up at once. His episcopal hat had fallen off during the execution, so the peasants got a hammer and nailed it back on before sticking the head on the end of a long pole. Then one of them held the pole aloft for everyone at the back to see.

'This is the predator's head,' he told the cheering crowd. 'Simon of Sudbury. The Chancellor of England.'

A ripple of applause followed the head as it was paraded through the streets, on its way to London Bridge. Later, reduced to a skull, it was removed from the bridge and returned to the Archbishop's hometown of Sudbury. His friends there hoped it might become a venerated relic, generating the sort of money that Thomas Becket was getting at Canterbury. When the anticipated revenue streams failed to materialise, the venture was abandoned and the skull was locked in a cupboard in Sudbury church, where it remains.

The peasants knew they had done it now. There could be no going back, after the murder of the Archbishop. Wat Tyler was acutely aware that he personally had no choice thereafter but to press on regardless, as the peasants' leader. Either victory or death awaited him as he rode away from Tower Hill to prepare for his meeting with King Richard next morning. There was nothing for him in between.

The meeting was held outside St Bartholomew's hospital, on the smooth field where the annual fair took place, and the Friday livestock auctions. Smithfield was also used for jousting tournaments and public gatherings in the summer. King Richard's advisers had chosen the place because it lay outside the city walls, well away from the crowded streets where the peasants were running riot.

The peasants were the first to arrive. Thousands of Kentishmen appeared at the appointed hour, carrying swords, pikes and bows and arrows as they assembled outside the hospital. Tyler rode on horseback at their head, a general in command of his troops. With all of London cowering before him, he was full of arrogance as he held up his hand and told his men to wait there for the King.

Richard II was a boy of 14. He had the mayor of London, William Walworth, and a few dozen horsemen with him as he rode up from Westminster Abbey, where he had been praying for help at the shrine of Edward the Confessor. He too ordered a halt when they arrived at Smithfield.

The two sides faced each other across the field. At Richard's command, one of his courtiers rode forward to fetch Wat Tyler and bring him to his monarch. Tyler saw it as a meeting of equals as he obligingly spurred his horse and went to meet the King.

He showed no deference when he arrived. When Adam delved and Eve span, who was then the gentleman? Wat Tyler was the one with a large army. King Richard was just a boy. Tyler saw no reason to doff his hat to a teenager.

'Why won't you go home?' Richard ignored Tyler's bad manners as the peasant seized hold of his horse's bridle. 'We have listened to the people's demands. They have been promised their freedom. You've done what you came to London to do. Why won't you go home now?'

'Not until we have everything in writing. We want all the promised reforms in letters patent before we go anywhere.'

'You should go. The letters will be prepared, in due course.'

'That may be, but we want to see it in writing. If you put it in writing, we'll know that you mean what you say. Give us the letters and then we'll go away.'

'How dare you talk to the King like that?' William Walworth was outraged.

'I'll talk to him as I please.' The success of the last few days had gone to Tyler's head. 'It's none of your business how I talk to him.'

Daggers were drawn at that. Walworth gave the order for Tyler to be arrested.

Tyler was preparing to defend himself when Walworth stabbed him in the head and knocked him off his horse.

Without even thinking about it, one of the King's esquires jumped off his own horse and finished the job with a sword. One quick thrust through the body was all it took to kill Wat Tyler. He was dead before he even knew what had hit him.

It was the peasants' turn to be outraged. Reaching for their weapons, they started forward at once. Their leader had been murdered, right in front of their eyes. They couldn't allow that to go unpunished.

But Richard II was their King, ordained by God. He didn't hesitate for a moment. Spurring his horse, he rode across the field to address his rebel subjects. It was the Black Prince's son who reined to a halt in front of them and spoke to them from the saddle.

'I am your King,' he told them. 'You have no other leader than me. On your loyalty as my subjects, I command you now to leave this place at once. Go in peace and you will all have my pardon for what you have done. Go now, and you will not be punished for your rebellion.'

The peasants went eventually, with considerable reluctance. A few were hanged or beheaded for particular offences, but the King was as good as his word. Peace returned after a few turbulent months. The reforms demanded by the peasants were not immediately implemented, but it was clear to everyone after the killing of the Archbishop and Wat Tyler that the days of serfdom were numbered.

Tyler's head replaced Simon of Sudbury's on London Bridge. He left a wife and son behind in Maidstone, both of them remembering a man of strong convictions as they mourned his passing. The son grew up to have sons of his own in due course, as did they in turn. Wat Tyler's descendants continued to live peacefully in Maidstone for the next three centuries.

It wasn't until 1723 that one of them, Ned Tyler, decided to try his luck in London again. Central to his thinking was the impending motherhood of a local maidservant, angrily pointing her finger at him. Rather than marry the girl, Ned Tyler left home very early one morning in March and hitched a lift to London with a local carter. The following day, he found himself in England's capital with no intention of ever returning to Maidstone.

Ned Tyler had no idea that he was descended from Wat as he paced the very same streets as his ancestor. He had never even heard of the Peasants' Revolt. All he knew for certain was that London was a very difficult place for a young man without any friends to make a living. A young man could starve to death without anyone even noticing.

It wasn't long before Ned Tyler found himself in trouble with the law. Within a week of his arrival in London, the little money he had brought with him was all gone. Within two, he had become a thief. Within three, he had been arrested for stealing a loaf of bread and eating it to hide the evidence. He cut a miserable figure as he stood in the dock at the Old Bailey, awaiting sentence for the crime.

'Prisoner at the bar.' The judge consulted his notes for the name. 'Tyler. You have been tried by your peers and found guilty of theft under the value of one shilling. Have you anything to say before I pass sentence?'

Ned shook his head. No use pointing out that he had been desperate for something to eat. No one would listen.

'Then it remains only for me to sentence you to transportation for seven years. You will be taken from here and transported to Philadelphia. You will remain in the colonies until you have served the full term of your sentence.'

Ned looked blank. Philadelphia? The colonies?

'And I must remind you,' the judge continued, 'that if you are found to have returned to these shores before your time is up, you will suffer the full rigour of the law. The penalty for transgression is fixed by the law. Set foot in England again any time in the next seven years, young man, and you will be hanged by the neck until you are dead.'

Ned was led away in shock to await the next shipment of convicts. The clerk of the court made a quick note of the case for the Old Bailey's records as he was taken down:

Edward Tyler, late of Maidstone in Kent, was indicted for feloniously stealing a Loaf of Bread, val 3d, the Goods of Benjamin Chandler, on the 6th of April last. It appear'd that the prisoner came to the Prosecutor's shop and went away with the Loaf, which was taken upon him as he tried to eat it. Guilty to the value of 3d. Transportation.

So it was that the first of Ezra Tyler's American ancestors left England for ever and arrived most unwillingly in the New World.

Chapter Seven

Geoffrey Chaucer and the Harlot of Mercery Lane

Tourism was booming in Canterbury. Thanks to St Thomas, the city had become the number one visitor destination in England. Several thousand people a week came to see the shrine and leave a donation before spending their money in Canterbury's taverns and souvenir shops. They were called pilgrims, but most of them were only tourists enjoying a bit of travel and the chance to spend some time away from home for a while.

They all needed somewhere to stay while they were in Canterbury. The cathedral authorities had decided to meet the demand by rebuilding the tourist hotel on Mercery Lane. It had been there for centuries, but it was no longer fit for purpose. The authorities knocked it down in 1392 and set about replacing it with a massive new hotel to cater for the ever-increasing tourist numbers who needed accommodation while they were in town.

The work took three years. The Chequers Inn was enormous when it was finished. Including the basement, it stood on four floors grouped around an inner courtyard. There were private bedrooms for the rich and a dormitory for the poor that could accommodate a hundred people in a single room. The inn was built along Mercery Lane, but the main entrance was through a small door on Canterbury's high street.

The monks were delighted when it opened. They would be cashing in, once the building and operating costs had been recouped. The income from tourist beds could be put towards the upkeep of the cathedral, perhaps even paying for a new central tower to replace the existing one.

The management organised a series of events to publicise the new hotel.

Chief among the attractions in the first few weeks was a reading of his works by the greatest writer of the age. Geoffrey Chaucer had once been a knight of the shire and the Member of Parliament for Kent. Persuading him to give a reading of his works at the Chequers Inn was an extraordinary coup for the cathedral authorities.

In fact, the great man was very happy to oblige. It was some time since he had last been to Canterbury, a place he always enjoyed visiting. Chaucer thought the cathedral was looking particularly lovely in the sunshine as he dismounted outside the inn and went in to drop his bags and discuss the arrangements for his talk.

The innkeeper was there to greet him. He came forward at once, full of welcome for Canterbury's distinguished visitor.

'Lovely to see you, sir. I'm so glad you're here. Did you have a comfortable ride? We've been looking forward to your visit all week.'

'Thank you. I'm glad to be here too. I must say, this is a splendid new inn.'

'It certainly is. We're very pleased with it. You won't find a better one in Canterbury.'

'May I see my room?'

'You can, sir. The porter will take your bags. We'll talk about your reading when you come down again.'

The porter took Chaucer's bags and carried them upstairs. 'I hear you're an author,' he said, on the way. 'Should I have heard of you?'

'Oh I don't think so,' said Chaucer. 'Not everyone has.'

The porter showed Chaucer to his room and gave him the key. After he had unpacked his things, Chaucer went downstairs again and found the innkeeper.

'About my reading,' he said.

'It's all arranged. Four of the clock this afternoon. We've got quite a crowd coming to hear you.'

'That's good news.'

'I'm sorry that we won't be able to pay you anything for it, but plenty of people will be there. I'm sure you'll enjoy reading your books to them.'

'I'm sure I shall,' said Chaucer. He had heard the bit about not being able to pay him many times before.

Four of the clock left ample time to look around the cathedral beforehand. Chaucer had lunch at the inn first. He ordered a tankard of ale with his meal. It was served by a blowsy barmaid who twinkled at him as she poured his drink.

'My name's Kit,' she told him. 'I'm at your service, sir. Anything you want, just ask.' She gave him a wink.

Good heavens. It was a long time since a barmaid had winked at Chaucer like that. He was a little disconcerted.

'That's very kind,' he said.

'I have a bed in the taproom. I lie there naked at night. I haven't had a man friend since my husband died.'

'I'm sorry to hear that. I'm sure you'll find another one.'

'Man friend or husband?'

'Whichever you're looking for.'

'I'd certainly like to find a friend,' said Kit. She winked again as she went to serve another customer.

Chaucer finished his lunch and set out to see the cathedral. It lay at the other end of Mercery Lane, not far away. He went up Burgate and in through the gate.

The cathedral was crowded with pilgrims. As always, they had gone to see the Martyrdom first, and then the shrine of St Thomas. Quite a few were crawling all the way between the two, shuffling along on their stomachs and hauling themselves up the steps to the shrine as best they could. Devout pilgrims knew no better way of demonstrating their reverence for the saint.

Chaucer didn't bother with any of that. Stepping past the people on their hands and knees, he made straight for St Thomas's shrine. A crowd was gathered around it, waiting for the signal to go forward together to present their offerings at the altar.

The ceremony was performed several times a day. Chaucer was just in time for the early afternoon show. He had only just arrived when a bell rang to alert the pilgrims that it was about to start. Everyone hurried forward to make sure that they were there in time to witness the raising of the canopy above the jewelled chest containing Becket's bones.

Two monks worked the pulley. The canopy rose and the chest was revealed in all its glory. The pilgrims gasped at the sight of all the jewels around it. There seemed to be more every year. King Louis' ruby was still the star attraction, but there were plenty of other gems as well.

Stepping forward, a priest pointed out all the more important ones with a white wand and told the audience their history. When he had finished, the pilgrims went forward with gifts of their own for St Thomas. They had all brought something with them: a brooch, a silver ring, a few coins wrapped in cloth. Most of them carried candles as well as they abased themselves before the shrine of St Thomas.

Chaucer didn't join them. He had been to the shrine before. Leaving the pilgrims to it, he went over to see the tomb of the Black Prince. Chaucer had worked for the Prince's brother earlier in his career. He was interested to see where the man was buried.

He went back to his hotel after admiring the tomb. He found Mercery Lane crowded with souvenir sellers as he returned. The lane was where they set out their stalls during business hours. They all tried to sell him something as he passed.

'Souvenir, sir? A pilgrim badge? A lapel pin? What would you like?'

'Nothing, thank you.' Chaucer despised the tourist trade in fake blood and pigs' bones alleged to be sacred relics. 'I'm not looking for a souvenir.'

'You ought to have something. I've got a nice token of St Thomas's murder. Or a phial of his blood, if you want. Whatever takes your fancy.'

'I hardly think you have any of the Martyr's blood, after all this time.'

'It has magical properties, sir. It wouldn't be St Thomas's blood if it didn't.'

'Not for me, all the same. Not unless you have a piece of the True Cross.'

Chaucer thought he was making a joke. He hadn't gone much further up the lane when running footsteps caught up with him. A shifty-looking trader appeared at his elbow.

'Are you serious?'

'What about?'

'A piece of the True Cross?'

'Good heavens. Why?'

'I could get you a piece, if you're serious.'

'A piece of the True Cross? That Our Lord died on?'

'It would only be a splinter. Pieces of the True Cross are very hard to come by. But I could get one for you, if you're serious.'

'I don't think so,' said Chaucer. 'I'll do without, thank you very much.'

He entered the inn. People were beginning to gather for the reading. The innkeeper was delighted with the turnout.

'The mayor is coming,' he told Chaucer. 'Most of the aldermen as well. All of Canterbury's best people. Everyone wants to hear you read from your books.'

The innkeeper was quite right. The room was full when Chaucer entered. Several hundred people were waiting eagerly to hear the great poet give a reading. Rapt anticipation was written all over their faces as he appeared.

He studied the audience before deciding which of his stories to give them. As usual, the gathering was composed mostly of middle-aged women whose children were off their hands at last. Without children to look after, they had nothing better to do with their time than go to their story club every week and listen to the latest tales while having a good gossip as well.

Chaucer was a prolific author. His books included *Troilus and Criseyde*, *The Book of the Duchess* and *The Parliament of Fowls*. He knew, though, that the audience at The Chequers wouldn't want to hear any of those. There was always only one book for them. It was *The Canterbury Tales* every time.

Chaucer knew exactly which tale too. *The Merchant's Tale* always went down a treat with middle-aged women. They never tired of hearing about adultery in the shrubbery.

He rose to his feet as soon as the innkeeper had finished introducing him.

'Good afternoon, Mr Mayor, ladies and gentlemen. It's wonderful to see you all and be back in Canterbury again. I'm going to begin this afternoon by reading *The Merchant's Tale* to you. I think it's a good place to start. After that, I shall be open to requests, if anybody has a particular favourite they'd like to hear.'

The women leaned forward expectantly as Chaucer began to read. He skipped the first part, knowing that they only wanted to get to the juicy bit in the story where May went behind her husband's back in the garden and succumbed to the charms of lovely Damian. A good rogering in the bushes! The women had all been there in their thoughts, if nowhere else.

There was enthusiastic applause when he had finished. The wives of Canterbury loved hearing about Damian. Chaucer read a few extracts from *The Reeve's Tale*, *The Miller's Tale*, and *The Wife of Bath* on request and then ended the reading by calling for questions from the floor.

They weren't slow in coming. 'Where d'you get your ideas from?' someone asked.

'If I knew the answer to that, I'd go there more often.' Chaucer always got a laugh with that. 'The ancients are a good source, and the French. And the Italians. I usually just start writing though and hope that something will come to me.'

'What are you working on now?'

'More of the same. I have a lot more to do before I've finished. I just hope I manage to get it all done in time.'

'Are you looking for ideas?' This came from a man at the back, a lugubrious-looking fellow with a long nose.

'I'm always open to suggestions. I get my inspiration wherever I can find it.'

The meeting broke up after the questions were over. Most people went home after shaking Chaucer's hand and congratulating him on his work, but quite a few stayed behind for a post-mortem at the bar. Chaucer was surrounded by admirers as they sat down and gave their orders.

'What d'you fancy, sir?' Kit the barmaid leaned over Chaucer. She had an ample bosom in a low-cut dress. She gave him another twinkle. 'You can have anything you like.'

Gracious. Chaucer had been celibate since his wife died. He led the sad, lonely life of a writer, squeezing out agonising couplets by candlelight while everyone else was in the tavern. And now here was this woman, waggling a couplet of her own at him. One of the perks of fame, he supposed.

'A jug of wine, please. Whatever you've got.'

Chaucer tried not to think of her as she went to fetch the drink. His attention was diverted by a tourist couple who had been at the reading. They were showing off their latest purchase, a souvenir that they had bought in Mercery Lane. If Chaucer had heard aright, the man was retired from the haulage business and was doing the sights with his wife now that they had plenty time on their hands.

'Here it is.' The man unwrapped a small piece of wood. 'I can't believe we've got this. It's from St Peter.'

'What is it?'

'It's from his boat. St Peter's fishing boat. The Sea of Galilee.'

'From St Peter's fishing boat?'

'The very one. From his fishing days. This bit of wood was probably touched by Our Lord more than a thousand years ago.'

The silence that followed was awestruck.

'Was it expensive?' Chaucer asked.

'I'll say.' The haulier was smug. 'Cost me a small fortune. Worth it, though. No one else has anything like this where we live.'

'I know exactly where I'm going to put it when we get home,' said his wife happily.

Kit arrived with the drinks. The gathering broke into groups. The lugubrious man from the reading came to sit next to Chaucer.

'I've got an idea for one of your stories,' he told him.

'Yes?'

'You'll love it. It's really good.'

Chaucer listened patiently as the man told him his idea. It was a riff on *The Miller's Tale*, not at all suitable for a family audience. It wasn't funny either, despite the man's repeated assertions to the contrary. Chaucer was glad when the story came to an end.

'That's very interesting,' he said. 'I'll have to give it some thought.'

'You should. I really think you could make something of it, with your talent.'

They sipped their drinks. The man drew closer.

'I saw you talking to Kit Beryn earlier,' he said.

'Is that her name?'

'It is. I wouldn't go there, if I was you.'

It was on the tip of Chaucer's tongue to deny any such intention, but curiosity got the better of him.

'Why ever not?'

'She's not a good woman. She isn't what she seems.'

'No?'

'She'll rob you, if she can. She just wants to take your cash without doing the business, if you know what I mean.'

'How d'you know?' Chaucer was disappointed to hear it.

'I'm a pardoner.' The man spoke in confidence. 'It's not much of a living, but I make a reasonable wage. I got fed up with the way they serve the food in here. The gentry are always served first, before anyone else. I hadn't had anything to eat and I hadn't had a drink either, because I was on my way to St Thomas's shrine. You're supposed to abstain from drink before you pray at the shrine.'

'Yes, I know.'

'Anyway, I was fed up, so I went to talk to Kit. She told me in confidence that she lay naked in bed at night and hadn't had a lover since her husband died.'

'Goodness.'

'So I went with everyone else to St Thomas's shrine. Stole a souvenir from Mercery Lane on the way back to the hotel. Then we all had a big party, everyone in our group. Plenty of beer and wine, now that we didn't have to fast anymore.'

'I can imagine.'

'The others all went out on the town afterwards, but I stayed behind. I wanted to sleep with Kit. I'd given her some money to buy a goose first, so we could have a good meal before we went to bed.'

'And?' Chaucer wasn't sure if he wanted to hear the rest of this.

'Well, I'll tell you. The woman wasn't alone when I arrived. She was in bed with someone else.'

'No!'

'Yes. She wasn't in the least bit embarrassed. She had a lover all along. They'd eaten my goose.'

'What happened then?'

'I hit the bloke on the nose with a frying pan. Really made his eyes water. Next thing I know, he's running down the corridor yelling "Stop, thief" at the top of his voice, trying to pretend that I was a burglar. Of course everyone came out of their rooms when they heard that.'

'What did you do?'

'What could I do? I had to make myself scarce. I tried to get back to my room, but the guard dog wouldn't let me past. Great big ferocious animal standing there, growling at me and snarling. There was no way I could get round the brute, so I ended up spending the rest of the night in its basket while it lay on my bed, comfortable as anything.'

'Oh dear.' Chaucer tried to keep a straight face. 'That's awful.'

'Yes, it was. And all because of Kit Beryn. None of it would have happened if it hadn't been for her.'

'So Kit was the cause of all the trouble?'

'Indeed, she was. The harlot of Mercery Lane. I'd steer well clear of her, if I was you, Mr Chaucer.'

'It's quite a funny story, though.'

'I suppose so,' conceded the pardoner. 'Perhaps you could use it in one of your prologues.'

'It's certainly an idea,' agreed Chaucer. 'I'm not sure I'm the right one to do it, though.'

Chapter Eight

Henry V Gives Thanks for Agincourt

Near the little castle of Azincourt, in northern France, a dreadful battle was raging. A ragged army of Englishmen – tired, dispirited, half-starved and riddled with dysentery – had been making its way back to Calais and safety, when its path was blocked by a much larger French force bent on its destruction. The battle was fought on 25 October 1415 and the slaughter was prodigious.

The fighting did not follow the usual course. It was a well-known military maxim that the army that made the first move in a battle always lost. The army that simply stood its ground always won.

The two sides accordingly faced each other across a field for three hours on the morning of the 25th, St Crispin's Day, without anybody moving. The standoff continued until the French commanders grew bored at length and began to fidget. With nothing else to do, they drifted off to talk to each other or see to the horses. Their troops began to relax as well. It was then that King Henry V of England decided to rewrite the rulebook.

Henry knew that his men would crack if they had to stand there much longer. Something would have to be done soon, even if it meant making the first move. Summoning his chaplains, he asked them to give the army their blessing before it went into battle.

'We're going to attack in a minute,' he told the priests. 'We want you to say a prayer for us first.'

The holy men crossed themselves at once and obliged.

'Remember us, O Lord,' implored one of them. 'Our enemies are gathered together and boast themselves in their excellence. Destroy their strength and scatter them. Have compassion upon us, and upon the crown of England.'

When the priests had finished, every man in the army fell to his knees and kissed the ground in front of him before symbolically placing a piece of earth in his mouth. Then they all picked up their weapons and followed the King towards the French.

If the soldiers had any qualms about making the first move in the battle, they kept their doubts to themselves as they went forward. They were all keen to get on with it, the archers in particular. Henry had told them quite untruthfully that the French were going to cut two fingers off their archery hands so that they could never draw a bow again. The archers weren't having that.

The English came to a stop within arrowshot of the French front line. There was a wood on either side of them now, so they couldn't be attacked from the flank. The newly-ploughed ground in front of them was ankle-deep in mud and surface water, very difficult for a cavalry charge. Henry knew that because he had sent scouts out before dawn to examine it.

The French army in front of them looked even more daunting as they came up to it. The French were much better fed, superbly equipped, armed to the teeth with swords, lances, crossbows, guns, catapults and all the engines of war. The English knew they were a sorry sight by comparison.

But the field was narrow and the ground soggy. The French cavalry struggled as the English archers let fly. There was terrible slaughter as horses and riders fell in every direction.

In the hand-to-hand fighting that followed, King Henry lost a fleur-de-lis from his crown, knocked off by a Burgundian taking a swipe at him. The fighting continued at close quarters for three dreadful hours. The English had taken so many prisoners by the end that the captured French among their ranks became a threat to their security.

'We'll have to kill them,' Henry decided. 'We can't have them running loose behind our lines.'

'The men won't like it, sire.' It was against the laws of chivalry to kill prisoners, especially if they were rich. The Frenchmen had been captured because they had money and could be ransomed for a small fortune.

'I don't care. They're too dangerous. They'll have to be killed. All except the very important ones.'

'As you wish, sire.'

'Do it now. Before they turn on us. Don't waste any time.'

The order was given and the deed was done.

'Sorry, mate.' An archer sitting on a Frenchman in a suit of armour drew a dagger and slit the man's throat. Others used heavy wooden mallets to club their prisoners to death. Before long, the French all lay dead and no longer posed any threat to the English.

Henry's men were so busy dispatching their prisoners that they couldn't spare anybody to protect their baggage train behind the army. While their backs were turned, the wagons were being attacked and looted by French marauders who had been eyeing the baggage train for hours from a safe distance. The robbers waited until the English were fully occupied elsewhere before stealing all King Henry's jewels, his piece of the True Cross and a lot else besides before making off with their booty.

The French army admitted defeat soon afterwards. Those who could, ran away. The rest awaited their fate at the hands of the English. It seemed to an exhausted King Henry V, as he surveyed all the bodies on the field, that he had comprehensively won his trial by battle, so establishing in the eyes of God that his cause was just. He summoned the English and French heralds to get their opinion.

The heralds were impartial observers, like judges at Wimbledon, who had watched the battle from the stands. Much against their inclination, the French heralds were forced to agree with the English that Henry had indeed gained the day. He had won the battle and the victory was his. It would be named after that little castle in the distance.

'Thank the Lord for that,' said Henry. 'I shall give thanks when we get home. The Lord has been wonderfully kind to us this day.'

It was a sensational victory. Half the chivalry of France, effectively the government of the country, lay dead on the battlefield. Despite the odds, the English had achieved a mighty success against their longest and most implacable of national opponents.

They had taken some very important prisoners too. Charles, Duke of Orléans, had escaped the slaughter by lying unnoticed under a heap of bodies as the fighting swirled around him. Clad in heavy armour, the twenty-year-old was unable to stand up without help. The English hauled him upright after the battle and took him to King Henry.

Charles was important because he was the leader of the Armagnacs in France. He was also one of the heirs to the French throne. Henry was very glad to have him captive.

'Welcome, cousin. I'm sorry the battle didn't go your way today.'

'Alas, God chose not to smile on France this time.'

'It's His judgment on your army, I'm afraid. Your people have been too proud and arrogant. Your soldiers have robbed churches, raped women and stolen from the countryside. You can't expect any help from God, if you behave like that.'

'What will happen to me now?'

'England, I fear. You will be our prisoner.'

'Will I be ransomed?'

'We must wait and see. I may have to keep you hostage, if you're in line for the throne.'

It was beginning to get dark as they spoke. Too late in the day for Henry's exhausted troops to go anywhere. Henry gave the order for them to make camp where they were, right in the middle of the battlefield, and settle down for the night. They were only too happy to obey.

They resumed the march to Calais next morning. There was a renewed spring in their step as they went. The men had all had a good feed before they set out, tucking into French army rations and keeping more food for later. They marched to Calais in battle order, but they were no longer expecting to be attacked. Henry allowed them to march without their heavy coats of arms, although they were told to remain on their guard at all times.

His army reached Calais in three days. Food, beer and medicine awaited them, sent over in advance from London. Henry spent the next fortnight organising ransoms and exchanges of prisoners before ordering his army back to England. It wasn't until the middle of November that the first of the victorious troops began to return across the Channel.

Henry himself returned to Dover on 16 November in the middle of a dreadful snowstorm. He was greeted by a reception committee of Cinque Port barons who waded into the freezing water to carry him ashore shoulder high.

Henry spent the night in Dover, allowing his companions time to recover from the sea sickness that they had all suffered during the crossing. He set off next morning for Canterbury, taking his prisoner Charles d'Orléans with him. The two men rode side by side for the fifteen-mile journey.

'We'll stay the night in Canterbury,' Henry told the young duke as they set out. 'There's plenty of time to get to London. I want to give thanks at the shrine of St Thomas first.'

A huge turnout awaited them along the road. Everyone in Kent had heard the wonderful news about Agincourt. Thousands of excited people hurried to the roadside to make sure of catching a glimpse of the victor as the great King Henry passed by.

At Barham Downs, a few miles short of Canterbury, the Cinque Port men-at-arms were drawn up beside the road to welcome the conquering hero. Barham was the traditional place for Kentish soldiers to greet a monarch returning from abroad. The men bristled with weapons as they prepared to give Henry a royal salute. They alarmed the Duke of Orléans when he spotted them.

'Are we about to go to war again?' he asked, only half-joking.

'Relax,' Henry told him. 'These are the children of my country. They've only come to welcome me home.'

The crowds grew even larger as they approached Canterbury. Henry and his retinue were joined by a mounted escort of local men for the last stretch. They were applauded all the way to the city gates, where Henry Chichele, Archbishop of Canterbury, was waiting with a cluster of dignitaries to welcome the King to their city.

The streets were full of cheering people as he made his way in procession to the cathedral. He was accompanied by hundreds of the nobles, knights, esquires, archers and pikemen who had fought alongside him at Agincourt. The fighting men all dumped their weapons in a great pile when they reached the gate and then followed their leader into the cathedral.

Henry was the picture of humility as they entered. He knew that he owed his miraculous victory against the odds to God, rather than his own military skills. If he was a great commander now, fit to be mentioned in the same breath as Richard the Lionheart, Edward I and the Black Prince, it was the Lord's doing, not his. Henry was suitably grateful as he prayed to St Thomas and made his offering at the shrine.

He went to see the Black Prince's tomb after the mass was over. That extraordinary young man had defeated a much larger French army at Crecy and Poitiers, just as Henry had at Agincourt. He spent some time in reflection at his great-uncle's tomb before turning to the Archbishop at length.

'And now for my father,' he told him.

The most important tomb had been left until last. Henry's father had been buried in the cathedral two years earlier. His tomb lay close to St Thomas's, just across the way from the Black Prince.

Henry IV had been expecting to die in Jerusalem, according to an ancient prophecy. He had fulfilled the prophecy by expiring in the Jerusalem Chamber at Westminster Abbey, rather than on a crusade, as he had imagined. His body had then been taken to Canterbury for burial.

The journey had been by water, rather than land. There had long been a rumour that the body had got no further than the river Thames before being thrown overboard in the middle of a storm. According to gossip, the boat had continued its journey to Kent when the weather improved. An empty coffin had then been given a ceremonious burial in the cathedral.

There was no truth in the story, although quite a few people had believed it for a while. Henry V paid it no mind as he knelt beside his father's tomb. He prayed in silence for a time, shielded from the throng by his people. When he had finished, he rose again and rejoined the Archbishop.

'All done, my Lord?' the Archbishop asked.

'I think so.' Henry nodded. 'It's been good to spend some time at my father's grave. I'm very glad I've been able to do that.'

The whole congregation rose to its feet as Henry left the cathedral. The archers and pikemen in the nave all bowed in respect as he passed. He was followed by the Archbishop, the other priests, the nobles and a long procession of knights and esquires as they formed up behind him and emerged triumphantly into the open air.

An admiring crowd was waiting to greet them. Trumpets sounded and Bell Harry rang out in celebration as King Henry appeared. The people of Canterbury gave him a loud roar of appreciation and prolonged applause as he returned to the cathedral gate. Henry V was king of England, monarch of them all, the greatest military commander of the age. They were determined to give him a time in their city that he would never forget.

The celebrations continued for the rest of the day. When all was done, Henry and his companions retired exhausted to St Augustine's abbey to stay the night before continuing to London next morning. They were in no hurry to reach the capital. The people of London needed time to complete the arrangements for a royal reception, now that they knew for certain that the King was coming.

The crowds were out again next morning to watch Henry depart. A long column of men-at-arms stood waiting outside the abbey's Fyndon Gate to escort him in style to London. Henry looked every inch a conquering hero as he emerged from the gate mounted on a fine steed and accompanied by the Duke of Orléans and his standard bearer. When all was ready, he raised his right hand and turned to look at the rest of his horsemen.

I see you stand like greyhounds in the slips,
Straining upon the start. The game's afoot:
Follow your spirit; and upon this charge
Cry 'God for Harry! England and Saint George!'

Unfortunately, the dramatist to turn Henry's fine thoughts into words had yet to appear. The command he actually gave his men at the Fyndon Gate was far more prosaic.

'Fellers,' he told them. 'Let's go.' It was the same order he had given at Agincourt.

Chapter Nine

Edward IV and the Wars of the Roses

Waddington Hall was a very good place to hide for a while. Just south of the Forest of Bowland, in the wildest part of Lancashire, the farmhouse lay well off the beaten track, hardly visited by anybody from one month to the next. A man with a price on his head could lie low there for years without the outside world ever knowing anything about it.

One day in July 1465, the occupants were enjoying a quiet dinner when they received a rude surprise. Armed men appeared at the door, demanding to be let in. The men were looking for a well-known fugitive. They had reason to believe that he was one of the people sitting down to dinner.

They were correct. The man they wanted was there, all right. He jumped up at once, terrified that he was going to be captured at long last.

'Quick!' One of his companions ushered him to the stairs. 'Up to your room. Out the window. We'll hold them off while you get away.'

The man did as he was told. It was a mile across the fields to the river Ribble. If he could get across the stepping stones before his pursuers caught up with him, he might just lose them in the woods the other side.

It was a forlorn hope. The man's pursuers were relentless. They caught up with him at the river and took him prisoner before he had a chance to vanish into the forest. He cut a pathetic figure as he struggled to regain his breath.

'Who are you?' they demanded, when he was able to talk.

'I'm a monk. Just a simple man of God. Why are you chasing me?'

'You're no monk. Who are you really?'

The man tried to bluff it out, but he soon saw that it was hopeless. His captors knew perfectly well who he was. He couldn't pretend otherwise.

'I am King Henry VI of England,' he conceded defiantly. 'The son of King

Henry V. I am the rightful ruler of this realm. I am your lord and sovereign.'

His captors weren't impressed. The country had a new sovereign now. King Edward IV of York had held the throne for the past four years, ever since the defeat of Henry's Lancastrians at the battle of Towton. One side in the civil war favoured a red rose as its emblem, the other white. The struggle for supremacy between the two cousins had been going on ever since the first bout of Henry VI's mental illness more than ten years earlier.

'Where are you taking me?' he demanded, as he was led away.

'That'll be for others to decide. London, probably. We're not going to kill you, if that's what you're wondering.'

It was splendid news that they had managed to track him down at last. Henry had been missing for the past twelve months, his whereabouts completely unknown. He had disappeared from public view after the battle of Hexham, wandering in disguise from place to place in the north of England while people loyal to his cause took it in turns to give him food and shelter. But the Yorkists had him now.

'We must tell King Edward,' one of them said. 'He'll want to know at once. Where is the King?'

'Down south somewhere. We'll have to get a message to him.'

A monk was appointed to the task. He was given a letter containing all the details of Henry VI's capture and told to take it straight to the King. On no account was he to give it to anyone else. He was to hand it to King Edward IV in person.

The monk set off. Several days of hard riding brought him to London. He made inquiries and was told that the King was in Canterbury with his new Queen. The monk went that way immediately, carrying the precious letter with him.

King Edward had arrived in Canterbury on 13 July, the same day as Henry VI was captured in Lancashire. He had his wife with him, Elizabeth Woodville, the woman he had recently married in great secrecy, to many people's annoyance. She had been crowned Queen by the Archbishop of Canterbury only six weeks previously.

The cathedral monks were curious to see the new Queen when she arrived. They had heard that Elizabeth Woodville was very beautiful, so good-looking that she had King Edward firmly under her thumb. The monks reasoned that she must be quite a woman to be able to do that. King Edward was no stranger to the ladies.

Queen Elizabeth was indeed a great beauty. A little past her best, but still a magnificent woman. The monks could quite see why the King was so taken with her, even though no one liked her much, or her grasping family.

The royal couple were in Canterbury for a visit to St Thomas's shrine. They were planning to stay for at least a week. They had been there for several days when the monk arrived from Lancashire. He told the King's people the reason for his visit and insisted that he would speak to no one but the monarch himself.

The monk was ushered into the royal presence. Dropping to one knee, he gave his letter to King Edward.

'Wonderful news, sire. I think you should read it.'

The King did. The news was wonderful indeed. His rival for the throne had been captured at last, after more than twelve months on the run. Henry was being taken even then to London for incarceration in the Tower.

'Who else knows about this?' Edward demanded.

'No one, sire. I haven't told a soul.'

'Keep it that way. I want it to be a secret for the moment. I'll see that you're rewarded.'

The monk nodded and withdrew. Edward could hardly contain himself as the man left. He would be much more secure on the throne if he had poor, sick Henry under lock and key. The house of Lancaster would have no one to rally to if Henry was permanently out of circulation.

It was almost time for mass. Edward quickly summoned the Archbishop and told him what had happened. They agreed that the news should be made public at once. The best way to do it would be to announce it from the pulpit, during the sermon.

The announcement was duly made. King Edward and Elizabeth Woodville were sitting in the choir to hear it. An audible ripple of excitement ran through the congregation as the implications sank in. King Henry a prisoner! It would surely mean the end of the war, if King Henry had been captured at last.

The monks of Canterbury cathedral hated the civil war. Red rose, white rose, what did it matter to them? They had done their best to keep the fighting out of the precincts, but they hadn't always succeeded. Both houses, York and Lancaster, wanted St Thomas on their side for the struggle. Both houses had presented jewels to his shrine to curry favour with the saint.

King Henry VI himself had been to the shrine before his overthrow. So had the Earl of Warwick, the one they called the king maker. And so had King Edward's brother Richard, the Duke of Gloucester.

The monks all remembered the King's brother. Such a contrast between the two of them. Edward was tall, handsome and commanding, an obvious leader of men. Richard was puny, physically handicapped by scoliosis of the spine. A hunchbacked little man, but a brave fighter, by all accounts.

The mass came to an end. The congregation was still buzzing with the news of Henry's capture as everyone filed out of the cathedral. All eyes were on King Edward as he emerged after the service. He was a lot safer on the throne, now that his cousin had been taken prisoner.

'What are you going to do with Henry?' his wife asked, as soon as they were alone.

'I'll keep him prisoner in the Tower for the moment. He'll be well looked after.'

'Aren't you going to kill him?'

'Not for now. There's no point.'

'Why not?'

'He's much more use alive. I can keep him as a hostage.'

'You should kill him now. Cut his head off before the Lancastrians rescue him.'

'No.' Edward shook his head. 'I'm not going to do that. Not while his son's alive.' King Henry's son and heir was safe in France with his mother, well beyond Edward's reach. 'The Lancastrians would only rally to the boy if the father was murdered.'

'So you're just going to keep Henry prisoner in the Tower?'

'For the moment. For as long as his son is still alive.'

'I think you should kill him. Do it now, while you have the chance.'

'Why?' Edward was puzzled. 'We have Henry safe as a prisoner. He can't do any harm in the Tower. Why are you so keen to see him dead?'

'You really want to know?'

'Yes, I do.'

'I'll tell you, then.' Queen Elizabeth Woodville slipped an arm through her new husband's. 'I'm pregnant, that's why. You're going to have an heir in a few months' time. The child will succeed you on the throne one day, just so long as there are no rivals around to dispute it.'

Chapter Ten

Henry VIII and the Boleyn Girl

For more than four weeks now, the Holy Roman Emperor had been stranded in the Spanish port of Corunna, waiting for a fair wind to England. Charles V was due to arrive at Sandwich on 15 May 1520 for a long-planned meeting with Henry VIII, but the weather stubbornly refused to shift. If it didn't change soon, the meeting would have to be abandoned and his chances of disrupting the alliance between England and France might be lost.

As Holy Roman Emperor, Charles was the successor to Charlemagne. He was King of Germany, Italy and Spain, Duke of Burgundy, Archduke of Austria and Lord of the Netherlands. Charles was the most powerful man in Europe after the Pope. But he wanted to destroy England's already shaky alliance with France for political reasons of his own.

The weather turned at last. The sails of the Emperor's ships were spotted off Dover on the evening of 26 May. Rather than continue to Sandwich, as originally planned, the Emperor headed straight in to Dover to make land as soon as possible.

It was a momentous occasion. No Holy Roman Emperor had ever set foot in England before. Cardinal Wolsey had been sent to Dover to greet him on behalf of the King. The Cardinal arranged to be rowed out from the harbour as the Emperor's ships lay becalmed just outside the port.

'Send a message to the King,' he told an aide, before he set out. 'You'll find him in Canterbury. Tell him the Emperor has arrived. We'll put him up at the castle tonight and take care of him until His Majesty gets here.'

Henry VIII hurried to Dover as soon as he got the message. His formal introduction to the Holy Roman Emperor took place at the castle next morning. The Emperor came down the staircase to greet his host and the two monarchs

73

exchanged courtesies while their staff looked on discreetly. They were all relieved that the Emperor had arrived in time to catch Henry while he was still in Kent.

It was a family occasion, as much as anything else. Henry's wife, Queen Catherine of Aragon, was the Emperor's aunt, the sister of his mother. The Emperor was looking forward to meeting her for the first time.

'The Queen is expecting you at Canterbury,' Henry told him warmly. 'She's looking forward to it too. We've got all sorts of entertainments lined up for you, now that you're here at last.'

A long cavalcade took the Canterbury road. The Holy Roman Emperor never went anywhere without a large retinue. He had brought hundreds of people with him from Spain, including two hundred Spanish ladies dressed in the latest Spanish fashions. They all joined the procession and settled down for the journey to the cathedral city.

The people of Canterbury watched with approval as Henry and his famous companion made their way to the cathedral. Cardinal Wolsey rode behind the two monarchs as they went in through the new Christ Church gate. The great stone archway had recently been built to allow a proper wheeled entrance into the cathedral precincts.

The new gate was further along the street from the old one. It had a postern for pedestrians beside the main carriage gate, two brick storeys above, and twin towers on either side that made it look like a giant H for Henry. The eighth monarch of that name was rather proud of it.

'Took years to build,' he told the Emperor. 'They're still putting the finishing touches to it at the top. It's very solid, though. Going to last a long time, this gate.'

They went into the precincts. The Archbishop welcomed them at the west door of the cathedral and escorted them inside. Their swords of state were carried solemnly in front of them amid a sprinkling of incense and holy water as they walked in procession up the nave for Whitsun mass in the choir.

After the service, the Archbishop took them to the Martyrdom, where Henry and his guest knelt down to pray at the site of St Thomas's murder. Then they straightened up and went to see the saint's shrine beyond the high altar.

Monks stood ready to show them St Thomas's hair shirt, his broken skull and other holy relics. King Henry and the Emperor Charles kissed each item in turn, as was expected of them. When they had finished, Henry pointed out all the jewels at the shrine, in particular the Régale de France, which had pride of place at the right of the altar.

'A gift from the French king of the time,' he told the Emperor. 'Magnificent, isn't it?'

'It certainly is.' The Emperor was impressed. 'I've never seen anything like it.'

'Neither have I. St Thomas is very lucky to have a ruby like that.'

The Archbishop's palace lay beside the west door of the cathedral, where they had come in. Queen Catherine was waiting there to meet her nephew after they had finished in church. The Archbishop led the way as they retraced their steps down the nave and went outside again. The door of the palace stood open to receive them.

The porch was lined with good-looking ladies from the English court. Among them was Mary Boleyn, the Queen's newly appointed maid-of-honour. The young woman was a highly decorative addition to the Queen's household, in King Henry's opinion. He gave her the suspicion of a wink as he escorted his guest into the palace.

The women all smiled and curtseyed as the Emperor passed. Inside, twenty young pages in gold brocade and crimson satin lined a long corridor leading to a marble staircase at the end. Queen Catherine stood at the top of the stairs, waiting to meet her nephew.

She wore pearls and a robe of gold cloth lined with ermine. She was all smiles as the Emperor came up the stairs to embrace her. Queen Catherine of Aragon was famous in England for her charm and sweet nature. Her nephew took to her at once.

There were tears as well as smiles as they went in to lunch. Catherine was an emotional woman. Without a son of her own, she was delighted to have such an impressive nephew coming to visit her. She only wished that her own child had been born a boy that her husband could cherish, instead of a daughter.

The lunch was private for the family, a chance for the Emperor and his hosts to get to know each other. King Henry threw a more public party for him that night, a splendid banquet at the palace with music and dancing that lasted until dawn. The arrangements had been supervised by Thomas More, the King's secretary.

'Put on a big splash,' Henry told his wife, as she decided which pearls and diamonds to wear for the occasion. 'Your nephew will expect the best. We want him to know that we favour him over every other monarch in Europe.'

'As you wish, my lord.' Catherine wore her grandest jewels and most sumptuous gown for the party. She sat with her nephew after the banquet, watching from the sidelines as everyone else took to the dance floor. One of the Spanish guests, a nobleman with a taste for the theatrical, became so smitten with the Englishwoman he was dancing with that he pretended to faint for love and had to be carried out of the room by his arms and legs.

King Henry was less smitten with the Spanish ladies, who weren't very pretty. They certainly couldn't compare with Mary Boleyn, batting her eyelashes at him from across the room. Henry plunged in nevertheless and joined the dancing with the rest. It was already getting light as the party broke up at last and they all went to bed.

There were more revels next day. It wasn't until the Tuesday afternoon that the two monarchs got together at the palace to discuss the reason for the Emperor's visit. He wanted England on his side in the coming war between France and the Holy Roman Empire.

'You should join forces with the empire,' he told Henry. 'You don't want to be an ally of the French. England would be much better off with us.'

'I'm not so sure.' Henry was non-committal. 'I think we'd be wiser to remain neutral, if there's going to be a war.'

'England and France aren't natural allies. When have your two realms ever been on the same side in a war?'

But Henry was not to be moved. He was on his way to France for a meeting with the French king. He wasn't going to commit his country to anything until he had heard both sides of the argument.

'I leave England in a couple of days,' he told the Emperor. 'I'm going to meet the French king in a field.'

'A field?'

'Somewhere near Calais. They're already putting the tents up for it. Using a lot of cloth of gold, from what Cardinal Wolsey tells me.'

Wolsey was the man for the Emperor to talk to, if he wanted to win Henry round. The sly cardinal was the power behind the throne, the man responsible for all of Henry's best ideas. The Emperor decided to have a word with him in private, as soon as he got the chance. Wolsey would see the advantages of an alliance with the empire, even if Henry couldn't.

The Emperor's chance came as he was leaving for Sandwich at the end of his visit. His ships were waiting there to take him to the Netherlands. Wolsey was to accompany him to the port and see him off. They would be able to talk in private on the road.

The Emperor said goodbye to his aunt before leaving. Queen Catherine was very sorry to see him go. So was King Henry, in his way. He accompanied the Emperor for the first five miles along the Sandwich road before turning off towards Dover, where he himself was going.

'We'll meet again,' Henry told him, as they parted at the turning. 'After I've talked to the French king, I'll come and see you in Flanders and tell you all about it. Or you can meet me in Calais, whichever you prefer.'

'I shall look forward to it,' said the Emperor.

He continued towards Sandwich, while Henry took the Dover road. The King was barely out of sight before Cardinal Wolsey was summoned forward to ride beside the Emperor. Spurring his horse, Wolsey did as he was told.

The Cardinal was a biddable man, said to be in the pay of the French. It was rumoured that he had been heavily bribed by the French king to make Henry do whatever France wanted. But two could play at that game. The Emperor had a proposal to put to the King of England's chief adviser.

'Well now, Cardinal. I've been thinking.'

'Yes, my lord?'

'You have been a good servant to your king these past few years. A good servant to the Church as well. On behalf of the Holy Roman Empire therefore, and after the good time I had in Canterbury, I think we ought to do something for you as a token of our appreciation.'

'That's very nice of you.' Wolsey wondered what was coming.

'The bishopric at Badajoz is vacant at the moment. There's an interest in the Palencia diocese coming up as well. I wonder if you'd be interested in them?'

'In Spain?'

'There are no actual duties. You don't have to go there. But there's a very good annual pension.'

'How much?'

'Five thousand ducats for Badajoz, two for Palencia. As a token of our appreciation for all your good work.'

Seven thousand ducats a year. Wolsey was impressed. 'And I don't have to do anything for it?' he asked.

The Emperor shook his head. 'It's a reward for everything you've done in the past.'

'Well, thank you very much. I'm delighted to accept.'

'There's something else we need to discuss as well.' The Emperor had saved the best for last. 'It's about the Pope.'

'Yes?'

'Leo can't last for ever. There'll be a vacancy when he dies.'

'Yes?' Wolsey's ears pricked up.

'The cardinals will have to choose a new Holy Father when the time comes. It'll be decided by a majority vote.'

Wolsey was aware of it.

'There are fourteen cardinals in the Holy Roman Empire,' the emperor told him. 'That's a substantial number, quite enough to swing the vote. I think the empire's cardinals could all be persuaded to elect you as the next Pope, if I asked them to.'

'Me?'

'If I asked them to.'

'As the next Pope?'

'You're a good man, Wolsey. We need someone we can trust in Rome.'

Wolsey didn't know what to say. He was an ambitious man, but he hadn't been expecting this.

'I think we understand each other,' the Emperor told him. 'You look after our interests with uncle Henry and we'll look after yours in Rome. It's time the English had another Pope.'

They rode on to Sandwich. On the other road, Henry continued towards Dover. He and Queen Catherine were due to sail from there to Calais for their summit conference with the French king.

It was going to be a magnificent occasion, something to be remembered for years to come. Henry was taking more than five thousand people to the field of cloth of gold with him, and half as many horses. Those who weren't already in France all had to be ferried across the Channel and brought safely in to Calais. It was no mean undertaking, even in good weather.

The preparations for departure were well under way as Henry arrived at the castle. The harbour was packed with shipping and the town was full of people waiting to accompany him to France. The *Great Harry*, his thousand-ton flagship, was magnificently fitted out with guns and cloth of gold sails for the voyage. The French had nothing like it in their navy.

Henry stayed the night at the castle with Queen Catherine. He was hardly up next morning when Thomas More popped his head in.

'The Cardinal is back. He's just got in from Sandwich.'

Cardinal Wolsey had ridden to Dover after seeing the Emperor off to the Netherlands. He reported to the King at once.

'All went well,' he told his monarch. 'The Emperor is looking forward to meeting you again in July. He was very pleased with his visit to Canterbury.'

'So he should be, after all the effort we put in.'

'We had an interesting talk on the way to Sandwich. I think we should work very closely with the Emperor in the future.'

'I thought you wanted to work with the French?'

'Them as well. But we must be careful never to do anything that might alienate the Emperor or his interests.'

'I'm surprised at you, Wolsey. You've always been very keen on the French.'

'Have I?'

'You certainly have. You're probably the only man in England who thinks an alliance with France is a good idea.'

'Oh well. We all make mistakes. I think we should be good friends with the Emperor from now on.'

Chapter Eleven

The Looting of Thomas Becket's Shrine

The break with Rome had come, and now the cathedral faced further indignity. By order of King Henry VIII, men were on their way to Canterbury to destroy the shrine of St Thomas and scatter it to the winds. One of the holiest sites in Christendom was about to come to an abrupt and very distressing end.

The warning signs had been there for some time. The national mood was changing under King Henry. Plenty of people still believed in the old religious ways and remained faithful to them. Others deplored the worship of statues, the purchase of fake relics and the sale of bogus pardons. They argued that what had once been honest piety was now simply a money-making racket for the church.

King Henry's men arrived in September 1538. They were led by Dr Richard Layton, a priest and lawyer. Layton was one of the Royal Commissioners for the Destruction of Shrines.

'Straight to the cathedral,' he told his men, as they arrived. 'You'll find St Thomas's shrine behind the altar. Go there at once, before the monks know what's happening, and put it under guard. Don't let anybody stand in your way.'

Layton was a determined man. He had worked for Cardinal Wolsey at the beginning of his career, and later for Thomas Cromwell. He had been a relentless inquisitor at the trials of Anne Boleyn and Sir Thomas More. He was making a good living out of destroying the country's shrines. Layton always made sure he got his cut before the rest of the valuables were taken to the Tower of London for safekeeping.

His men headed for the cathedral. The building had changed in recent years. It had a new central tower now, constructed to house the cathedral bells. Bell Harry stood an astonishing 250 feet tall and loomed majestically over the city.

It was an extraordinary sight in the sunlight, but wasted on Layton's men as they pushed into the cathedral and proceeded at once to St Thomas's shrine.

No one dared to stop them. Against the rules, Layton's men had brought their weapons with them into the cathedral. The monks could only watch helplessly as a force of armed men climbed the steps from the nave and hurried past the altar towards the shrine at the east end of the cathedral.

'There it is,' one of them yelled. 'There's St Thomas's tomb. That's where the traitor lies.'

The men quickly surrounded it. The monks on duty fled. So did the pilgrims who had been patiently awaiting their turn with the saint. Nobody offered any resistance as Layton's men shoved them aside and seized control of the shrine.

St Thomas's tomb was still the most extraordinary sight in the cathedral. A golden angel now pointed dramatically towards the Régale de France, Louis VII's great ruby. The innumerable pearls, diamonds, sapphires, emeralds and amethysts surrounding the great jewel were as lustrous as ever.

The gold at the tomb weighed 4,999 ¾ ounces, according to the weigh book. The gilt weighed almost as much and the plain silver far more. St Thomas's was easily the most opulent shrine in the kingdom.

The holy relics had multiplied as well. There were more than four hundred sacred relics now, everything from skulls, jaws, teeth, hands, fingers and old bones to an arm of St George, still with the flesh on it, that was available for pilgrims to kiss, if they could afford it. There were filthy old bits of rag that might once have belonged to a saint and phials of St Thomas's blood that looked suspiciously like red ochre mixed with water. Dr Layton and his fellow Royal Commissioners had no compunction in shutting the whole circus down at once.

'Tear it all to bits,' Layton ordered. 'Everything. All the relics. I want to see the whole lot broken up and destroyed before we've finished.'

'Even St Thomas's bones?'

'Especially his bones. Pile them up with everything else. We'll make a bonfire of the lot, right next to the tomb.'

'They'll call it sacrilege in Rome.'

'They can call it what they want. We're not answerable to the Pope anymore. We have our own church now.'

Layton's men went to work. If any of them remained Roman Catholic in their hearts, they showed no sign of it as they began to dismantle the shrine. Pikemen stood guard as the rest wielded their tools. Their first task was to disconnect the iron chest containing Becket's bones and take it down from the top of the shrine.

It took them a considerable time to lever the chest out of its compartment. The chest was carefully handed down to the people waiting below. Several men struggled under its weight as they carried the saint's jewel-encrusted coffin away from the shrine and laid it down on the flagstones nearby. Layton's goldsmith was waiting for it.

'Get the jewels out first,' Layton told him. 'Prise them all out of their settings. Once you've done that, we can break the coffin open and see what's inside.'

The goldsmith nodded. Kneeling down beside the chest, he started work at once. The others took their sledgehammers and began to demolish the tomb.

The cathedral's monks watched appalled from a distance. Their whole world was falling to pieces. They had already been forced to sign an agreement accepting King Henry VIII as head of their church, rather than the Pope. Now they had to stand and watch as the King's men stormed into the cathedral and destroyed everything they held most sacred. The monks were in despair.

'They can't do this.' Brother Francis was a young monk, full of idealism. 'Surely they can't? Isn't there anybody who can stop it?'

'Who?' Father Robert was his older friend. 'Who can stop the King?'

'Somebody must be able to. It's sacrilege. He can't just send his men in here and destroy the Martyr's tomb. Nobody can do that.'

They watched helplessly as the demolition continued.

'We have to stop it,' Francis insisted. 'We can't allow them to just walk in here and smash everything. We have to stop them somehow.'

'How, though? What can we do?'

'Where's the Prior? It's his job. Why isn't Prior Goldwell here? He's the man in charge.'

Prior Goldwell was the senior figure among the monks. He shared their disgust at what was happening, but he had reasons of his own for not doing anything about it. Prior Goldwell was nowhere to be seen as Brother Francis went in search of him.

It was a while before the goldsmith had managed to prise all the jewels off the iron chest. He stuffed them into bags when he had finished. Then Layton told the rest of the men to smash the chest open with crowbars.

They did so at once. The chest was quickly forced open and the contents spilled out. In no time at all, the bones of St Thomas the Martyr had seen the light of day for the first time in almost three centuries and lay strewn all over the cathedral floor.

'There he is.' Layton kicked the bits with his boot. 'The remains of Thomas Becket. The man who was a traitor to his king.'

The skeleton wasn't complete. There was no skull, for a start. Other parts were missing too. All that remained were a few mouldering old bones amid a heap of detritus on the flagstones.

'Now for everything else,' Layton ordered. 'All the other relics. Make a pile of them on the floor.'

The relics were displayed at various points around the cathedral. Layton's men collected all the bits and pieces and stacked them up on top of Becket's bones. When everything was ready, Layton took a lighted taper from one of the tall candlesticks beside the shrine.

'No!' Brother Francis had found Prior Goldwell in hiding and brought the reluctant man to the shrine. 'You can't do that. You cannot burn St Thomas's bones. You have no authority to do that.'

'We have all the authority we need.' Layton flourished his commission. 'We have our authority from the King himself. What we do is by order of the King's Majesty.'

'It's a crime against God. The King will be excommunicated by the Pope if you burn St Thomas's bones.'

'What the Pope does is his affair, but St Thomas is certainly going to be burned. All the other bones too. This whole relic business has gone on far too long.'

Brother Francis turned desperately to the Prior. 'Tell him,' he implored. 'Tell him he can't burn St Thomas. It simply isn't possible.'

Prior Goldwell said nothing. The priory was going to lose all its lands and income under the King's reforms. There would be pensions in compensation, for those who held their tongues. The Prior needed a pension, if he was going to lose everything else.

'We'll never get the bones back if they're destroyed now,' Brother Francis told him distraughtly. 'They'll be gone for ever, once they've been burned.'

'I'm afraid it's God's will,' Goldwell shrugged. 'There's nothing we can do about it.'

'Of course there is. We can try to stop it.'

'Too late now,' Father Robert pointed out. 'The bones have already been scattered.'

But Francis wasn't having that. Stepping forward, he confronted Layton once more.

'You will be damned for all eternity if you do this.' He pointed to the lighted taper. 'Your soul will remain in hellfire for evermore if you set fire to St Thomas now.'

Layton wasn't impressed.

'You monks,' he said. 'It's the same wherever we go. You live off the people. You're dreadful landlords. You take everyone's money and spend it on whores and idle distractions. And then you claim you're doing God's work, when actually you're just living off other people's earnings.'

He lit the pile before Francis could reply. It took a while to catch. The monks watched in horror as the flames took hold at last and the relics began to burn. Brother Francis was in tears as the smoke drifted slowly upwards towards the vast roof of the cathedral.

'Hellfire,' he told Layton's men. 'You will all burn in hellfire for this.'

'Like St Thomas?' The men laughed.

They stood watching the fire for a while and then went back to demolishing the shrine. It was hard work, even with sledgehammers. The men took several hours to reduce Becket's tomb to an enormous pile of stone and rubble lying forlornly on the flagstones in the middle of the cathedral.

'Hellfire,' repeated Francis. 'You're going to regret what you've done on the Day of Judgment.'

'Come away,' Father Robert urged him. 'No point watching anymore. We've seen everything there is to see.'

Still tearful, Brother Francis allowed himself to be led away. Prior Goldwell went too, and the other monks. None of them could bear to watch as the King's men laid waste everything they held dear.

The process took several days by the time the relics had been reduced to ash and all trace of the shrine had been removed. The jewels had to be bagged up as well, and all the gold and silver taken down from the shrine. A column of wagons was parked outside the cathedral door, waiting to carry the valuables to London as soon as everything had been done.

Layton had a visitor on the third day, a fat little man with a sly face. The man kept his distance from the shrine, preferring not to get too closely involved. He stood watching from afar, waiting for Layton to spot him. Layton hurried over as soon as he did.

'Who's that?' Francis asked Father Robert.

'The Lord Privy Seal.'

84

'Who?'

'Thomas Cromwell. The King's man. He's King Henry's eyes and ears in the cathedral.'

They all knew the King was somewhere close by. He had been seen going in and out of St Augustine's abbey, one of his new possessions. Henry was planning to demolish the abbey, now that it belonged to him. He was going to turn the rest of the place into a royal palace with accompanying deer park.

'The King isn't coming himself?'

'It doesn't look like it. He was here last year with Jane Seymour. I imagine he's staying away this time, in case there's any trouble.'

'About the shrine?'

Father Robert nodded. 'He's keeping a low profile. The King wouldn't want to be involved, if there were any protests about the shrine.'

'So he's sent Cromwell instead to see how it's all going?'

'It certainly seems that way. Cromwell will report everything back to the King, like he always does.'

The Lord Privy Seal returned next morning. He was there to watch as the loot from St Thomas's shrine was carried outside to the waiting carts. Two wagons were needed just for the jewels alone.

Everything else – the gold, the silver, a wooden throne, four precious mitres and Becket's ornamented crozier – was loaded onto the other wagons. The convoy stretched half the length of the cathedral, waiting to transport everything to the Tower of London.

The treasure was loaded aboard and secured with rope and tarpaulins. Layton gave the signal to move when all was ready. Armed guards shouldered their pikes and walked alongside as the wagons started off, rumbling through the Christ Church gate and out into the city. Brother Francis couldn't bring himself to watch as they disappeared in the direction of London.

He turned on Prior Goldwell as soon as the convoy had vanished.

'You should have done something,' he accused him. 'You're the Prior. It was your duty. You should have stood up to them when you had the chance.'

Goldwell sighed. 'If only it was that simple.'

'We've lost St Thomas now. We'll never get him back. We've lost our saint for ever and it's all your fault.'

'That's a bit hard,' said Father Robert. 'There was nothing the Prior could do.'

'He could have tried! He could have made the effort. He just stood there and let the King's men do what they wanted. He didn't even try to stop them.'

The Prior was about to say something in reply, but thought better of it. He remained silent instead.

'I don't think I want to be a monk anymore.' Francis was visibly distressed. 'Not here, anyway. How could you all just stand there while St Thomas's bones were burned in front of your eyes? I can't believe you did that.'

The monks looked uncomfortable. They were all a bit shamefaced. It was the Prior who spoke at length.

'We have to make the best of it,' he told Francis. 'None of us likes what has happened, but there's nothing we can do. We just have to put it behind us now and carry on as best we can.'

'Not me,' said Francis. 'I don't think I can. Not after what has happened.'

He was still upset next day, and the day after. He was rude to the Prior again, and to the senior monks. Francis had all the certainty of youth in his disdain for his colleagues and their failure to stand up to Layton and his men. When he continued to show his contempt for them all, Father Robert decided to take him aside and have a quiet word in his ear.

'There's something you ought know,' Robert told him.

'What?'

'About St Thomas.'

'What about him?'

'Promise me on the Holy Cross that you won't breathe a word of what I'm about to tell you.'

'All right.'

'You swear you won't tell a soul?'

'I swear.'

'All right, then. St Thomas's bones haven't been burned.'

'Yes, they have. I saw them.'

'No, you didn't. St Thomas is quite safe.'

Francis was swift to grasp the implications. 'You mean somebody else's bones were burned instead?'

Robert nodded. 'We knew this was coming,' he said. 'It was only a matter of time. The bones were switched quite some time ago. That's why Prior Goldwell wasn't bothered when the shrine was attacked. He knew it wasn't St Thomas who was being destroyed.'

Francis was stunned. There was more to Prior Goldwell than he had realised.

'So where are the bones now?' he asked.

'They're safe. Still here in the cathedral. They've been hidden where no one will ever find them.'

'And you're not going to tell me where?'

Robert shook his head. 'It's a secret. Only two or three people know. I'm not one of them.'

Francis was enormously relieved to hear it. St Thomas was safe! Hidden somewhere in the cathedral. All his anger and bitterness had been for nothing.

He was still feeling embarrassed about his behaviour when Dr Layton reappeared the following day. He had Thomas Cromwell with him. They demanded to see Prior Goldwell at once.

'The Régale de France,' Layton told the Prior, as soon as he came.

'Yes?'

'King Louis's great ruby, the one from the shrine.'

'Yes?'

'It's gone missing.'

'Missing?'

'It isn't with the other jewels. We've searched through everything on the wagons that left the cathedral, but we couldn't find it anywhere.'

'Oh dear. I'm sorry to hear that.' The Prior was shocked. 'It was certainly put on one of the wagons. One of your people must have stolen it.'

'We don't think so. We don't think the ruby ever left the cathedral. We think it's still here somewhere. We think one of your monks has taken it and hidden it from us.'

Goldwell was outraged. 'That's a terrible thing to say,' he told Layton. 'Our monks would never do anything like that. If somebody has stolen the French king's ruby, I can assure you, it certainly wasn't one of us.'

Chapter Twelve

Christopher Marlowe and Queen Elizabeth's Birthday Party

Queen Elizabeth was due to turn forty in September 1573. The daughter of Henry VIII and Anne Boleyn had decided to celebrate her birthday in Canterbury, during her annual summer progress through the realm. Even without St Thomas's shrine, Canterbury was still the best place in Kent for a big birthday party.

Archbishop Parker had rashly agreed to host the event at his palace beside the cathedral. It had seemed a splendid idea when he first suggested it. As the day drew nearer though, Parker was beginning to have serious doubts. He was a worried man as he approached the Queen's high treasurer for advice on how to handle it.

'You'll certainly have to push the boat out for her,' Lord Burghley warned him. 'She likes a splash. The Queen's Majesty will be expecting something pretty spectacular for her fortieth birthday.'

'I'm an old man. I don't know much about parties.'

'No worries. Just find out how everyone else entertained her in the past and do it much more lavishly. The Queen will love that.'

'Where is she going to stay?'

'St Augustine's, I imagine.' The Queen had leased the abbey to Lord Cobham, but still kept rooms there for her own use. 'That's probably best.'

'She could stay with me, if she wanted.'

'In the Archbishop's palace?'

'It's right by the cathedral. I'm not sure it's suitable, though. It would be difficult for ordinary people to see her there. I could have you and the Earl of Leicester too, if you brought your own furnishings.'

'St Augustine's would be better,' said Burghley.

The Queen was due to arrive on 3 September. An advance party arrived twelve days earlier to take over the abbey and prepare it for her occupation. Her household staff needed that long to tidy the place up, make any necessary repairs and ensure that everything was properly arranged, ready for Her Majesty's arrival.

The advance party booked every spare bed in the city as well, to accommodate all the people who were accompanying her on the visit. It wasn't just the Queen who was coming to Canterbury for two weeks summer holiday. It was her court too, and most of the government.

'We're expecting about 350 people in all,' one of them warned the Archbishop. 'And more than two thousand horses. A lot of the courtiers are very particular about where they sleep. It's going to be a nightmare, trying to fit them all in.'

'We'll manage,' the Archbishop said. 'We shall have to, somehow.'

Preparations in his own household had begun in July. Large quantities of wine and beer had been brought in, ready for the party. The Archbishop had spent a lot of his private money on the palace over the years, doing it up and making it a fit place to entertain a queen. It looked as if his investment was going to pay off at last.

'We'd better take that picture of Cranmer down,' he told one of his staff, as they went through the arrangements for the Queen's reception. 'Her Majesty won't want to see it. Or at least, I don't want her to.'

Poor Cranmer. Parker's predecessor as archbishop had been burned at the stake for heresy during the reign of Queen Mary, Elizabeth's older sister. He had died bravely, thrusting his guilty hand into the flames without flinching. Parker didn't want to put ideas into the present Queen's head.

Elizabeth was coming to Canterbury from Dover. She had arranged a meeting at the port with a delegation from France. A marriage between Elizabeth and the King of France's brother had been proposed. Elizabeth had gone to Dover to meet the young Duke d'Alençon off the boat and see if there was any possibility of the marriage happening.

In the event, the Duke hadn't turned up. The French had sent an ambassador instead. The Comte de Retz and his whole party were so ill from the sea crossing that the meeting had had to be postponed. Elizabeth had told the French to come and see her in Canterbury in a few days' time, after they had recovered from their ordeal.

She herself set off for Canterbury on 3 September, as arranged. Her progress via Sandwich made for an astonishing sight. The column of carts and coaches bearing her courtiers and their luggage was fully a mile long. There were more than 400 wheeled vehicles in all, escorted by outriders and heralded by trumpets and flying banners. Queen Elizabeth of England never travelled lightly when showing herself off to her people.

She was bringing all her servants with her, whether she needed them or not. Heralds, trumpeters, messengers, coachmen, footmen, porters, drummers, flautists, musicians, tipstaffs, sergeants at arms, a yeoman of the bottles, a surveyor of the ways, a bear master for bear-baiting and Walter, the court jester. Her staff could all be maintained at Canterbury's expense while they were staying in the city.

The Queen was expected to reach Canterbury at about three in the afternoon. The Archbishop and his senior priests gathered at the west door of the cathedral to await her arrival. Heralded by a fanfare, she appeared soon after the hour, riding on horseback through the Christ Church gate. Parker went down on one knee as she came to a stop in front of him.

'Welcome, Your Majesty. Welcome to our fine city.'

A boy from the King's School in the precincts was standing at his elbow, ready to greet the Queen in Latin. Elizabeth remained in the saddle as the boy gave her the traditional oration. When he had finished, she dismounted and joined the Archbishop and the other priests in a psalm and a prayer of thanksgiving for her safe arrival. Then they all rose to their feet again and went into the cathedral for evensong.

Four knights carried a canopy over the Queen's head as she made her way in procession along the nave. Music played and the choir sang as she took her place for the service. The cathedral was full of people who had come to catch a glimpse of her in all her finery.

Queen Elizabeth went to her quarters in St Augustine's after the service was over. Bidding farewell to the Archbishop, she asked him to come and see her later, adding that she was looking forward to her birthday party at his palace on the 7th. The rest of her court was looking forward to it as well.

'We've invited the French ambassador,' she told Parker. 'The Comte de Retz. He'll be in Canterbury with his officials, so we ought to have them at the banquet. You don't mind, do you?'

'Of course not, Your Majesty. Any guests of yours are guests of mine. It will be an honour.'

The next three days flew by as the Archbishop prepared his palace for the party. The house was not particularly grand, a palace in name only, but he was determined that the Queen should have a good time while she was a guest under his roof. He wanted her birthday party in Canterbury to be an event that she would never forget.

'The Queen is only going to be forty once,' he told his staff. 'We must make it a great occasion. We must give her a party here that she will remember for the rest of her life.'

The staff needed no urging. They were all delighted that the Queen was coming. Her birthday party was going to be an occasion that they would never forget either. They were determined to give her a splendid time when she came.

The high point was to be the banquet in the hall. The Queen was to sit in the Archbishop's marble chair under a golden canopy, looking down the room. The French ambassador was to sit beside her with her ladies-in-waiting. Everyone else would sit at the other tables stretching the full length of the hall.

It was going to be a tight squeeze to fit them all in. The numbers had been daunting enough before the Queen invited the French ambassador as well. They became a lot worse when it emerged how many of his officials the Comte de Retz was proposing to bring with him.

'How many?' The Archbishop couldn't believe the number.

'A hundred, Your Grace.'

'He wants to bring a hundred Frenchmen to the party?'

'He does, I'm afraid. They all want to be there.'

'A hundred Frenchmen?'

'I fear so. He says they're all nobles and ought to be invited.'

'Have we got room for them?'

'Only if we turn the Kentish nobility away. Or the mayor of Canterbury and the aldermen.'

'Well, we can't. Tell the ambassador he can bring some of his people, but not all of them.'

It wasn't just the extra guests. It was the additional expense as well. More food, more drink, more everything. The people of Canterbury were helping with the costs of the Queen's stay in their city. So were the cathedral's dean and chapter. But the Archbishop's birthday party for her was his own idea.

He alone was picking up the bill for all the food and entertainment at his palace. The Archbishop had already had the Privy Council to dinner, and various members of the royal court on different nights. Now he was throwing a huge party as well, at enormous cost to himself. The expense of entertaining a monarch and her entourage in the manner to which they were accustomed was ruinous.

'We shall manage,' Parker assured his staff, wishing he could believe it. 'Of course we shall. We only have to do it this once, thank the Lord.'

The Queen was invited for early afternoon. Crowds gathered expectantly as she set off from St Augustine's abbey. It was only a few hundred yards from there to the Christ Church gate, where the Archbishop was waiting to welcome her to his palace for her birthday party.

Christopher Marlowe and his family watched the excitement from Mercery Lane. Christopher's uncle had a draper's shop in the lane, directly opposite the cathedral gate. Nine-year-old Christopher had been looking forward all day to seeing the Queen. In the event, he and his family only caught a brief glimpse of her through the window as the coach rumbled down Burgate Street without stopping and turned into the cathedral.

The Queen was shimmering with jewels as she got out beside the palace. The Archbishop bowed low and welcomed her to his home.

'Here we are,' he told her. 'Very many congratulations on your birthday, Your Majesty. May I wish you every happiness on this great occasion?'

'You may.' The Queen was in an excellent mood. 'We were born at exactly this hour, if you remember.' Parker had been chaplain to the Queen's mother at the time. 'Greenwich Palace. We shall be sitting down to eat at precisely the time we came into the world.'

'I do remember, Your Majesty. It was a wonderful day. Everyone was delighted when you were born.'

They went into the hall. All was ready for the banquet. The Queen washed her hands first, then took her seat on the marble throne. The others followed suit; her courtiers, the Privy Council, the French diplomats, the Kentish nobility, the mayor of Canterbury and all the other important people who had managed to secure an invitation to the feast. They all found their seats and waited for the Archbishop to say grace before sitting down and tucking in.

The food was magnificent. A long row of meat dishes was laid before Queen Elizabeth and another of fish. A row of cakes followed. Beer was poured and wine flowed. The Archbishop's servants stood ready at every table to ensure that drinking vessels were full and no plate was empty. Everything was being done to ensure that the banquet would be a success.

As was customary, the ordinary people of Canterbury were allowed in to watch the fun. A crowd of onlookers gathered in the middle of the hall, most of them gaping unashamedly at the Queen. There were so many of them that they obscured her view of the room.

'Tell everyone to move,' she said irritably. 'Tell them to stand to the side so that I can see what's happening.'

The onlookers shuffled obediently to the side walls. The banquet continued. The Queen turned to her ladies-in-waiting and sat chatting with them for most of the meal. She was watched carefully by the French ambassador at her side. He was waiting for the right moment to raise the subject of her marriage to the Duke d'Alençon.

It was an unlikely match. The French king's brother was still only eighteen, small and weedy, his face pitted with smallpox. Forty-year-old Queen Elizabeth didn't want to marry him or anyone else. She was well aware, though, that flirting with the French would greatly upset the Spanish. The French ambassador was aware of it too.

His moment came after the banquet was over. The plates were cleared away and the tables were removed by the Archbishop's staff. Musicians came in and the dancing began. The ambassador sat with the Queen as the rest of her court took to the floor.

'Lovely party,' he told her. 'The music in England is exquisite.'

'You think so?'

'I don't believe any prince in Europe has heard anything like the music we heard in the cathedral the other day. Or the Holy Father, either, for that matter. It was sublime.'

'I hope you're not comparing that Romish rascal to our great Queen.' A young nobleman nearby did not care for the Pope.

The ambassador was annoyed. He was about to rise to the Pope's defence before he thought better of it. The English weren't Roman Catholic anymore. Best just to bite his lip and let it lie.

'Come and have a talk,' the Queen told him. 'We have lots to discuss.'

There was a private door to the Archbishop's gallery. They could watch the dancing from there. The Queen sat by the window with the ambassador and chatted with him almost until nightfall. She listened without comment as de Retz extolled the Duke d'Alençon's virtues. She hadn't committed herself to anything when the party came to an end at length and it was time to leave.

Queen Elizabeth went first, as protocol demanded. She was still in a splendid mood as the Archbishop escorted her to her carriage.

'A marvellous banquet.' The Queen was full of congratulations. 'It was everything we could possibly have wished for. We enjoyed ourselves immensely at our birthday party.'

'Thank you, Your Majesty. I'm very pleased to hear it.'

'We shan't forget the sight of the Privy Council dancing the galliard in a hurry.'

'No indeed. All those lords a-leaping!'

The rest of the guests left soon after the Queen. They too were agreed that it had been a wonderful party. They all wanted to shake the Archbishop's hand and thank him profusely as they called for their coaches. Nobody had ever attended a banquet quite like it before.

The Queen stayed in Canterbury for another nine days. It was a relief to everyone when she left at last, taking her entourage with her. She went to Faversham first, and thence by stages to London. She left behind indelible memories of a fabulous royal personage decked out for every occasion in beautiful clothes and brilliant jewels. In Queen Elizabeth, the people of England at last had the monarch they craved.

The Archbishop gave her a golden salt cellar inlaid with agates before she left. He also tipped her personal staff, distributing five hundred gold pieces among the servants and attendants of the royal household. It pained him to part with so much money, but there was no alternative. The Queen's staff expected to be tipped.

The Archbishop had kept open house for the two weeks of her visit. He had had her officials continually in his house for breakfast, lunch and dinner, all of them cheerfully freeloading at his expense. Even so, he found after their departure that he had over-ordered on the food. So much remained that he invited the poor of Canterbury to come and eat at his palace until it had all gone.

Parker was substantially out of pocket by the time everyone had finished browsing and sluicing. He consoled himself with the thought that it would never happen again. The Queen was careful to make her royal progress through a different part of the country every summer. She wouldn't be returning to Canterbury for the foreseeable future.

He himself left for London a few days later. He arrived at Lambeth Palace to discover that news of the Queen's birthday party had preceded him. Everyone had heard about it and wanted to congratulate him on his great success.

'I hear that it was the party of the century,' someone told him. 'They're saying at court that no one will throw another one like it for at least a hundred years.'

'I should certainly hope not,' said Parker. 'The expense was ruinous. I'd be a pauper if I had to do it all again.'

The talk in London was of nothing but the party for the next few days.

The Archbishop basked in all the praise. Everywhere he went, people wanted to discuss it with him and hear all the details. It was generally agreed that his hospitality in Canterbury had set the standard for all the royal parties to come.

He was at his desk in Lambeth, looking across the river to the Houses of Parliament, when two of his secretaries burst in. They brought wonderful tidings.

'We've just had word from the court,' they told him. 'About your party.'

'Yes?' The Archbishop wondered if the Queen had said something.

'Her Majesty enjoyed it so much that she wants to have another one next year. She's decided to come to Canterbury next September so that she can celebrate her birthday with you again, at the palace.'

'You're not serious?'

'We certainly are. She wants to do it all again.'

'In my house?'

The secretaries nodded enthusiastically. What a coup for the Archbishop! The Queen never spent her birthday in the same place twice running.

'Oh dear Lord.' The Archbishop rose from his desk. Going across to the window, he peered out in despair. He was ruined. Another party like the last one would destroy his finances for ever. He couldn't possibly afford to host the Queen again.

He would have to resign as Archbishop. Either that, or plead sickness, or find some other excuse. Anything to avoid entertaining the Queen in his house again. He would be doomed if he spent any more money on her.

But then the Archbishop caught sight of the secretaries' faces. Both were corpsing with laughter.

'That wasn't funny,' he told them sharply. 'Don't make jokes like that again.'

Chapter Thirteen

A Pilgrim Father Charters the *Mayflower*

For weeks, someone had been going around Canterbury pinning libellous notices to church doors. The libels were religious tracts attacking the Church of England. It was clear from the tone that they had been written by a dissenter, one of the new breed of Puritans opposed to all the ritual and dogma accompanying Christian worship in England.

It was November 1603 before the authorities managed to identify the author. Robert Cushman was an apprentice grocer, active in the Puritan movement. He was hauled before the court on charges of writing the tracts and failing to attend church, as the law required.

Cushman refused to confess to the libels, even though the evidence was overwhelming, but he couldn't deny his failure to attend service on the Sabbath. The Church of England, with all its pomp and ceremony, wasn't for him anymore.

'The singing of hymns is an abomination,' he told the court. 'It's a corruption of God's word. So is the Book of Common Prayer. Where is it written in the Bible that there should be bishops, living fat and sleek off their flock?'

'That's no reason to nail *Lord have mercy upon us* to the church door.'

'God's chosen are few. Scarcely one in a hundred will be saved if they don't repent.'

Unimpressed, the court sentenced Cushman to a brief spell in the prison at the West Gate to bring him to his senses. He emerged more determined than ever to live like a Puritan. He wanted to be free for the rest of his life from all the bowing and scraping of the Church of the England. Cushman wanted to worship the Lord in his own particular way.

He was due to marry Sarah Reader when he had completed his apprenticeship. Sarah lived in the cathedral precincts. She and her brother Helkiah were active Puritans. Helkiah Reader had done time in the West Gate for distributing Cushman's libellous tracts.

Cushman went to see Sarah in her lodgings beside the cathedral. Like him, Sarah knew the building well, but could never bring herself to worship there. Beginning with the statue of Jesus over the Christ Church gate, Canterbury cathedral represented everything they hated most about the way religion was conducted in England. Statues of Jesus were idolatrous.

Cushman found Sarah at home and sat in the parlour with her, discussing their future in an unsympathetic country. It looked more and more as if they would have to submit to the Church of England for the rest of their days if they couldn't find an acceptable alternative. Neither of them was happy about that.

'King James is the problem,' Cushman told his fiancée. 'There are a thousand Puritan clergy in the realm. Some of them went to see the King the other day. They asked him to make a few small changes to the Church of England, but he refused to listen. He wouldn't help us at all.'

'Not even changes to the creed?'

'Nothing. The King wouldn't hear of it. He says he will make Puritans conform to the established Church or else harry us out of the land. That's what he told his court.'

'Is he serious?'

'I fear so. We must bow to the Church of England for the rest of our lives or find another country to live in. That's the only choice we have.'

It was a daunting prospect. Neither of them wanted to move abroad. They would both much rather just stay where they were and worship as they wished.

'We aren't alone,' Cushman said. 'There are people like us in other parts of the realm. They feel as we do. We could all go together if we could find somewhere else to live.'

'It's a big step.' Sarah Reader wasn't sure that she was ready to move to another country. 'Perhaps the King will change his mind.'

'Or perhaps he won't. He's never going to be our friend.'

'Where would we go?'

'That's the big question. We must find somewhere where they will allow us to worship as we please. It won't be easy, but there must be somewhere. We shall have to find out where.'

Holland was the obvious place. Dutch Protestants would take the Puritans in. But getting to the Netherlands was easier said than done. The Puritans needed official permission to travel abroad. It was never granted to religious nonconformists.

'The sheriff's men will try to stop us,' Cushman warned. 'So will the coast guard. We'll have to go secretly. We must find a ship's captain prepared to take us, no questions asked.'

It was 1609 before Robert and Sarah Cushman managed to get to Holland. They went to Amsterdam first, and then to Leiden to join a group of like-minded English Puritans who had settled in the town. Cushman worked as a wool-comber and became a deacon of the Puritan community.

But the English never took to Holland. Dutch ways were alien and different. A truce between Holland and Spain was due to come to an end in 1619, which meant that the Puritans might find themselves subject to the horrors of the Spanish Inquisition if the war was renewed. In 1617 therefore, Cushman was sent back to England to find another home for the Puritans, somewhere English this time.

The proposed destination was north America. A consortium of London businessmen calling themselves the Merchant Adventurers was getting together to fund a trading settlement at the mouth of the Hudson river. Fur and cod were to be the main commodities. If the Puritans were prepared to do the work, the businessmen would put up the money and finance their voyage to the New World.

Cushman was sent to organise it. He returned to Canterbury and rented a room in Palace Street. From there he made frequent trips to London to meet the adventurers and negotiate the business arrangements for the voyage. It took him two years to reach an agreement acceptable to both sides.

A friend in Canterbury advised him against the enterprise. He told Cushman that the Puritans were mad even to think about it.

'America is full of savages,' he pointed out. 'They flay white men alive with seashells. They cut off their members and broil them on hot coals. They won't allow you to live peacefully in their land, let alone practise religion as you wish.'

'They will,' Cushman assured him. 'Once they've heard the word of God. We must teach them the errors of their ways.'

Trading goods would buy the savages off. There were all sorts of commodities the Puritans could bring with them to exchange for valuable furs. The word of God could come later, after the savages had become dependent on their benefactors for all the manufactured goods that came with them.

The English flag was coming too. The Puritans planned to plant it on fresh soil, next to the colony of Virginia, where no flag had flown before. It would benefit everyone, white man and savage alike, to live under the protection of the English flag. The Puritans meant to bring the best of England to the New World, while leaving the worst behind.

'The Merchant Adventurers are chartering the vessel,' Cushman told his friend. 'My job is to fill it with everything we need for the crossing. I have to get a lot of other stuff as well to help us start a new life in a new land.'

'What d'you need?'

'Everything. Beer, wine, beef, pork. Hard tack and dried peas. Clothes, tools, muskets, fishing tackle. Trade goods for the savages. I'm looking for a screw jack as well. It'll come in useful for lifting heavy weights.'

'And you sail when?'

'Spring next year, if the Adventurers have found us a ship. We want to reach the New World before the winter storms at sea.'

The voyage was certainly not for the faint-hearted. The risks were so great that several financial backers had decided to pull out after thinking about it. They preferred to invest their capital in something less hazardous. Quite a few Puritans had withdrawn too, dismayed at the prospect of a perilous sea crossing and an unknowable life thereafter. Cushman understood their concerns.

'None of us really knows what we're doing,' he confessed to his friend. 'We're all of us learning as we go. There's no one to tell us what we should do. We just have to muddle through and hope the Lord will provide in the end.'

The worst moment came in June 1620. The Puritans were ready to leave, but the Adventurers still hadn't managed to find a ship for the voyage. The Puritans needed to sail almost at once if they were to cross the ocean before the bad weather. They knew their plans would come to nothing if they didn't leave England soon.

A flurry of correspondence followed as they tried to resolve the problem. It resulted in the Puritans pooling their resources to buy a small ship of their own. The *Speedwell* lay in the Dutch port of Delfshaven. She was less than fifty feet long and rated only sixty tons. It would be a miracle if they managed to sail such a tiny craft across the Atlantic and arrive in one piece. But they could use her for fishing if they did.

The Puritans clearly needed a bigger ship as well. The two vessels could rendezvous in Southampton and set out together. There would be safety in numbers, if they remained in contact throughout the voyage.

'I wish I could be sure it was going to happen,' Cushman confessed. 'There's been so much confusion. If we don't go soon, we'll have eaten half our food before we even leave England.'

Others shared his pessimism. There had been incessant arguments among the Puritans, as well as confusion. Everyone was at loggerheads with everyone else. The Puritans were very close to abandoning the whole enterprise when better news arrived from London. The backers had managed to charter a ship at last.

'She's already on her way to Southampton,' Cushman told his friend. He was cockahoop as he came to say goodbye. 'I'm off there too. It looks as if we're really going to leave England at last.'

'What kind of ship?'

'She's a three-decker apparently. Much bigger than the *Speedwell*. About a hundred feet long. She can carry 180 tons of cargo as well.'

'That sounds promising.'

'It does. We'll certainly need the space. There'll be a hundred passengers on board, if we can fit them all in.'

'That many?'

Cushman nodded. 'It'll be a tight squeeze, but it does look as if everybody who wants to go to America will be able to, now that we have a bigger ship.'

'So you're really on your way?'

'Yes, we are, at long last. She's called the *Mayflower*. I think she's going to be just what we need for the voyage.'

Chapter Fourteen

King Charles I Consummates his Marriage

There was something distinctly dubious about the two bearded men and their attendant taking the ferry across the river Thames on a cold February morning in 1623. Their beards looked false, for one thing. They were very furtive, for another. The men clearly wanted to keep a low profile as they paid the fare from Tilbury and wrapped themselves in hooded cloaks for the journey across the river to Gravesend on the south bank.

They were both young men, calling themselves Tom and John Smith. They didn't have the right money for the crossing, so they gave the ferryman a gold piece instead. He looked at it in disbelief.

'I can't change that. It's far too much.'

'Don't worry. You can keep the change. It's no bother to us.'

The ferryman's suspicions were aroused at once. Nobody threw cash around like that. Not unless they had something to hide. The men were on their way to Dover. The ferryman wondered if they were fugitives from justice, fleeing abroad before the law could catch up with them.

His suspicions were confirmed when the men asked to be taken to the outskirts of Gravesend, rather than the usual landing stage. They clearly had something to hide if they didn't want to be seen in the town.

The ferryman rowed himself to the landing stage as soon as he had deposited them. Tying up his boat, he went ashore in search of a magistrate.

'The men are going abroad under false names,' he told the official. 'I think they might be going to fight a duel. Someone should stop them, if they are.'

'A duel?'

'Something. I don't know what. They're up to no good, whatever it is.'

'Where are they now?'

'On their way to Rochester. They've hired post-horses.'

The magistrate mulled it over. 'You're right,' he decided, after a while. 'We should know what they're up to. I'll send someone to Rochester. The magistrate there can find out what's going on.'

A post-boy was despatched at once. He arrived in Rochester to discover that the two men and their attendant had only just passed through, en route to Dover. The post-boy hurried after them.

The men weren't far ahead when they ran into a problem coming the other way. It was a royal carriage escorted by horsemen. Whoever was in the carriage, John Smith and his companions didn't want to meet them for fear of being recognised.

'We'll have to go across country,' Smith decided. 'Come on. Over the fields.'

Turning off the road, the three men spurred their horses across the fields, making a wide detour behind the hedges to avoid being seen by the royal cavalcade. They had only just disappeared when the post-boy arrived. Reining in, he asked the royal party on the road if they had seen the three men anywhere.

'Why?' asked the man in charge of the escort. 'What have they done?'

The post-boy explained. Sir Henry Mainwaring listened carefully. As the Lieutenant of Dover Castle, he was escorting the Flemish ambassador to London in the coach. He didn't want anything to happen to the ambassador while the man was in his charge.

The idea of the two men going abroad in disguise to fight a duel seemed far-fetched to Mainwaring. He came up with another explanation instead.

'They're not duellists,' he decided, after listening to a description of the men. 'They're that Dutchman's sons. What was his name? The one who was beheaded.'

Johan van Oldenbarnevelt had been a Dutch leader in the fight for independence from Spain. His execution for alleged crimes against the government had caused outrage in England. The trial had recently been a play on the London stage.

'They're his sons,' Mainwaring declared. 'That's who they are. They're on their way to Holland to assassinate the Prince of Orange and avenge their father's death. We must stop them before they do.'

Scribbling a note authorising their arrest, Mainwaring handed it to one of his own people.

'Ride like hell,' he told him. 'Canterbury first, then Dover if you have to. Alert the authorities and tell them what's happening. Make sure the men are intercepted before they have a chance to leave England.'

The man did as he was told. He had the advantage of the road as he started off. The three suspects were still hacking across country on inferior horses. By the time they had returned to the road, they were some way behind him as he reached Canterbury and demanded to see the mayor at once.

He handed him Mainwaring's note. The mayor read it carefully. Sir Henry was the Member of Parliament for Dover as well as Lieutenant of the Castle. His signature on the document was all the authority the mayor needed to make an arrest.

'Right.' The mayor summoned the watch. 'We're looking for three suspects,' he told them. 'Possible assassins. They'll have to change horses here if they're heading for Dover. We'll check the post inn first.'

The White Hart lay on the London road, just outside the West Gate. The mayor led the way as they hurried down the High Street.

He wasn't a moment too soon. Three men answering the right description had just hired fresh mounts at the inn and were preparing to saddle up. The mayor stepped in to stop them.

'Who are you?' he demanded. 'What are you doing in Canterbury?'

'We're on our way to Dover.' The older of the two Smiths spoke. He was a flamboyant man in his late twenties, obviously an aristocrat. 'What's it to you?'

'I'm the mayor of Canterbury. I'm responsible for law and order in the city.'

'Well, good for you. We're not doing anything wrong, so we'll be on our way, if you don't mind.'

'I do mind. I want to know your business. What are you doing here?'

The elder Smith was about to reply but changed his mind. It was the younger Smith who spoke.

'What we're doing is none of your business,' he said. The younger Smith was a small man, just over five feet tall. He spoke with a stutter. 'We don't have to tell you, if we don't want to.'

'Right, take them in.' The mayor wasn't going to be spoken to like that, not in his own city. 'We'll soon see if it's my business or not.'

The watch arrested the two Smiths and their attendant. They were frogmarched to a room at the inn where they could be questioned properly. The mayor took a seat while the three suspects stood in front of him under close guard.

'All right, then,' the mayor said. 'What's this all about?'

'What do you mean?'

'The false beards, for a start. Why are you in disguise?'

It was a hard one to answer. The elder Smith blustered for a while, then abandoned the attempt and tore his beard off.

'We're travelling incognito,' he told the mayor.

'I can see that. Why?'

'We don't want anyone to know who we are.' It was the younger Smith who answered.

'Wait your turn,' the mayor told him sharply. 'I wasn't talking to you.'

'We have reasons for not wanting anyone to know.' The older Smith didn't want to say any more. 'You shouldn't speak to my companion like that.'

'I'll speak to him however I please. I'm the mayor here.'

'And I'm the Marquess of Buckingham. We're travelling on official state business.'

Oh Lord. The mayor reeled. He hoped it wasn't true. The Marquess of Buckingham was King James's very special friend.

'I'm the King's admiral,' the Marquess went on. 'I'm on my way with my companions to Dover to inspect the fleet. We want to assess the navy's state of readiness in the Narrow Seas.'

'Is that so?' It was the mayor's turn to bluster. 'And who is your companion then?'

The younger Smith had had enough of this. He too took off his beard.

'I am Charles Stuart, Prince of Wales,' he told the mayor. 'I'm the King's son.'

And heir. The mayor had just arrested the future King of England. Oh dear God! The mayor fell immediately to one knee and cringed in submission, waiting for the earth to swallow him up.

'I'm so sorry,' he apologised. 'I had no idea. Believe me, my Lords. If only I'd known.'

'You had no reason to arrest us.'

'Of course I didn't. I see that now. I shouldn't have done it. I can only apologise.'

England's future King didn't seem mollified. Neither did the Marquess of Buckingham. Both were very irritated at their arrest.

'We're not breaking any law. We're on a secret mission.'

'I understand that. I should never have interfered. I'd been given wrong information.'

'Well.' Prince Charles struggled with his stammer when he was cross. 'See that it never happens again.'

'It won't. Of course it won't. I shall make sure that it never does.'

'And see that you don't tell anyone about this. You've caused us enough trouble already. There are very good reasons why we're travelling incognito.'

'Not a word, my Lords. Not to anyone.'

The prisoners were released. Bowing repeatedly, the mayor escorted them outside to their horses. The three men mounted up, gave him a look of contempt, and resumed their journey. Clattering across the drawbridge, they rode through the West Gate and disappeared up Canterbury High Street in the direction of Dover.

They were on a secret mission, but it wasn't to inspect the fleet. They were going to Spain to inspect the Spanish king's daughter. If the negotiations went well, Charles was planning to marry her. But that was no business of the mayor of Canterbury's.

The negotiations didn't go well. The idea was abandoned after much discussion and Charles decided to marry the King of France's daughter instead. His next visit to Canterbury, two years later, was to receive his new bride and welcome her to England after her arrival from France.

A great deal had changed by the time Charles returned to Canterbury in June 1625. His father had just died and he was the King now. He had no need of a cloak or a false beard as he arrived by coach from Rochester. Church bells rang out in every village and people turned out in large numbers to cheer him on his way.

The mayor of Canterbury was no longer in office. He kept his head down and maintained a very low profile as the King arrived. It was John Finch, recorder of the city and Member of Parliament, who swept off his hat and welcomed the monarch back to Canterbury.

'The people of the city must humbly ask your pardon,' he told the King, on bended knee. 'We know what happened, the last time you were here. We're all very embarrassed about it. I hope you will find it in your heart to forgive us. One gracious look from Your Majesty is all we wish for.'

The King did his best, but he couldn't hide his lack of enthusiasm for Canterbury. It was obvious that the incident still rankled. The mayor who had arrested him was wise to remain out of sight for the duration of his visit.

Charles stayed two nights at St Augustine's before continuing to Dover to collect his bride. Fifteen-year-old Henrietta Maria was on her way from France but delayed by sickness and bad weather.

The two of them had never met, but they were already married. The ceremony had taken place at Notre Dame in Paris, with a proxy standing in for the groom. All that remained now was for the new Queen to come to England and commence married life with her husband.

Henrietta arrived at length and was introduced to Charles at Dover Castle. His courtiers were relieved to see that she was tiny, almost a head shorter than him. It would have been awkward if she had towered over the King, as some women at court did.

'I'm standing on my own feet,' she told Charles in French, to emphasise the point. She indicated her shoes. 'This is how high I am. Neither taller nor shorter.'

They set out for Canterbury after lunch. The coach stopped at Barham Downs on the way, the traditional Kentish greeting place for a monarch. Tents and a picnic tea awaited them. The route thereafter was strewn with flowers and crowded with sightseers as Charles and Henrietta drove on in state towards the cathedral city.

All the bells were ringing as they arrived. The new mayor and his aldermen were waiting at the West Gate to receive them. Henrietta spoke no English. She didn't understand a word as the mayor formally welcomed her to Canterbury and wished her every happiness for the future.

They drove to St Augustine's after the ceremony. The streets were still full of people as they went. Everyone in the city had turned out to watch the procession. Henrietta was relieved to reach the abbey at last after a long day of travelling through her strange and unfamiliar new country.

She went to bed early that night. The King followed after a polite interval. Two of his attendants helped him into his nightshirt before themselves retiring discreetly. The last noise they heard was the sound of the King bolting the door firmly behind them as they withdrew.

He was famously an early riser, but it was past seven o'clock before he got up next morning. The two sentries outside his chamber exchanged knowing glances as they patrolled their beats.

'Aye aye,' one of them said. 'I wonder what keeps the King abed so late on a lovely summer morning.'

His companion sniggered.

Charles was in a splendid mood when he appeared at last. Married life evidently agreed with him. He was still in fine fettle when he attended cathedral later that day. People in the congregation remarked on how happy he looked as he led his new wife up the nave for the service. If nothing else, it surely meant that he had forgiven Canterbury at last for the mayor's dreadful mistake at the White Hart.

Chapter Fifteen

Roundheads Storm the Cathedral

The war had begun at last, the civil war between King and Parliament. King Charles had raised his standard at Nottingham on 22 August 1642, calling for his subjects everywhere to rally to his side. Thousands were doing so, now that talk had finally turned to action. It was official from here on in. The country was at war.

Unfortunately for him, King Charles had timed his call very badly. Most of the country's cities and ports were controlled by forces sympathetic to Parliament. So were most of the stocks of arms and ammunition needed for the fight. As soon as the King raised his standard, the Parliamentarians moved quickly to secure everything else in an attempt to avert a disastrous struggle before it could even begin.

Commanded by Colonel Edwin Sandys, five hundred Parliamentary horsemen left London for Kent on 19 August. Their mission was to capture Rochester Castle and seize the dockyard at Chatham, where the navy's heavy guns were stored. After that, they were to continue to Dover to capture the castle there and take control of the port.

The troops reached Canterbury on Friday night, a week after they had set out. The city's walls had recently been strengthened and its gates bolted against any attack. Canterbury's gentry and the cathedral clergy were Royalist almost to a man, unsympathetic to any rebellion against the King. But there were plenty of Parliamentarians among the townspeople.

The gates were quickly unlocked and the troopers welcomed with open arms. A detachment made straight for the cathedral to put a guard on it and post sentries around the precincts. As soon as that had been done, Sergeant-Major Cockaine went to find the Dean to ask him where the cathedral's supply of arms and powder was stored.

He found the Dean's wife and son at home, but the man himself away. It was Thomas Paske, a royal chaplain, who very reluctantly led the Roundhead to fourteen barrels of gunpowder which had been stored in the precincts for safekeeping.

'Here you are,' Paske told him. 'The powder is all perfectly secure. We're always careful to keep it locked up. We have some muskets as well.'

'Give me the keys, then. We'll look after everything from now on.'

The cathedral's clergy spent a very uneasy night, knowing that there were Parliamentary troops all around them. The Roundheads had had a good war so far, pillaging and looting all the way from London. The troops were perfectly capable of breaking into private homes in the middle of the night, if they felt like it. There was no one in Canterbury to stop them.

The clergy were relieved therefore when dawn broke without further incident, but their relief was short-lived. They found the doors guarded when they went to unlock the cathedral for morning prayers. Roundhead sentries refused to let them in.

'This is an outrage,' Paske told one of them. 'We're men of God. You can't ban us from the cathedral.'

'Nothing to do with me,' said the sentry. 'I'm just obeying my orders.'

Canterbury cathedral was an offensive sight to zealous Puritans, especially the tower of Bell Harry. It stood so high and mighty, so pleased with itself, so Popish. The King had climbed all the way to the top to enjoy the view during his last visit to Canterbury in 1641.

The Puritans, on the other hand, would pull the whole lot down and use the stones for something else, if they had their way. That was all a cathedral was any good for, in their opinion. That, and stabling horses.

The clergy were still wondering what to do when Sir Michael Livesey appeared. He was a Kentish man, a local Puritan commander and a zealot. He demanded the keys to the cathedral.

'Tell your steward to hand them over,' he told Paske. 'We want access to all areas.'

'Why? What are you going to do in there?'

'That's for us to decide. Just give them to us at once.'

Paske was reluctant, but Livesey insisted. 'Hand them over,' he told the chaplain. 'In the name of Parliament, give me the keys to the cathedral. I won't ask again.'

The keys were on an iron ring. Paske nodded unwillingly to the steward, who surrendered them without enthusiasm. The Roundheads immediately unlocked the cathedral's doors and rushed in.

Livesey himself didn't go with them. He was on his way to Dover for the next phase of the operation. 'The men have orders to conduct themselves civilly,' he assured Paske as he left. 'They'll behave themselves in the cathedral. There's nothing for you to worry about.'

Paske wished he could believe it. He and the steward followed the troops into the cathedral after an interval. They watched from a discreet distance as the men began to tear the place apart, pulling down and destroying anything of value that couldn't be stolen or taken away.

The Roundheads went for the altar rails first. Altar rails were a Popish idea, hated by Puritans. Parliament had ordered their removal from churches, but Canterbury's rails were still defiantly in place. The Roundheads tore them down at once and broke them up so that they couldn't be used again.

The soldiers went for the communion table next. They kicked it over and ripped the velvet cloth that covered it. Some smashed the cathedral's seats while others defaced screens and stone monuments. They smashed the organ as well and did their best to break the brass eagle supporting the Bible on the lectern.

When they were bored with that, the Roundheads turned to the cupboards where the choristers' surplices and prayer books were kept. Forcing the doors open, they trampled on the surplices and gowns, ripped the pages out of the prayer books and scattered them indiscriminately all over the floor. The mess by the time they had finished was indescribable.

'Madness.' Paske watched in horror. 'The Devil's work. They don't know what they're doing.'

Not all of the troops were involved. Quite a few shared Paske's disgust and took no part in the destruction. It was the zealots among them who were the most active, the Puritan extremists who hated idolatry in every shape or form. There was no stopping them as they fell upon a large tapestry of Jesus in the choir and began to attack it.

'Here's Christ,' one of them shouted, as he waved his sword. 'Watch me stab him.'

'I'll rip his bowels out.' Another joined in. Between them they cut the tapestry to pieces, yelling in triumph as they did so. Everyone else cheered.

'This can't go on,' Paske told the steward. 'We have to stop it somehow.'

Three Roundheads in lobster-tailed helmets had found the entrance to the crypt. Paske watched in alarm as they rushed in. There was something in the crypt that the soldiers mustn't be allowed to discover.

'Get help,' he told the steward urgently. 'Come back with some men, quick as you can.'

The steward went for reinforcements. Paske followed the three soldiers into the crypt. They had found a door set into the far wall. It led down stone steps to a small stream flowing through the foundations under the cathedral.

The soldiers were looking for church ornaments. They wondered if there was something valuable behind the door. It was heavily locked, so they began to break it down to find out.

Paske knew exactly what lay behind the door. It was where the cathedral's secret was kept. The secret was entrusted to only two or three clergy at any one time. It dated from the days of Henry VIII and the despoiling of St Thomas's shrine.

'Please, Lord,' Paske prayed. 'Please stop those men. Don't let them find what's hidden down there. Steer them down a different path instead.'

The Roundheads had just succeeded in forcing the door open when the steward returned. He had five burly men with him. They all carried weapons as they hurried into the crypt.

Paske briefed his steward as the three Roundheads disappeared down the stone steps. He told him exactly what would have to be done to preserve the secret hidden under the crypt. The steward nodded grimly and went after the Roundheads with his men.

Paske decided not to wait for the outcome. It might be unseemly for a clergyman to be present. Leaving the crypt, he returned to the main body of the cathedral.

He found the nave in a dreadful state as he emerged. Everything had been smashed, all the way along. Scarcely daring to look, Paske made his way out of the cathedral through the south door and took a deep gulp of fresh air in the sunshine outside.

The Roundheads had got there before him. A group of them were standing outside the Christ Church gate with their muskets. They were amusing themselves by taking pot shots at the statue of Christ over the gate.

Paske couldn't believe it. There the men were, shooting at Christ himself. They were making a competition of it, seeing who could be the first to knock the head off the statue. The soldiers were cheering like yokels at a country fair every time anyone came close.

'Lord have mercy,' Paske told himself. 'They're trying to crucify him. It's the Crucifixion all over again.'

Some of the men seemed to be drunk as they took aim. The statue was visibly disintegrating under their fusillade. The Roundheads had fired perhaps forty shots in all when Colonel Sandys appeared, drawn by the sound of the shooting. He was outraged when he saw what his men were up to.

'Stop that,' he ordered. 'Stop it at once. What in Heaven's name d'you think you're doing?'

The men lowered their muskets reluctantly. They would have preferred to go on. A statue of Christ was idolatrous. There was no harm in trying to destroy it.

Sandys turned to Paske. 'I'm sorry about that,' he told the priest. 'The men shouldn't have done it. I don't know what came over them.'

'The statue is ruined now.' Paske pointed up at its broken face. 'We'll have to take it down and remove it. There's nothing else we can do. A statue of Christ.'

'It shouldn't have happened. The men had strict orders. They were told to behave themselves when they came to the cathedral.'

'Your soldiers have been a miserable spectacle to all eyes.'

'Indeed, they have.' Sandys shared Paske's annoyance. 'I can only apologise again. We're going to Dover now. I'll get them on the road as quickly as I can and we'll be on our way.'

The Roundheads left Canterbury soon afterwards. They reached Dover that afternoon and took control of the port. The men proved no more popular in Dover than they had been in the precincts of the cathedral.

As soon as the Roundheads had gone, Paske summoned witnesses to see the mess they had left behind. John Nutt and Sir Edward Masters were Canterbury's two Members of Parliament. They shared Paske's anger as they surveyed the devastation in the choir.

'It's appalling,' Nutt said. 'It should never have been allowed to happen.'

'Your troops smashed everything they couldn't carry away.' Paske still couldn't believe it. 'They ran through the cathedral completely out of control.'

Sir Edward agreed. 'Something obviously went wrong somewhere.'

'You must tell Parliament. Tell them what's being done in their name.'

'Yes, we must. We'll have to make sure it never happens again.'

Sir Michael Livesey reappeared the following day. He too was embarrassed when he saw what the troops had done. He had promised Paske that they would behave themselves in the cathedral.

Livesey went in search of Paske to offer his apologies. He found the priest in the crypt, supervising the repairs to the broken door.

'We're having the doorway to the stream bricked in,' Paske told him. 'Your troops will find it much harder to break down if it's made of solid stone.'

The job was almost completed. Paske and Livesey stood admiring the workmanship as the last brick was carefully cemented into place.

'That'll hold,' Paske said. 'It looks just like the rest of the stonework. No one will even know that there was ever a door there.'

They made polite conversation. Sir Michael Livesey expressed the hope that the war wouldn't last long, if the King would only come to his senses and make a reasonable accommodation with Parliament. Paske made no comment.

'We lost three of our troopers while we were here,' Livesey went on. 'They were absent when we called the roll. They haven't turned up since.'

'No?'

'I don't suppose you've seen them anywhere? Three Parliamentary troopers in helmets. We're wondering what happened to them.'

'Deserted, probably. It's harvest time on the farm.'

'I suppose so.'

'Or maybe they didn't like what their comrades were doing in the cathedral.'

'Maybe. Anyway, if you see them, you will let us know, won't you?'

'I'll think about it,' said Paske.

Chapter Sixteen

The Restoration of Charles II

England was a monarchy again. Eleven years after his father's execution at the end of a devastating civil war, King Charles II was returning from foreign exile to reclaim the throne of his ancestors.

The country was delighted to have him back. The decade of Parliamentary rule under Oliver Cromwell and his major-generals had not been a success. The English were not a republican people. They wanted a King on the throne, not a gang of sanctimonious Roundheads imposing their ideas on everyone else. Now, at last, they had one again.

The new King arrived at Dover on 25 May 1660. The clifftops were black with sightseers as he was rowed ashore after his voyage from Holland. He stepped onto dry land early in the afternoon to a thunderous salute from the harbour's guns. Charles dropped to his knees at once and gave thanks to God for his momentous restoration to his native land.

General Monck was waiting to greet him on behalf of the nation. Monck had fought for Parliament in the Civil War, but he was no republican. He recognised the need for a monarch to fill the void left by the death of Oliver Cromwell. It was George Monck who had negotiated Charles's safe return and formally invited him back to England to take the throne.

'Welcome home, Your Majesty.' General Monck went down on one knee as the King approached. He took Charles's hand and kissed it.

'Father!' Charles kissed him on both cheeks in return after he had got to his feet again.

'God save the King!' shouted everyone else. There was a great roar of acclaim from an ecstatic crowd as Charles was escorted under a canopy to meet the mayor and aldermen of Dover before setting off for Canterbury, where he was to stay for the next few days.

Samuel Pepys had come ashore with the King. He watched as the mayor presented Charles with his white staff of office and a beautiful Bible bound in leather. Charles immediately returned the staff to the mayor but kept the Bible, a gift to him from the people of Dover.

'A Bible is the thing I love above all things in the world,' he assured them, not entirely truthfully.

The King started off immediately for Canterbury. He was accompanied by General Monck and the noblemen who had shared his exile. A long column of coaches was waiting beside the harbour to carry everyone up the hill from the seafront.

The column was escorted by a troop of the King's life guards in splendid uniforms. As soon as it had set off, a beacon was lit at the top of the hill behind Dover Castle. The bonfire was quickly followed by others across the country, hilltop to hilltop, each one fuelled with tar and damp hay to make dark smoke in the sunshine. The King was on his way at last and the people of England were delighted to hear it.

By ancient custom, the convoy stopped at Barham Downs en route to Canterbury. Thousands of people were waiting at the traditional place to receive their monarch, just as their ancestors had received his father and mother in 1625 and Henry V after Agincourt. Now it was Charles II's turn after his recall from a long and bitter exile abroad.

The Kentish nobility were all there, wearing the colours of the King in their hats. So were the ordinary folk for miles around. Squadrons of cavalry and several columns of Kentish militia had been drawn up for Charles's inspection. They all stiffened in anticipation as trumpets and distant cheering announced his imminent arrival.

The troops came to attention as their new monarch appeared. They had been loyal to Parliament for years, but they were the King's men now. There was a flurry of movement as every officer raised his sword and gave Charles a royal salute as he passed down the line.

A few of the officers retained secret Roundhead sympathies, but there was no disguising the enthusiasm of the men at the sight of their new King. Some of them broke ranks and surged forward as he came past. They cheered madly as they set eyes on a monarch for the first time.

'God save the King!' they cried. 'God save Your Majesty! Welcome back to England.'

Charles acknowledged graciously. He was a little dazed at his reception so far. It had been nothing but gun salutes and loud applause all the way, very different from his time during the Civil War. He had had to disguise himself as a servant during the war, hiding in a tree to escape detection. The people of England appeared to have changed their minds since then. They seemed genuinely pleased to see him this time.

'The mayor will be there when we reach Canterbury,' Monck told him, after the inspection was over. 'He'll be waiting for you at the West Gate. That's where royalty traditionally enter the city. The mayor and aldermen will welcome you at the gate and take you on to St Augustine's to stay the night.'

'I'll like that. It's where my parents stayed when they first met.'

'It is, sir. St Augustine's is a very fit place for royalty.'

The Barham troops joined forces with the King's life guards for the remainder of the journey to Canterbury. Bell Harry began to ring as soon as the cavalcade came into view. The rest of the city's church bells followed suit as the long column of horsemen jingled around the ancient walls before coming to a stop at last outside the West Gate.

It was evening by the time they arrived. The mayor of Canterbury made a brief speech of welcome before presenting the King with a tankard of solid gold worth £250. Then he produced a ceremonial sword. Holding it upright in front of him, the mayor led Charles and the rest of the procession through streets full of cheering people to the gates of St Augustine's, the other side of the city.

'Here we are, Your Majesty,' the mayor told the King when they reached the abbey. 'I hope you'll enjoy your stay at the abbey. It had very happy memories for your parents.'

'I'm sure I shall,' Charles said. 'It'll be wonderful just to be sleeping in England again.'

The Fyndon Gate closed behind him. Charles wasn't seen again for the rest of that day. Some of his companions from exile stayed the night at the abbey with him, but most found accommodation in the city. Every inn was busy and every hotel room was taken as they celebrated their long-awaited return to England before finally bedding down for the night.

Next morning, there was a service of thanksgiving for the King's restoration. The cathedral was crammed for the occasion. All of Canterbury was there to welcome the King and point him out to their children. Hundreds of people had come from elsewhere as well. It had been a very long time since anybody had seen a monarch in Canterbury. Nobody wanted to miss it as the King arrived from St Augustine's and took pride of place in the choir.

He was a fine-looking man as he sat down. Twenty-nine years old, much taller than his parents, splendidly dressed for the occasion. Charles looked every inch a king as he knelt to say his prayers before the service began.

The cathedral, by contrast, was a very sorry sight. Years of neglect had taken a heavy toll. After the miseries of Parliamentary rule, Canterbury cathedral looked more like one of Henry VIII's ruined monasteries than the foremost place of worship in the kingdom.

The roof had been badly damaged, for a start. So much lead had been stolen that the timbers were rotting and snow lay thick on the floor of the nave in winter time. The stained glass windows had been smashed, as had much of the pipework. The choir had been stripped of all its tapestries. The organ, communion table and altar rails had not been repaired since their destruction during the Civil War eighteen years earlier. And the monuments were still defaced.

On top of all that, the cathedral's books and furniture had long ago been sold. The records and paperwork had been scattered and lost. Everything else of any value had been smashed or stolen, right down to the brasses and iron bars around the monuments. The place was so derelict that Parliament had discussed the possibility of taking Bell Harry's tower down brick by brick and leaving the middle of the cathedral open to the sky.

But that was in the past now. The King was back, which must surely mean that the cathedral would be restored in due course. The outlawed Book of Common Prayer was back as well. It was in open use during the service. The congregation told each other happily that there would probably be hymns again too, once a new organ had been installed.

'An excellent service,' Charles told General Monck, after it was over. He was very gratified at his reception in the cathedral. 'It's splendid to be in an English church again.'

'You have been in exile too long, sir. It'll all be different from now on.'

They returned to St Augustine's after the service. The King was going to hold the first court of his reign there. He had invited the local gentry to meet him at the abbey and kiss his hand, as was the custom. Other people were coming as well, everybody who felt that they had a claim on the King's attention, now that he was back in England at last.

'There are rather a lot of them,' Monck warned, as the King waited to receive his subjects. 'It looks as if it'll take quite some time for you to see them all.'

'What do they want?'

'Some of them fought for Parliament during the rebellion. They want to apologise for that and receive your pardon in exchange.'

'Others?'

'They fought for your father. They lost their estates or were forced into exile. They're asking for compensation, if they can get it.'

The queue of people seemed never-ending. Everyone had a petition or grievance of some kind. The new king was forced to remain standing for hours as they all waited in line to kiss his hand and tell him their story. He was exhausted by the time the last of them had gone and he was free to relax again.

'I'm afraid there's more,' Monck told him. 'I've made a list of people you may want to appoint to the Privy Council.' He handed it over. 'I believe you're going to hold a meeting of the council later?'

'Tonight.' Charles put the list in his pocket. 'After we've had a rest.'

The King read the list as soon as he was alone. He was appalled to see that only two of the names belonged to Royalists. About forty of the remainder were Presbyterians or former Roundheads. They were Monck's choices, not his. The man was trying to pack the council with people loyal to Parliament.

Charles decided to appoint only a few councillors that day and leave the rest for later. He mollified Monck by appointing him a Knight of the Garter at the beginning of the council meeting. Taking up a sword, Charles dubbed the Roundhead general gently on the shoulder.

'This is for your famous actions in military commands,' he told him. 'By your wisdom, courage and loyalty, you have acted principally in our restoration without effusion of blood. Your actions have no precedent or parallel.'

'Well, thank you, Your Majesty. I'm very happy that no blood has been shed during your return. There's been far too much of that already.'

Only a handful of Privy Councillors were present for their first meeting at St Augustine's abbey. Monck wore the insignia of the Garter around his neck as they got down to business.

'The most important item on the agenda is Your Majesty's arrival in London,' he told the King. 'You go to Rochester from Canterbury. You'll visit the royal dockyards at Chatham before spending the night in Rochester. Then on to London next day.'

'What kind of reception will we have when we get there?'

'The same as you've had already. Great rejoicing all the way.'

'Are you sure about that?'

'Quite sure, Your Majesty. Everyone will be very pleased to see you.'

The other councillors nodded in agreement. The country was celebrating the end of Roundhead rule as much as the reappearance of the King after his enforced absence. It was going to be a new beginning for the realm in every way.

'And when we get to London?'

'You'll ride across London Bridge, then down past St Paul's and along the Strand. There'll be a huge procession all the way to Whitehall. The members of both Houses of Parliament will be assembled there to greet you.'

'I can hardly wait,' Charles said wryly.

'You'll find Parliament much changed,' another councillor assured him quickly. 'The members all know that dreadful mistakes were made in the past. They're determined to work sensibly with the King from now on. Monarch and Parliament both need each other.'

'I suppose they do,' Charles conceded reluctantly. 'We shall all have to let bygones be bygones if we want to live together in peace. Except for regicides, of course.'

They nodded again. It had been agreed as part of the King's return from exile that former Roundheads should not be punished for their conduct during the Civil War, so long as they took an oath of loyalty to him. The only exception was for the Parliamentarians who had signed the warrant for Charles I's execution. There was to be no mercy for the people who had killed the new King's father.

'Where is Sir Michael Livesey now?' Charles asked. Livesey was the man who had demanded the keys to Canterbury cathedral in 1642. He had later been one of those who signed Charles I's death warrant.

'Nobody knows. On the run somewhere. He'll be hanged, drawn and quartered if he dares to show his face.'

'Let's make sure that he is. Whatever mistakes my father made, he didn't deserve to be butchered in public.'

They turned to the next item on the agenda. There was a lot of business to get through. Charles was astonished at quite how much. He had found it one thing after another ever since his arrival at Dover the previous day. Charles had hardly had a moment to himself since setting foot back in England.

He was on the move again a day later, leaving Canterbury for Rochester. The crowds gathered again to watch him go. They gave him an enormous cheer as he got into his carriage at St Augustine's and set off along the High Street towards the West Gate. The people of Canterbury were going to miss their new

King after all the buzz and excitement of the past three days. It was wonderful to have a monarch on the throne again.

Chapter Seventeen

Wolfgang Mozart and the Infant Prodigy

'Are we there yet?' Wolfgang Mozart was a fidgety child, only nine years old. He was always bored on long coach journeys. 'Will we get there soon?'

'Quite soon,' his father assured him. 'Not much further now.'

The coach rattled on. The Mozart family was travelling from London to Canterbury. Leopold Mozart, his wife Anna Maria, their thirteen-year-old daughter Nannerl and young Wolfgang had lived in England for the past year, but they were going home now. After one last performance in Canterbury, they were off back to Europe and their real home in Salzburg.

It had been a splendid year for the family. Young Wolfgang, a composer since the age of six, had been a huge sensation in London. Within a few days of the family's arrival in April 1764, he had been invited to Buckingham House to play the clavier for King George III and Queen Charlotte. The Mozarts hadn't looked back after that.

A week after the performance, the four of them were walking in St James's Park when the King spotted them from his carriage, even though they were wearing different clothes. He leaned out of the window at once, nodding to the family and waving at them as he drove past, while onlookers gaped in astonishment. A king saluting a small boy didn't happen every day in the park.

Where the King led, everyone else followed. The Mozarts had been invited everywhere during their stay in London. Wolfgang's father and sister were talented musicians in their own right. Often playing as a trio, the three of them had taken the capital by storm.

They had twice returned to Buckingham House to entertain the King and Queen again. At her request, Wolfgang had dedicated six of his newly composed sonatas to the Queen in return for a 50 guinea fee. The Mozarts had given public recitals as well, raking money in as the aristocracy flocked to hear them. There were no mountains that they hadn't conquered during their fourteen months in the capital.

But the time had come to leave, if only because London was no place for children to grow up. England's capital was the biggest, most powerful city in the world, but it was also expensive, dirty, unhealthy and full of vice. The Mozarts yearned for Salzburg after so long a time away from home.

'We'll spend a night in Canterbury before we go,' Leopold told the children. 'Nannerl and Wolfgang are booked to give a performance in the town hall. After that, we've been invited to stay in the country for a few days until our ship is due to sail.'

'The country?'

'Bourne Park. A Mr Mann has invited us. I believe he's an English milord of some kind.'

They drove on. Canterbury was looking lovely when they reached it. Their first sight of the city was through the window as their coach rounded a bend near Harbledown. The city lay in the valley ahead of them, dominated by the tower of Bell Harry. Leopold pointed it out to his children.

'See that? That's the Hauptkirch. Canterbury cathedral.'

A few minutes later, they arrived at their inn on the High Street. The inn lay across the road from the town hall, where the children were to give their recital next morning. As soon as they had unpacked, Leopold Mozart went across to the hall to discuss the arrangements for the performance.

'I'm afraid we have bad news,' he was told. 'It looks as if it may have to be cancelled.'

'Why?'

'We haven't sold enough tickets.'

'Not enough?' Leopold was shocked. 'Why ever not?'

'Nobody wants to come.'

'But we always sell tickets for Wolfgang's performances.'

'Not in Canterbury, you don't. There isn't much demand, I'm afraid.'

'Did you advertise it properly? Tell people he was coming?'

'We did, yes. We put an advertisement in last Saturday's newspaper.'

A copy of the Kentish Post for 20 July 1765 was produced. Leopold scanned it in disbelief:

On Thursday July 25 at Eleven in the Forenoon will be A MUSICAL

PERFORMANCE at the TOWN HALL in Canterbury FOR the BENEFIT of Master MOZART, the celebrated German Boy aged nine years and his Sister who have exhibited with universal Applause to the Nobility and Gentry in London. The Compositions and extempore Performances of this little boy are the Astonishment of all Judges of Music. Admission 2s 6d.

'Yet you haven't sold enough tickets?'

'I fear not. Unless there's a last-minute rush, we'll have to cancel the whole performance.'

Leopold was outraged. 'Wolfgang and Nannerl performed for the King and Queen in London,' he pointed out. 'They're very talented. Everyone wants to hear them play.'

'Not in Canterbury, they don't. It's probably because of the races.'

'The races?'

'There's a race meeting at Barham this week. Horse racing. There's cock fighting too. People would much rather watch a cock fight than see your children perform.'

Leopold Mozart knew about the race meeting. Horatio Mann had invited his family to attend when they came to stay. He hadn't realised it would interfere with the recital.

'So the performance is cancelled?'

'We won't know for sure until tomorrow morning. There may be a last-minute rush, now that everyone knows you're here.'

There was no rush. The performance was duly cancelled and the Mozarts were left at a loose end for the morning. After they had got over their annoyance, they wondered what to do until it was time to go to Mr Mann. Mrs Mozart suggested they should look around the Hauptkirch, since they were in Canterbury.

'We might as well,' she told her family. 'We won't get the chance again.'

They went to the Martyrdom first and then wandered around the rest of the cathedral. Disappointed at the cancellation of the performance, Wolfgang Mozart trailed disconsolately after his parents until they came at length to the organ loft beside the choir. He perked up when he saw the organ, sitting high in the loft. It was a mighty instrument, with three manuals and fourteen stops. He eyed it with professional interest.

'Think you could play that?' his father asked him. There was no more complex piece of machinery in the world than a church organ.

'Of course I could, if anybody in Canterbury wanted to listen.'

They returned to the inn after their visit to the cathedral. The innkeeper came at once to tell them that they had had a visitor in their absence.

'The Dutch ambassador,' he told Leopold Mozart. 'He's waiting for you in the tap room.'

'The Dutch ambassador?' Leopold was puzzled. What did a diplomat want with the Mozarts?

He went to find out. The ambassador leapt to his feet as soon as he came in.

'I'm so glad I found you,' he told Leopold. 'I've been following you all the way from London. I thought I was going to miss you before you went to France.'

'Well, now that you're here, what can I do for you?'

'I have a request for you from the Princess of Weilburg.'

'Who's she?'

'The Prince of Orange's sister. In Holland. She's very keen to meet your son.'

'Yes?'

'She wants you to come to The Hague before you go home so that she can hear him play.'

'At The Hague?'

'She's heard so much about Wolfgang. She wants to see him for herself.'

Leopold sighed. He had already refused several invitations from the Prince of Orange to visit Holland. Now the Prince's sister was asking him as well.

'She's with child,' the ambassador told him. 'She'd count it as a very special favour if she could hear Wolfgang play before her confinement. The Princess would certainly make it worth your while, if you all came to Holland.'

'How much?'

The ambassador named a sum. The Princess's offer was very generous.

'All right,' Leopold agreed wearily. 'I suppose we shall have to give in. We'll come. We can hardly refuse a woman if she's pregnant.'

'That's very good of you. You won't regret it. The Princess will make your family very welcome in The Hague.'

The ambassador departed after lunch. He was visibly relieved as he bade the Mozarts farewell and returned to London. The family settled their bill at the inn and hired a coach to take them to Bourne Park. It was a large country estate just outside Canterbury, near Barham Downs.

Their host wasn't quite an English milord. Horatio Mann was merely the heir to a baronetcy. He was a rich young man of 21, recently married to the Earl of Gainsborough's daughter Lucy. They were in the first flush of wedded bliss as they welcomed the Mozarts to their magnificent home across the road from the racecourse on the Downs.

Bourne House stood in its own extensive grounds. The estate included an ice house, a bridge over the river feeding the lake and a paddock that was currently being transformed into a cricket pitch. Horatio Mann – Horace, to his friends — was an enthusiastic sportsman. He had big ambitions for cricket in Kent.

Mann had his dog with him as the Mozarts appeared up the drive. He made no secret of his delight as a footman opened the carriage door.

'Here you are at last! I'm so glad you could come. It's lovely to have you all here.'

'Thank you for inviting us,' said Leopold.

'Think nothing of it. I heard your son play when I was in London. You must be very proud of him.'

Mann led the way to the house. The Mozarts were impressed. The house was very grand and the grounds were sublime. Nannerl was particularly enchanted by the view across the lake.

'You have a wonderful garden,' she told Lady Lucy. 'It's really beautiful.'

'Thank you. We do rather pride ourselves on our gardens in England.'

The Mozarts didn't take long to settle in. English country life was unfamiliar to them, but Bourne was lovely and the Manns were attentive hosts. They did everything they could to put their guests at ease.

After breakfast next morning, the ladies went for a stroll in the garden. Fetching bat and ball, Horace Mann took Leopold and Wolfgang down to the paddock to have a look at his new cricket pitch. He returned later with devastating news.

'I'm afraid your son will never make a cricketer, Mrs Mozart. He has no eye for the game at all.'

'Oh dear.' Mrs Mozart took the news philosophically. She was just happy that her son was enjoying himself at Bourne. With no performances to prepare for, Wolfgang was off the leash for a while. He was free to be a little boy of nine again, tearing around the garden and waving his arms, throwing sticks, shouting to his heart's content. He was having a wonderful time.

Wolfgang had learned some English during his year in London. His favourite words were poo, bum and piss. Nobody was sure if he even knew what the words meant, but he used them all the time. The Manns forebore to comment. What might have been objectionable in an English child was obviously pardonable in a foreigner.

The Manns were greatly looking forward to the race meeting at the end of the Mozarts' stay. The racecourse had been built on Barham Downs, the flat pasture where soldiers used to gather to greet the sovereign. The three-day meet at Barham was one of the highlights of the summer calendar in Kent.

'Everyone will be there for it,' Horace Mann told the Mozarts. 'Everyone we know. We're having a lunch party beforehand. I've asked our friends here to meet you. We'll all have lunch at the house and then go on to the races together.'

The Mozarts were as excited as the Manns at the prospect. It was all very different to what they were used to. The family were in their best summer clothes as the guests' carriages began to roll up the drive soon after midday. The sun was so hot that everyone went straight indoors for a cooling drink before gathering in the dining room for lunch.

Among the guests was Mrs Reynard. She had brought her son with her. George was a chubby boy of four, unprepossessing to look at, but clearly the apple of his mother's eye.

'I couldn't bear to part with him,' she told the Manns. 'You don't mind, do you? George gets very upset if I leave him with his nurse.'

'Not at all,' said Lucy Mann graciously. 'George is most welcome. We don't mind a bit.'

George was something of an infant prodigy, according to his mother. His first words, his first footsteps, his every new tooth had all been hailed as extraordinary milestones in his development. Mrs Reynard felt that it reflected very creditably on her, having such a remarkable child for a son.

'He's very advanced,' she told Mrs Mozart, as they sat together. 'Extraordinarily so. George is very forward for his age.'

'Is he?'

Mrs Reynard nodded. 'He's wonderfully gifted. I've never seen anything like it.'

'Gifted?'

Mrs Reynard nodded again. 'Quite astonishing. It's too soon to tell, of course, but I rather suspect we have a young genius on our hands.'

She dominated the conversation for the next ten minutes, telling everyone about George's phenomenal abilities. No one else could get a word in edgeways as she prattled on. She was still extolling her son's virtues when there was a sudden burst of shouting in the garden.

Mrs Reynard transferred her gaze from her astounding son to the uncouth child on the lawn outside. Wolfgang Mozart was running around the flower beds, yelling obscenities as he beheaded all the flowers with a cricket bat.

Mrs Reynard watched him sourly. She felt all the satisfaction of a mother mentally comparing her own little angel to somebody else's perfectly ghastly small boy. Then she remembered her manners.

'What about your son, Mrs Mozart? I hear he plays the piano?'

'He does. He composes as well. As a matter of fact, the Queen…'

'George will play the piano too when he's older. He'll delight us all with his wonderful music when he's grown up. Won't you, pumpkin?'

The infant prodigy beamed at his mother.

'Poo, bum, piss,' said Mozart.

Chapter Eighteen

John Adams, Future U.S. President

Boston, Massachusetts was a foot deep in snow on the night of 5 March 1770. There were no streetlights, but the moon was out as a gang of unruly Americans headed towards the British army post near the Custom House on King Street. There were at least a dozen of them, mainly apprentices or young thugs armed with cudgels, and they were spoiling for a fight.

Trouble had been brewing ever since the British government sent troops to Massachusetts in an attempt to enforce law and order. The sight of Redcoats on the streets had only inflamed the situation. The people of Boston didn't like the idea of a standing army on their soil. They didn't like the soldiers supplementing their pay by taking part-time jobs from local people. And they certainly didn't like them picking up American girls in their fancy uniforms.

'Let's get them,' the Americans told each other, as they arrived in King Street. 'Bloody lobsterbacks. Let's find a few of the bastards and beat them up.'

The only soldier in sight as the gang closed in was Private White of the 29th Regiment. He was on sentry duty outside the Custom House, where the tax revenues were kept. The Americans surrounded him at once and began to taunt him.

They provoked him into swinging his musket and hitting one of the apprentices on the side of the head. The boy reeled in pain. His friends immediately began to pelt White with stones and snowballs, challenging him to come out of his sentry box and fight like a man.

White loaded his musket in self-defence and ostentatiously fixed the bayonet. The Americans, more than fifty of them by now, jeered. They knew White wouldn't dare fire. One of them told him he would be hanged for murder if he did.

'Damn them.' White glared at the gang. 'If they molest me, I'll fire all right.'

'Go on, then!' the Americans yelled. 'Fire, damn you! Fire!'

'They're only boys,' an onlooker advised White. 'Just kids. They won't hurt you.'

'Kill him,' the gang shouted in response. 'Kill him. Knock him down.'

White banged on the Custom House door, but couldn't get in. He yelled for help, calling for the main guard down the street to come to his aid. At the same time, a church bell began to ring, the signal for a public emergency in the streets.

The people spilling out of their houses at the sound were quickly drawn to the commotion at the Custom House. Before long, a crowd of several hundred had joined the gang around Private White. His life was clearly in danger as his officer, Captain Preston, dithered about how to save him.

Preston was an Irishman and a good soldier, but he was hampered by the law. Troops were forbidden to quell civil disturbances without a specific request from the civic authority. There would be outrage if he ignored the law and fought the mob without an order from a magistrate. But White would be killed if he didn't.

Preston didn't hesitate for long. Summoning the only available troops, he went to White's rescue. Six privates and a corporal formed up with their muskets at the shoulder and followed him as he led the way along the street to the Custom House.

The soldiers were heavily outnumbered when they arrived. The same man who had advised White not to fire now came out of the crowd again and warned Preston not to either.

'For God's sake, take care of your men,' he told him. 'If they fire, you'll all die.'

'I'm aware of it,' Preston replied.

White was rescued. Turning his men around, Preston marched them back towards the main guard post beside the State House. A howling mob threw rubbish at them and tried to block their path. The troops had reached the State House when Preston told the crowd to disperse. The crowd dared him to open fire in return. They knew Preston would never give the order.

'Put your weapons down and fight us,' they mocked him. 'Go on. Either fire at us or fight.'

Preston knew better than to be provoked. Unfortunately for him, someone came out of the darkness and hit Private Montgomery with a heavy club. The soldier slipped on the ice and fell over. Another missile hit him just as he was getting up.

'Damn you,' Montgomery shouted. 'Fire!'

He took his own advice, but the shot didn't hit anybody. There was a brief, shocked silence before the rest of the soldiers opened up as well. They all

128

discharged their muskets and reloaded at once. By the time they had finished firing, five people in the mob that had been taunting them a minute earlier lay dead or dying in the snow. The rest were running away.

Preston was appalled. 'Stop it,' he ordered his men, as soon as he got the chance. 'Stop firing. Who told you to start firing?'

'You did, sir.'

'No, I didn't.'

'Someone did. We heard someone telling us to.'

There was no use arguing about it. The damage had been done. Five Americans had been killed by the British army. Nothing would ever bring them back. The bodies lying in the snow were eloquent testament to that.

The mob returned cautiously after the shooting had stopped. The crowd doubled in size as the news spread, but there was no more trouble that night. Massachusetts's Lieutenant-Governor addressed the people from the balcony of the State House and told them all to go home quietly. He promised them that the soldiers would be put on trial for the shooting and he would see to it that justice was done.

The Lieutenant-Governor was as good as his word. The soldiers were arrested at once to await trial for murder. They would be sentenced to death if they were found guilty.

Nobody wanted to defend them when they came to court. Every lawyer in Boston knew that it would be commercial death to take the case. It might be real death too, if the lawyers' houses were burned down by an angry crowd or they were physically attacked in the street.

In the end, John Adams, a lawyer with political ambitions, reluctantly agreed to lead the defence team. He didn't like it any more than anyone else, but he was a lawyer first and foremost. Men standing trial for murder were entitled to a fair trial. That meant having a lawyer to defend them.

'It's in Magna Carta,' he told his critics, when they accused him of lacking patriotism.

'What is?'

'The right to a fair trial. *No free man shall be seized or imprisoned except by the lawful judgment of his peers.* It's in Magna Carta. The bedrock of justice.'

Tempers had cooled by the time the trial took place. The Americans killed in the so-called Boston massacre had been asking for trouble when they deliberately provoked the troops. They had gone out looking for a fight that night and they had found one. Adams had little sympathy for them as he addressed the jury.

'They were a mob,' he told the jurors. 'In plain English, gentlemen, a motley rabble of saucy boys, negroes and mulattoes, Irish teagues and outlandish jack tars. Why should we scruple to call such a set of people a mob?'

Adams warmed to his theme as he defended the soldier who had fired the first shot.

'In regard to the soldier Montgomery, the evidence is clear enough that he had been assaulted and knocked down before he rose and fired. How much was he supposed to bear before retaliating?

'When the multitude was shouting and huzzaing, and threatening life, the bells ringing, the mob whistling, screaming and rendering an Indian yell, the people from all quarters throwing every species of rubbish they could pick up in the street, Montgomery in particular smote with a club and knocked down, and as soon as he could rise and take up his firelock, another club from afar, struck his breast or shoulder. What could he do?'

Adams told the court that the British had only fired in self-defence, and then only by accident. A jury packed with Crown loyalists agreed. They found two of the soldiers guilty of manslaughter, to be branded on their thumbs as punishment. The rest were found not guilty and walked free.

Adams's career didn't suffer as he had feared. Instead, his insistence on upholding the law against his own inclinations increased his standing in Massachusetts. He became one of his country's founding fathers when he signed the American Declaration of Independence. He later went to France as one of the American representatives negotiating the Treaty of Paris that brought the war with Britain to an end in September 1783.

The treaty was very favourable to the United States. Recognising the inevitable, the pragmatic British offered generous terms in return for commercial arrangements that would benefit both sides. If they didn't own the colonies anymore, the British could still make money by trading with them. The Americans could pay their own defence costs against the Redskins from now on.

The peace was signed in Paris on 3 September. Adams immediately began to plan a trip to England to explore the trading possibilities. It was safe for him to visit at last, now that the two countries were no longer at war.

He was greatly looking forward to the trip. Despite everything that had happened, England was still the mother country. English law, English language, English literature. English ideas and inventions. Adams knew where his ancestors had come from. He didn't want to die without seeing England first.

His wife Abigail was home in America, but his son, John Quincy Adams, was in France. The two of them went to England together.

'We'll stay the night at Abbeville,' Adams told his son, as they left Paris. 'We'll go on to Calais and sail from there to Dover.'

The passage across the Channel lasted eighteen hours. Adams and his son arrived dreadfully seasick in the small hours of 24 October. They were taken through the darkness to the Royal Hotel at the foot of the Dover cliffs and collapsed thankfully into bed. It wasn't until much later in the day that they surfaced again and were able to take stock of their new surroundings.

Adams was appalled at the sight of the cliffs above his head. So high and perpendicular. He wondered if parts ever broke off and destroyed the houses below.

He and his son decided to explore them. They climbed the coach road to the top of the cliffs. It was a foggy day, but they still had a good view of the harbour from the heights, and the nearest of the ships out to sea. What impressed them most, though, was the size of the sheep on the clifftops. They had never seen such fat sheep before, or such green grass.

'They're enormous.' John Quincy Adams could hardly believe it. 'Much bigger than anything in France.'

'It's the grass. England has the climate for sheep. The Speaker in the House of Lords sits on a big sack of wool to remind him where the country's prosperity comes from.'

It wasn't until next morning that Adams and his son set off for London. They travelled in a post chaise and pair and made their first change of horses at the coaching inn in Canterbury. The tower of Bell Harry was the first thing they saw of the city as they came in along the Dover Road.

'I wonder what that is,' said John Quincy.

'It's the cathedral tower. Canterbury is the chief see in England.'

'Can we go see it?'

John Adams shook his head. 'There isn't time. We have to get to Dartford tonight.'

They stayed at the inn only long enough to change horses and use the chamber pot. It seemed a shame that they didn't have a chance to look around at all. There was a lot to see in the cathedral.

'Hey, landlord,' said John Adams.

'Sir?'

'Can you tell me something about the cathedral? Am I right in thinking that they keep a copy of Magna Carta in there?'

'King John's Magna Carta?'

'That's the one.'

'Oh, bless you, sir. I believe they did have a copy years ago. I think it got damaged in a fire.'

'So it's not there anymore?'

'I don't think so. Someone took it away.'

'That's a shame,' said Adams.

He and his son returned to their post chaise and continued to London. A few months later, once he was settled in the capital, Adams sent for his wife from America. Abigail came soon afterwards, arriving at Deal on 20 July 1784.

She too admired the sheep as she travelled inland. But Abigail Adams, wife of one future American President and mother of another, wasn't particularly impressed by her first sight of a cathedral city. She told her sister so in a letter home:

Canteburry is a larger town than Boston, it contains a Number of old Gothick Cathedrals, which are all of stone very heavy, with but few windows which are grated with large Bars of Iron, and look more like jails for criminals than places designd for the worship of the deity.

One would Suppose from the manner in which they are Gaurded, that they apprehended devotion would be stolen. They have a most gloomy appearance and realy made me shudder.

Chapter Nineteen

Napoleon's Troops in the Precincts

One of Napoleon's invasion barges had just been captured. It had been intercepted in the English Channel and towed in to Deal, complete with soldiers and crew. The Frenchmen didn't look happy as they floated fifty yards offshore, while everyone stared at them from the beach.

The Prime Minister hired a rowing boat and went out to have a closer look. William Pitt had a farm near Deal and was Warden of the Cinque Ports. He commanded the Cinque Port Volunteers, a ragbag collection of ploughboys and fishermen armed mostly with pikes and pitchforks. In November 1803, they were all that stood between London and Napoleon's Grand Army if the invasion troops ever managed to come ashore.

Pitt had his niece with him as they approached the captured barge. Lady Hester Stanhope lived with her bachelor uncle at Walmer Castle and acted as his hostess at dinner. She often accompanied him on his inspection tours of the Volunteers, sometimes riding more than twenty miles at a stretch.

The barge was an ungainly craft, flat-bottomed, about thirty feet long. It had two large guns on board, four sailors, and thirty soldiers. They stared back defiantly as Pitt and his niece inspected them from the rowing boat.

'Picked men,' Lady Hester whispered to her uncle. 'They're obviously good troops. You only have to look at them to see that.'

Pitt agreed. His heart sank at the sight of the French. General Bonaparte's troops were a lot more professional than the amateurish Englishmen opposing them. The men of the Grand Army were properly trained and superbly equipped, much more so than their British counterparts.

'I suppose you were practising for the invasion when you were captured?' he asked the prisoners.

They nodded.

'Well, you're our prisoners now. You won't go back to France. You'll be taken ashore instead and kept in confinement.'

'Not for long,' one of them retorted. He was a small man in a cocked hat. 'Why?'

'We'll be rescued as soon as the invasion starts. It won't be long now. A couple of months at most. We'll all be free again after that.'

The man was probably right, Pitt knew. There would be no stopping the French, once they had a foothold on British soil. Bonaparte had more than a hundred thousand troops across the Channel, ready to invade at any moment. Their tents had turned the clifftops white, all the way from Calais to Boulogne.

But the French hadn't arrived yet. They never would, if the Royal Navy had anything to do with it. The British were as strong at sea as the French were on land. The navy wouldn't allow the French to come ashore without a fight.

'I shouldn't count on an invasion, if I were you,' Pitt told the Frenchman. 'It'll be a lot more than a couple of months before you're free again.'

He and Hester returned to shore. Pitt wondered if he should tell London about the invasion barge. The telegraph station stood on the seafront. Its operators claimed they could get a message to the Admiralty in ten minutes flat, with good visibility.

He decided not to bother. One captured barge didn't make an invasion. Hundreds would have been a different matter.

'It all depends on the Royal Navy,' he told Hester, as they returned to their horses. 'As long as the navy can hold the French off for a while, we'll be all right.'

'And if they can't?'

'We'll fight them with everything we have. We can't give in to Bonaparte. The man's a dictator.'

Hester agreed. She was greatly enjoying the invasion crisis so far. It was thrilling to be at the centre of events, following the Prime Minister around and entertaining all the generals and admirals at dinner as they discussed the situation. Hester had looked at France through a telescope and seen the Grand Army's tents on the cliffs. She was excited to think of the beastly French storming ashore in Kent while her uncle's Volunteers hacked at them with gardening tools in a battle to the death.

Hester had recently had some excitement of her own at the hands of some troopers from the Royal Horse Guards. Five of them, half-drunk, had spotted her in the street at Ramsgate and followed her to her door. They had chased her upstairs and grabbed hold of her dress.

The men were about to do their worst when Hester punched the nearest one so hard that he fell down the stairs, his sword rattling against the bannisters. The others retreated too. Hester had been a sensation for the next few days, everyone pointing her out in the street as the woman who had given a trooper of the Blues an enormous black eye.

'What will happen to the Frenchmen in the barge?' she asked her uncle, as they mounted up. 'Are they going to be put in prison somewhere?'

'They'll be questioned first and then taken inland. They'll be split up and dispersed in different places where they can't be a nuisance.'

'Inland?'

'Well away from the sea. We don't want their own people rescuing them if there's an invasion.'

Pitt and Hester rode back to Walmer Castle. The Prime Minister was a very worried man as they went. The threat from General Bonaparte was the greatest military crisis the country had faced since the Spanish Armada of 1588. Pitt knew better than anyone that there was very little to stop the French once they had their army on dry land. He could hardly bear to think about it as he and Hester returned to the castle.

Behind them, the Frenchmen in the barge came ashore in their turn and were taken to the town hall for questioning. A hostile crowd gathered to watch, but the men were still defiant as they were led along the street. They knew that they belonged to the most powerful and highly trained army in the world. They had nothing to fear from the English.

'We won't talk,' the man in the cocked hat told his interrogators, when they reached the town hall. 'We've nothing to say to you. The rest of our army will be here soon, and General Bonaparte too. That's all you need to know.'

'In a couple of months, you say?'

'Certainly no longer than that. Our troops are all ready to go. There's nothing to stop them.'

'Apart from the Royal Navy.'

'Pah!' The Frenchman shrugged. He was a supercilious fellow. 'Your navy won't stop us. Nothing will. Nothing can.'

The other soldiers agreed. The Grand Army was invincible. General Bonaparte's troops would roll the English up in no time at all, once they had their boots on the ground. All the troops needed was a fair wind and a calm sea for a few hours and England would become a province of France. There was nothing more to be said.

The prisoners spent the night under guard at Deal before being divided into groups and taken inland next morning. A dozen of them were sent to the cathedral gaol in Canterbury. The man in the cocked hat was among them as they set off under escort. They arrived in Canterbury that afternoon, still defiant as they entered the city and were led through the streets to the prison.

It lay among the old monastic buildings on the north side of the cathedral. The prison had been used in pilgrim times for the detention of minor offenders in the precincts. It had lain empty for years after Henry VIII got rid of the priory but had recently been called back into service for the imprisonment of Frenchmen captured in the war.

Curious eyes followed the Deal captives as they marched along Palace Street. The men turned into the Mint Yard and passed through the King's School to the Green Court gate, the old monastic entrance to the priory. The prison lay next to the gate, underneath a row of Norman arches.

The Frenchmen halted at the entrance as they waited to be admitted. On the wall next to them, someone had carved the date 1649 in large numerals to mark the execution of King Charles I. The date meant nothing to the men as they studied it. Louis XVI was the only monarch they knew anything about.

'All right, Frenchies.' A sergeant from the Canterbury garrison came forward to receive them. 'This is going to be your home in England for the foreseeable future. It's where you'll all stay until we've beaten your General Bonaparte.'

He led them through the gate. The prisoners were dismayed to see that the cathedral gaol was tiny, much smaller than they had expected. It had been designed to house the occasional drunk or petty thief caught stealing in the precincts, not a boatload of troops from France.

They looked around with sinking hearts. There was a small courtyard outside the prison. At one end stood the Norman staircase, an external stone stairway that had been there since Thomas Becket's time. At the other, they could see the tower of Bell Harry looming over the prison fence. That was all the space they had.

'Merde!' The French were deeply disheartened. They were still in shock at their sudden reversal of fortune. Two days ago they had been part of a mighty army, full of self-confidence as they prepared to invade their ancient enemies across the Channel. Now they were prisoners of the English, clapped ignominiously into gaol like common criminals. Some of them still had laundry to collect in Boulogne, and girls waiting for them in the town.

'It won't be for long.' The man in the cocked hat tried to rally his comrades.

'Only for a few months. We'll be out of here by the spring at the latest, on our way to London.'

They all hoped he was right. The sooner the Grand Army came to their rescue the better. None of them wanted to be a prisoner of the English for any longer than could be helped.

The soldiers weren't the only people in the prison. They were shocked to discover that a group of French sailors had got there before them and had been captive since June. The cathedral gaol was going to be even more cramped than they had thought.

The old lags weren't pleased to see them either, if it meant losing some of their bed space. The sailors clustered around, nevertheless, as soon as the newcomers had settled in. They were desperate for news from home.

'So General Bonaparte is going to invade England?' was their first, all-important question.

'Bien sur. Any day now. The army is only waiting for a fair wind.'

'Where is it going to land?'

'In Kent, somewhere. We've been training for months.'

The sailors were sceptical. There was more to landing flat-bottomed invasion barges in Kent than met the eye. It would need several days of good weather, for one thing, and the weather in the Channel was notoriously unreliable. They wondered how much General Bonaparte knew about the difficult conditions at sea.

There were other problems too.

'What about the Royal Navy?' one of them asked. 'It'll take several high tides just to get the invasion barges out of harbour. The English won't just stand by and watch, if they see us trying to invade.'

'Don't worry about the English.' The man with the cockade was full of confidence. 'General Bonaparte will take care of their navy. He knows what he's doing.'

The sailors certainly hoped so. They were all in favour of being liberated, if it could be done. They just hoped that whoever was in charge of the French invasion knew as much about the Channel's shifting sands and treacherous cross-currents as the English did.

'So he'll be here soon?'

'With a hundred thousand troops. It's the biggest army anyone has ever seen.'

The newcomers settled down impatiently to await rescue by their fellow countrymen. They found that life in the shadow of Bell Harry wasn't too bad, once they had got used to their cramped surroundings. They were guarded by English soldiers from the barracks just outside the town. The sentries were decent men. As time went on, they began to tease the French about General Bonaparte's continued failure to appear in Canterbury, as promised.

'Where is he then, Johnny?' All Frenchmen were Johnny Crapaud to the English. 'Where's your precious General Bonaparte? Shouldn't he have been here by now?'

'He'll be here, soon enough. You'll all know about it when he arrives.'

The Frenchman in the hat was Bonaparte's greatest admirer. The man had joined the French army for revolutionary reasons and wore the national cockade with pride. He saw it as his patriotic duty to subvert the English soldiers and bring them round to a revolutionary way of thinking.

'You should be with us, not against us,' he told one of the sentries. 'We're fighting for the brotherhood of man, after all. We've got rid of our king and the aristocrats and priests. Parasites, every one. You could easily do the same, if you wanted.'

'Cut all their throats, you mean?'

The Frenchman nodded. 'That's how to deal with them.'

'Well, I'll tell you what, mate.' The sentry had a grasp of political theory unusual in a private soldier. 'Why don't you just keep your revolution and we'll keep our King? That'll be best for everybody.'

The Frenchman shrugged.

'Parasites,' he repeated. 'That's how to deal with them.'

'Not here it isn't.' The sentry waved an arm around the peaceful, beautiful precincts of Canterbury cathedral. 'No Englishman around here is going to have his throat cut by a Frenchman in the name of the revolution. Your Mr Bonaparte will find that out, if he ever dares to show his face.'

'We'll see,' said the Frenchman.

Chapter Twenty

Jane Austen and Lady Hamilton's Enormous Behind

Jane Austen was staying with her brother Edward at Godmersham, his country estate near Canterbury. It was a lovely place in the Stour valley with a deer park of its own and good shooting in the woods. Jane always liked to spend a few weeks there every summer. It was where she did some of her best writing.

Jane was still unpublished in September 1805, but that was only because she insisted on endlessly revising her work. She had already written several novels and other bits and pieces, but she wasn't ready yet to show anything to a publisher. Jane was waiting until she had her books exactly right before she did that.

It was an exciting time at Godmersham. The French were still poised to invade, if they could somehow get past the Royal Navy. Edward commanded the local volunteers and drilled them endlessly in the park, ready to put up a good fight when they came. The feeling in the country was that the crisis must surely come to a head soon. The French would have to invade England by the end of the year or abandon the idea for ever.

For the moment, though, the weather was glorious and there wasn't a Frenchman in sight. Edward had some business to attend to in Canterbury. He invited Jane to come with him for the ride.

'You could do a bit of shopping while I do my business,' he suggested. 'Then we could have lunch or something. Look round the cathedral.'

'Oh yes, I'd like that.' Jane always enjoyed her visits to Canterbury. 'Yes, let's do that. It'll be fun.'

Jane did like Canterbury. She had found it dull in the past, but it had come alive during the invasion scare. It was full of people from Dover and other coastal towns, taking refuge inland until the danger from the French had passed. The city was full of soldiers too, handsome officers from the Foot Guards and other smart regiments. No ball at the assembly rooms was complete without a few officers in dashing uniforms lining up for the cotillion.

They went into Canterbury. After Edward had finished his business, they had lunch before going to see the cathedral. There was something in particular that Jane wanted to look at in the precincts.

'I have a mind to see the King's School. Our friend George Lefroy, the vicar at Ashe, he was a boy there.'

'Yes?'

'He said to look out for the school if ever I was in the cathedral precincts. His brother was there too.'

It was the brother's son who interested Jane. Tom Lefroy had grown up in Ireland, a clever young man with a degree from Trinity College, Dublin. Jane had met him when he was staying with his uncle at Ashe. She had been smitten at once.

Tom Lefroy had taken to her too, but nothing had come of it. Instead, Jane had worked furiously at her novel, a fanciful tale involving a rich landowner with a French-Irish surname falling in love with a poor but clever girl from a large family. It was her experience that love affairs always worked out much more satisfactorily on paper than in real life.

The King's School occupied the Mint Yard. It didn't take long to look around. Jane and Edward admired the old Almonry building where Christopher Marlowe had been a pupil and then moved on through the Green Court gate. They found the French soldiers still there, still captive in the prison beside the Norman staircase. A Frenchman in a cocked hat gazed forlornly at them as they peered over the fence.

'Rowlandson was here last year,' Edward told Jane.

'The artist?'

Edward nodded. 'He did a picture of the prisoners by the Norman staircase. You can get a copy in the High Street.'

They moved on again and turned to look at the cathedral. Bell Harry towered above them across the Green Court. Jane shaded her eyes to look at the great belfry, so very high in the sky.

'You can see France from the top,' Edward told her.

'Can you?'

'On a clear day. The French coast is less than forty miles away.'

'So you could watch the invasion from there?'

'I imagine so. If the weather was right.'

They had a strong personal interest in the invasion. Two of their brothers were serving in the Royal Navy. Frank Austen was the flag-captain aboard HMS *Canopus*, part of Lord Nelson's fleet. He would be in the thick of the action if the French navy ever put to sea.

'Do you suppose Frank's balloons will ever work?' Jane asked.

Both Britain and France were employing the latest military technology in the war. General Bonaparte, now calling himself the Emperor Napoleon, was contemplating the use of hot-air balloons to ferry his army across the Channel above the heads of the Royal Navy. Frank Austen had a plan for an early warning system that involved balloons tethered to Royal Navy ships in the middle of the Channel. Both ideas seemed a bit fanciful to Jane and Edward.

'I can't see a lot of Frenchmen flying over here and landing on the Green Court,' Edward said. 'It's too extraordinary for words.'

'Interesting to watch, though. A fleet of Bonaparte's balloons coming over Bell Harry to attack us from the air!'

They moved on towards the cathedral. The covered passageway ahead was known as the Dark Entry. Christopher Marlowe had gone to the cathedral that way during his schooldays.

'He mentioned it in one of his plays,' Edward said. '*The Jew of Malta*, I think.'

'A dark entry where they take it in,' Jane quoted. 'Something something neither see the messenger nor make inquiry. I've forgotten the rest. It wasn't his mightiest line.'

They continued towards the cloisters. They had almost arrived when Jane spotted someone coming towards them along the brick walk. Her heart sank when she saw who it was.

'Quick,' she told Edward. 'It's Miss Milles. Let's move on before she sees us.'

They were too late. Miss Milles had spotted them too. She came hurrying over at once.

'Is that really you, Miss Austen? I thought it was. How very nice to see you.'

'And you,' said Jane, not entirely truthfully.

Miss Milles lived with her mother in a cathedral property at the other end of the brick walk. Master Homer's house was more than five hundred years old. Edward IV had held a council meeting there during the Wars of the Roses. For the past fifty years, the house had been rented out to Mrs Milles, who was increasingly unable to keep up the payments. She and her daughter didn't have a penny between them.

They were nice people, but dreadfully poor and dull. Miss Milles in particular could prattle on for hours without ever saying anything interesting. Jane was thinking of putting her in a book.

'I'm so glad I found you,' Miss Milles told her. 'I have some astonishing news for you.'

Here we go, Jane thought. Someone has caught a cold. Her mother has lost her knitting again. She has had a letter and wants to read it to me.

Jane did Miss Milles an injustice. The news was indeed sensational.

'Lady Hamilton is here!'

'Lord Nelson's friend?'

Miss Milles nodded. 'The friend of his bosom. She's come to see his brother. Her carriage arrived not half an hour ago.'

Jane looked over Miss Milles's shoulder. There it was, right enough. Admiral Nelson's carriage, with his arms emblazoned on the side. It was parked outside Canon Nelson's house, next door to Master Homer's.

Canon Nelson was a pale shadow of his famous brother. He would have been a simple country parson if it hadn't been for the Hero of the Nile. He had traded on his brother's reputation to acquire a good living as a prebendary of Canterbury cathedral. He was angling to become Dean as soon as the job became vacant.

Lord Nelson had recently sailed from England to join the fleet off Cadiz. His orders were to bring the French fleet to battle and destroy it once and for all, so putting an end to Bonaparte's invasion plans. The whole country was cheering him on as he sailed towards his destiny.

Emma Hamilton was his mistress and the mother of his child, but she wasn't his wife. With few friends of her own, she had been distraught at his departure from their home at Merton. Unable to bear it for long, she had come to stay with Canon Nelson for a few days in case he had any crumbs of comfort to offer.

'We must see her,' Jane told Edward. 'I'd very much like to catch a glimpse of the notorious Lady Hamilton.'

'As you wish.' Edward was amused. 'I confess, I'd quite like to see her myself.'

They weren't the only ones. A crowd gathered outside the house as the word spread. They didn't have long to wait before Lady Hamilton appeared, with Canon Nelson in tow. They were going to take a turn around the cathedral.

142

'There she is,' Jane said, as her ladyship emerged. 'The woman who has Lord Nelson's heart.'

The crowd gasped at the sight. Lady Hamilton wasn't the person they had been expecting. She had been a great beauty in her youth, painted by all the best artists, but her youth had been long ago. Age and motherhood had taken their toll. It was obvious to everyone in the crowd that Lady Hamilton had lost her fabled good looks.

'Great Heavens,' Edward said, before he could stop himself. 'What a huge arse.'

'Oh hush!' Jane giggled. She had seen it too. 'That's a terrible thing to say.'

It was true, though. Lady Hamilton's rear end was beyond substantial. Pert did not describe it.

They watched as it disappeared into the cathedral, accompanied by Canon Nelson. It seemed rude to follow, so they returned to their carriage after a while and went back to Godmersham, delighted with their day out in Canterbury. Edward and Jane Austen were both very pleased to have set eyes on Lady Hamilton during their visit. It was something for them to talk about at dinner parties when they got home.

Emma Hamilton prayed for Nelson every morning in the cathedral during her stay in Canterbury. Out at sea, the man himself had arrived off the Spanish coast to discover that the fleet was running short of fresh water. He immediately summoned Rear-Admiral Louis and Flag-Captain Frank Austen to his cabin aboard HMS *Victory*.

'I want you to take six ships-of-the-line to Gibraltar,' he told them. 'Fill up with food and water and come back as quick as you can.'

'We'll miss the battle if we do,' Louis protested. 'The French are bound to come out of harbour if they know six ships have been detached from the fleet.'

'That's the whole idea,' Nelson said. 'There'll be plenty of time for you to get back before they do. That's why I'm sending you now.'

The battle was fought off the cape of Tarif-al-Ghar on the morning of 21 October. The guns were so loud that they were heard in Cadiz to the north and Morocco to the south. They spelled despair for Frank Austen, on his way back from Gibraltar with 300 tons of water for the fleet. Despite Nelson's promise, he had missed the battle and all the promotion and prize money that went with it.

Nelson himself lived just long enough to hear of the great victory before dying of his wounds. The despatch containing both good and terrible news reached England on 4 November and was carried at once to London by post chaise. A muddy naval lieutenant delivered it to the Admiralty after midnight two days later.

In Canterbury, the rumours of a sea battle had been circulating for days, but nobody knew anything for certain. All eyes were on Bell Harry as the waiting continued. The great bell would certainly ring out across the fields if there had been a victory over the French, the glorious triumph that everyone in Canterbury was hoping for. But Bell Harry remained stubbornly silent. If there was good news, it hadn't reached Canterbury yet.

The best place to find out what was happening was Mr Bristow's reading room on the Parade. Bristow always had the news before anyone else. The newspapers arrived from London on the mail coach and were delivered straight to the reading room at the end of the High Street. If anyone knew what was happening in the wider world, it was Mr Bristow.

Canon Nelson was a regular at the reading room. He went there at eight every morning to scan the newspapers and see if there was anything in them about his brother. He had been doing so for weeks, but still knew no more than anyone else about what was happening at sea.

It wasn't long before the news arrived at last. The coachman delivering the papers told Bristow glumly that it was good and bad. 'We have won a great victory,' he said. 'The French have been utterly defeated at sea. There'll be no invasion now.'

'And the bad?'

'Lord Nelson is dead. He was killed during the fight.'

Bad news indeed. Disastrous for Canon Nelson. Bristow reeled as he undid the newspapers and read the full story for himself.

'Canon Nelson will have to be told,' he announced, when he had finished. 'The poor man can't just come in here and read it in the paper, like a member of the public. I'll have to tell him in private.'

Bristow set off at once, hurrying down Mercery Lane. He knew where Nelson lived. He had got no further than the Christ Church gate when he spotted the man himself, just inside the gate. Bristow took him aside and told him gently what had happened.

Canon Nelson reeled in his turn. He immediately burst into tears, pulling out a handkerchief to dry his eyes. He stood by the gate, weeping openly as he struggled to cope with the news that he had dreaded for so long. His famous brother's luck had run out at last.

Bristow tried to comfort him. 'At least it was a wonderful victory,' he said. 'The French can never invade us now.'

'That won't bring my brother back.'

'You can be very proud of him, though. He has done our country a great service.'

But Canon Nelson was not to be consoled. No triumph against the French was worth the death of his brother. He was in tears as he went back to his house to break the news to his family. He was still in tears as Bell Harry began to peal, ringing out across Canterbury for a famous victory.

Chapter Twenty-One

Sir Thomas Picton Returns from Waterloo

Bonaparte was back. The man had escaped from Elba and returned to France at the head of his supporters. He was in Paris now, raising an army to make war again across Europe. His enemies were raising another to stop him.

The British and Dutch-Belgian forces were commanded by the Duke of Wellington. He was in Brussels, preparing for the fight that lay ahead. He had asked Lieutenant-General Sir Thomas Picton, his old colleague from the Peninsula campaign, to return to the army and join him in Belgium as a division commander.

Picton was delighted to accept. He had retired to Wales, but he dropped everything to return to the colours. He travelled to London first, and then down to Ramsgate, in Kent, where a ship had been chartered to ferry him and his staff across the Channel to Ostend.

The general dined with friends in Canterbury on the way. The Fountain Inn lay just off the High Street, opposite Mercery Lane. Picton and his companions had a very convivial dinner there before he continued to Ramsgate with his aide-de-camp. The hotel ostler wished them well as they set off again.

'Good luck, sirs. I hope you have success. I think we've all had as much as we can take of General Bonaparte and the French.'

'I think we have.' Picton tipped his hat. 'More than enough. We must stop the man once and for all this time.'

They rattled on to Ramsgate. From there they sailed to Ostend, before travelling inland to Brussels. They arrived in the city on the morning of 15 June 1815. At exactly the same moment, Napoleon Bonaparte was launching his army across the French border towards the Belgian capital. The war had begun.

Picton called for breakfast as soon as he reached his hotel. He was halfway

146

through the meal when he received a summons from the Duke of Wellington. The Duke wanted to see him immediately.

Picton put his napkin down. He found Wellington in the park, walking with the Duke of Richmond, commander of the army's reserve forces.

'I'm glad you've arrived,' he told Picton. 'The sooner you're on horseback the better. There's no time to lose. I want you to take command of your troops at once.'

News of Napoleon's invasion reached Brussels at three that afternoon. Wellington immediately issued a warning order to the army, telling everyone to be ready to move at a moment's notice. Further instructions would follow after he had consulted his senior officers and devised a plan of action.

Wellington had been invited to the Duchess of Richmond's ball that evening. So had Picton and the other senior officers. Rather than cancel the engagement and chase around Brussels in search of the individual generals, Wellington decided that they might just as well attend the ball. The Richmonds' house was as good a place as any for them all to meet for a conference.

It would send a message to the Belgians too, showing that the British weren't panicking, just because Napoleon had crossed the frontier. There was plenty of time for them to attend the ball and still defeat the tyrant in the days to come.

The Richmonds had rented a modest house in the Rue des Cendres, suitable for their needs while they were in Brussels. The ball was to be held in an adjoining coach house, about the size of a large garage. It was just about big enough to accommodate the two hundred guests who had been invited.

Wellington put on a brave front as he chatted with the Duchess, but he was a worried man in private. He didn't know exactly where Napoleon's army was, or where its main thrust would come. He was enlightened by two messages that he received during the ball.

The first told him that their Prussian allies had clashed with the French near Fleurus. The second said that the French were pushing straight up the road from the border to Brussels and had already reached the crossroads at Quatre Bras. They were advancing into Belgium along two different routes.

After continuing his dinner party chat for a few minutes to show his lack of concern, Wellington decided to abandon the ball and return to his headquarters. On the way out, he had a quiet word with his host, the Duke of Richmond.

'Have you a good map in the house?'

The Duke took Wellington to his study. They spread the map out. Wellington was aghast at the speed and skill of Napoleon's operation. The man was moving incredibly quickly, and along two different lines of approach.

'Bonaparte has humbugged me, by God. He has gained twenty-four hours' march on me.'

'What are we going to do about it?'

'I've ordered the army to concentrate at Quatre Bras. If we don't stop the French there, we'll have to stop them here.' Wellington jabbed his thumb at a point further up the road, just south of Waterloo.

The ball went rapidly downhill after Wellington's departure. The rest of the officers soon slipped away as well, quietly returning to their duties. Their wives were distraught, fearing that they would never see them again. A few thoughtless girls danced on, but it wasn't much fun without their partners. This was no time for dancing, with all the handsome young men departing for what was bound to be a very bloody battle.

The army marched before first light. Picton had been hoping for a good night's sleep after his arrival in Brussels the previous morning. Instead, he found himself in the park at four a.m., reviewing the men of his new command. They included the green-jacketed troops of the Rifle Brigade and kilted Scotsmen from the Gordon Highlanders. Some of the Gordons had given a display of Highland dancing at the ball only a few hours previously.

The troops stopped for breakfast at the small village of Waterloo, and then resumed their march south. Wellington rode east to find the Prussian army and confer with Marshal Blücher, their commander. The two generals had a look at the French through their telescopes and were rewarded with the sight of Napoleon, clearly identifiable by his hat, who appeared to be looking back at them.

Picton continued to the crossroads at Quatre Bras. A very confused battle occupied the rest of the day as both sides brought up reinforcements and struggled to win the road. The French advance was eventually halted, but not before Picton had been wounded in the hip by a burst of grapeshot that also broke two ribs and probably damaged his internal organs as well.

He was in great pain as the army camped on the battlefield for the night. His servant wanted him to get medical help, but Picton wouldn't hear of it.

'No one must know,' he told the man. 'Just bind me up and don't say a word to anyone. Nobody must know that I've been hit.'

Wellington ordered a withdrawal towards Waterloo next morning. The Duke proposed to stand his army at the crossroads south of the village and prevent the French from advancing any further into Belgium. The position seemed indefensible to Picton when he examined it, but Wellington had previously reconnoitred the ground and was more sanguine.

'The French will have to advance up the slope to attack us,' he pointed out. 'They won't even be able to see our troops until they arrive at the top.'

'What about the forest behind? An army should never have its back to a thick forest.'

'There's very little undergrowth. The troops will be able to slip through it like rain through a grate, if they have to.'

Picton slept badly that night. He was in more pain than ever as his servant helped him dress next morning. He wore civilian clothes for the coming battle: a low-crowned beaver hat and a blue coat so shabby that some officers mistook him for a sightseer from Brussels rather than a British general. But there was no mistaking Picton's resolution as he formed his troops up just east of the crossroads, ready for the French attack when it came.

The ground was muddy after a night of heavy rain. Napoleon allowed time for it to dry out before ordering his artillery to open fire. Riding a white horse, he showed himself to his troops first, acknowledging their cheers amid a great roll of drums and fanfare of trumpets as the French nerved themselves for the fight. The British and their allies watched in stony silence from the ridge above.

The battle of Waterloo began at 11:30 in the morning and lasted furiously for the rest of the day. Napoleon's first thrust was to the west, the other side of the road from Picton and his troops. It wasn't until about two in the afternoon that Napoleon gave the order for the main body of infantry to advance straight up the road towards Brussels. Eighteen thousand men stepped forward at once.

As Napoleon had intended, they looked terrifying as they came up the slope. Their ranks were twenty-seven deep in places. They were all carrying muskets with a bayonet on the end. Their colours were flying and their drummer boys were beating out the *pas de charge* at a frenzied pace. It seemed that nothing could stop the mighty juggernaut as it reached the British lines at length and prepared to fall on its enemies.

Napoleon had often used the tactic before. The aim was to frighten the enemy into turning tail and running for their lives before the great phalanx had even arrived. Napoleon's generals, the ones who had fought in the Peninsula, had advised him that the tactic would never work against the British. They had warned him repeatedly that the British wouldn't turn tail and run, as others did. The British would stand and fight instead.

Napoleon had ignored their advice, but the generals were right. The British troops stood their ground as the French arrived. Shoulder to shoulder, in ranks only two or three men deep, they opened fire as soon as the French were within range. The target was so enormous that they could hardly miss.

As well as gunfire, the French had run into a thick hedge along the side of the road. They had to break formation to get through it. Seizing their chance, the Black Watch and Gordon Highlanders rushed forward to attack them at bayonet point before they were able to regroup.

The Scots were heavily outnumbered, so Picton ordered the rest of his troops to attack as well. Waving his sword, he led the assault himself.

'Charge!' he shouted, spurring his horse forward. 'Hurrah, hurrah! Rally the Highlanders!'

Picton plunged into the fray. He had only gone a few yards when he was hit in the head by a musket ball and slumped forward in his saddle. Picton's aide-de-camp hurried to help him down from his horse, but too late. Picton was already dead.

There was no time to worry about it. The aide dragged Picton's body to a nearby tree, to be recovered later, and rejoined the battle. The French were in retreat now, driven off by a timely charge from the British cavalry. Some of the Gordon Highlanders grabbed hold of the Royal Scots Greys' stirrups and hitched a ride down the slope as they chased the French back to their starting point.

It wasn't until that evening, after Napoleon had fled from the field, that they were able to recover Picton's body. He was the oldest general in the British army and the most senior officer to have been killed. It was decided therefore that his body should not be buried where it had fallen, like everyone else's. It should be taken back to England instead and given a proper funeral, suitable for a British general.

The thick oaken chest containing his remains came ashore at Deal on 25 June, exactly a week after the battle. It was taken to Canterbury that evening and kept for the night at the Fountain Inn, in the same room where Picton had enjoyed his dinner a fortnight previously. A guard of honour stood watch over it throughout the hours of darkness.

'I shook his hand,' the ostler kept telling anyone who would listen, as the men maintained their vigil. 'Only two weeks ago, I shook General Picton's hand. Right here, on this very spot.'

At six o'clock next morning, the coffin continued its mournful journey to London. Soldiers from the 52nd Regiment, which had fought at Waterloo, were waiting outside the inn to escort the gun carriage to the city boundary. Forming up around the vehicle, they set off along St Margaret's Street, slow-marching with their arms reversed while a band played Handel's *Dead March* from *Saul*.

The cortege turned into the High Street. The people of Canterbury removed their hats as it appeared. They watched in respectful silence as the coffin was ceremonially conveyed through the city to the boundary at the West Gate.

The band came to a halt there. The slow march was abandoned and Picton's body continued at a brisker pace along the road to London. Bell Harry had rung from the cathedral for the great victory at Waterloo. There were no bells for Sir Thomas Picton as his cortege left the West Gate behind and set off in funeral pomp for the rest of the journey to the capital.

Chapter Twenty-Two

George Stephenson's New Steam Engine on Wheels

On 15 April 1830, a cargo ship slipped out of Newcastle and set sail for Whitstable, the little fishing village on the north coast of Kent. The ship was carrying an astonishing piece of machinery, revolutionary in design, for delivery to the Canterbury & Whitstable Railway Company. Nothing like it had ever been seen in Kent before.

The machine was a steam-powered locomotive engine. It was a strange contraption with cylinders, a boiler and a stack at one end, mounted on metal carriage wheels. It had been specially designed by George Stephenson & Son of Newcastle to pull a long train of passenger carriages down a pre-laid track.

Such a sight was not to be missed. All of Whitstable was there to see it as the ship came in. The villagers watched in wonder as the extraordinary device was unloaded and deposited gingerly on the quayside in front of them. The whole operation was supervised by Edward Fletcher, the mechanic who had accompanied the new engine from Newcastle.

'She's called *Invicta*,' he told the villagers, once the machine was safely ashore. 'We've named her after the White Horse of Kent. We thought that would be appropriate.'

'A machine that can do what a horse does?'

'Ten horses.' Fletcher patted the cylinder proudly. 'She can pull as much as ten horses when she gets going. Maybe even twelve.'

The villagers reserved judgment. They would believe it when they saw it. A machine that could do the work of twelve horses sounded far too good to be true.

The trials began a few days later. The track for the new venture had already been laid down. It covered the seven miles from Whitstable to Canterbury, which was as far as most people in the village had ever been. The plan was to connect the two places by a railway so that they could travel from one to the other every day. If it worked, it would be the first passenger railway service in the world.

The trials were conducted by George Stephenson's son Robert. He had designed the steam engine, with some oversight from his father. George had made a brief visit to Canterbury to inspect the proposed line, but he was too busy with other railway projects in the north of England to supervise the construction. He had left that to his son.

'We'll try her out on the flat first,' Robert Stephenson told Fletcher, as they discussed the experiment. '*Invicta* isn't so good at gradients. We'll run her as fast as we can on the flat and see how we go.'

A suitable stretch of line had been identified between Church Street and Clowes Wood. Stephenson joined Fletcher on the footplate as soon as steam had been raised. The two men produced pocket watches and compared the time. Counting down the seconds, Stephenson nodded to Fletcher to begin.

Fletcher pulled a lever. *Invicta* surged forward at once in a hiss of steam and smoke. Startled spectators fell back as the engine hurtled precariously along the track. Nobody wanted to be too close to it if the thing suddenly veered out of control.

'Don't go all out,' Stephenson warned Fletcher, as they picked up speed. 'We don't want to overdo it. Just take it steady for a while and don't strain the engine.'

Fletcher nodded. *Invicta* chugged on. They left Whitstable behind and pressed on quickly through open countryside. Almost before they knew it, they reached Clowes Wood, where the gradient began. Fletcher brought the engine to a stop at the agreed spot and the two men compared watches again.

'Seven minutes,' Stephenson announced in triumph. 'Seven minutes to go two miles.'

'We could have gone faster. Could have done it in less.'

'Seven minutes is good enough. That's seventeen miles per hour, if you think about it.'

It was an astonishing technical feat. Both men were very proud of their achievement. The only problem was the series of slight inclines from Clowes Wood to Canterbury, on higher ground inland. The new engine wasn't powerful enough to haul a train of carriages up even a modest slope.

Instead, two stationary engines were going to be used for that part of the line. The engines would wind in a long cable hooked to the passenger train.

One engine house had been built for the purpose at Clowes Wood, another at Tyler Hill, just outside Canterbury. Between them, the two winding engines would cover that part of the journey that *Invicta* couldn't manage.

It was an exciting venture. Canterbury would become a seaport in all but name, once it had a rail connection to Whitstable. London was easily reached by boat from Whitstable. So were lots of other places. The opportunities for trade were obvious for anyone to see.

'The line will be able to carry coal at half the price of a horse and cart,' Robert Stephenson told the villagers proudly. 'That's what my father's railway has done. Stockton to Darlington. It takes coal straight from the collieries to the seaport. We can do that here too, only we'll be taking people instead of coal.'

'Has that ever been tried before?'

'Not by steam engine it hasn't. This is going to be the first time.'

The date for the grand opening of the railway line was set for 3 May 1830. The plan was for the inaugural train to leave Canterbury at mid-morning, travelling by fits and starts from Tyler Hill to Clowes Wood, where the steam engine *Invicta* would be waiting to take it the rest of the way to Whitstable. The passengers – all of them local worthies — would then have lunch by the sea before returning to Canterbury in time for a celebratory dinner at the King's Head, if everything went to schedule.

'I just hope everything does,' Stephenson confided to Fletcher, as they made their preparations. 'The newspapers will all be there to watch us. We don't want anything going wrong on the day.'

'Nothing will go wrong, Mr Stephenson. It'll all be just fine.'

The whole of Canterbury turned out to see the train set off. The city had been decorated for the occasion. Bunting hung from windows and flags flew from public buildings. A banner proclaiming 'Prosperity to the City' had been draped across the entrance to the new railway terminus. Thousands of people gathered to join the party as the great machine prepared to set off on its epic journey to Whitstable.

The train was supposed to leave at eleven a.m., but it was a quarter past by the time everyone had taken their seats in the procession. The directors of the railway company sat in the first carriage, sporting white rosettes on their coats. The engineers sat with them, wearing crimson rosettes.

The aldermen of Canterbury sat behind them in an enclosed coach. The remaining carriages were occupied by friends, wives, local gentry and a small band of musicians. There were almost three hundred passengers in all, cheered on by thousands of onlookers as they waited for the journey to begin.

When all was ready, a flag was waved to the engineer at Tyler Hill. The cable between the railway lines immediately jerked into life as the steam engine at Tyler Hill began to reel it in. With a jolt, the whole train started forward and the passengers were on their way.

At the same time, Bell Harry began to peal, announcing the good news across the city. Cannons boomed from the West Gate. The sound of the guns was almost drowned by an enormous roar from the crowd as it watched the train disappearing in the direction of Tyler Hill. Nothing remotely like it had ever been seen in Canterbury before.

To Stephenson's relief, everything went according to plan. The train passed through the new tunnel at Tyler Hill without mishap and was hauled by cable all the way to the winding station at Clowes Wood. There, it was unhooked from the cable and attached to *Invicta*. The steam engine started off at once, towing all the carriages behind it for the last leg of the journey to Whitstable.

The sea lay blue and inviting in front of them as they arrived. Everyone in Whitstable was waiting to welcome them. *Invicta* came in slowly towards the end of the line and was surrounded by delighted fisher folk as soon as they were quite sure that the engine had stopped at last.

'Forty-one and a half minutes,' Stephenson announced. He waved his watch in triumph as he jumped down from the train. 'That's how long the journey took. Actual travelling time was less than three quarters of an hour to get the whole way from Canterbury to Whitstable.'

The passengers shared his enthusiasm. They were all very pleased to have arrived so successfully. Climbing out of the carriages, they flocked to the seafront in excited groups and took a stroll along the shore before lunch. A splendid meal had been arranged for them at the Duke of Cumberland pub.

The return to Canterbury that afternoon was just as exhilarating. The passengers all cheered as the train entered the tunnel at Tyler Hill. Fortified by a good lunch, they tested the tunnel's acoustics for the full half mile of unaccustomed darkness before emerging into the sunlight once more at the other end.

'There they are!' A man on the roof of Bell Harry was looking out for the train. He yelled to the bell ringers. 'They've come back. They're coming into the station now.'

Bell Harry began to ring at once. All across the city, people dropped what they were doing and hurried to the station again to greet the travellers' return. The crowds seemed even larger than they had been that morning as the train arrived at the end of its ground-breaking journey. Everyone wanted to hear about it as the passengers disembarked in triumph at the terminus and began to tell their stories.

'So far so good,' Stephenson told Fletcher quietly as they watched the passengers departing. 'Now for the hard part. I have to make a speech at the dinner tonight.'

'You'll be all right. Just tell them there's a great future in railways.'

The King's Head was an easy walk from the terminus. One hundred and fifty people had been invited to celebrate the grand opening of the railway line. Stephenson was an engineer, not a speech maker, but he knew he couldn't avoid saying something at the dinner. The line's investors wouldn't be happy if the designer of *Invicta* didn't give them a speech of some sort.

It was a very convivial occasion. Wine flowed and waiters bustled about. The band played throughout the meal. Singers came on at the end. The guests were all in a splendid mood by the time the tablecloths had been cleared away at last and the railway chairman rose with a glass in his hand to propose the loyal toast.

'Ladies and gentlemen,' he told everyone. 'The King.'

'The King.' They all got up and drank to the King's health. Then they raised their glasses again and toasted the health of the various railway people who had brought the Canterbury-Whitstable line into being.

When it was Stephenson's turn, he mumbled a few words of thanks in reply, but spoke in such a low voice that the newspaper reporters couldn't hear him. The gist of it was that *Invicta* had come up to all his expectations. Stephenson was glad to sit down again as soon as he decently could.

He was much more expansive talking to the railway directors sitting at his table. They called for more wine and sat listening as he told them about his father's ideas for the development of the railways.

'My father is very concerned about the gauge of the railway tracks,' he told them. 'The width between the two lines is four foot, eight and a half inches here. It's the same between Stockton and Darlington. It'll be the same when the line between Liverpool and Manchester opens. My father thinks that ought to be the standard gauge everywhere.'

'Why?'

'He says the lines will all be joined up one day. Not today and not tomorrow, but one day. He thinks it'll be possible to travel all over the country by railway train. The gauges would all have to be the same width for that to happen.'

'Your father really thinks that would be possible?'

'He does. But only if there's a standard gauge, so that the same wheels work on every track.'

156

The directors mulled it over while a waiter refilled their glasses. George Stephenson's suggestion made perfect sense, but they knew it would be a long time yet before the country was covered in railway lines. The directors had found it hard enough building a single line from Canterbury to Whitstable.

'I have an idea about selling passenger tickets,' one of them told the others.

'Yes?'

'It seems to me that people might want to go to Whitstable every day during the summer season. We could sell tickets to regular travellers at a discounted price.'

'What d'you mean?'

'If they undertook to make the journey five times a week, we could sell them five tickets for the price of four. A ticket for the whole season.'

The directors nodded in agreement. The idea was commercially sound. The railway business was full of interesting new possibilities that they looked forward to exploring in due course. Someone else had suggested that it might even be possible to live in one place and work in another, if there was a railway connecting the two.

But that was for the future. For the moment, the directors were simply relieved that the day had been such a success. They were exhilarated as the party broke up at last and they went their separate ways. Behind them, the waiters at the King's Head began to clear up and put everything away before they too finished for the day. The men compared notes as they worked.

'We had a right one on our table,' one of them said. 'I couldn't believe what I was hearing.'

'What did he say?'

'He said the country would be covered in railway lines one day. Not just this one to Whitstable, but everywhere.'

'All over the country?'

'That's what he said. The whole country would be connected by railway lines. They'd all join up. You could go from one end of England to the other on a railway train.'

Absurd. The waiters at the King's Head shook their heads. They knew a stupid idea when they heard one.

'Why stop at England?' one of them pointed out. 'Why not the rest of the world as well?'

They all fell about at that. Then they put the lights out and went to bed.

Chapter Twenty-Three

Charles Dickens and *David Copperfield*

Charles Dickens's American publisher had come to stay. James Fields and his wife were in England on the first leg of a grand tour of Europe. Dickens had invited them to spend a week at Gad's Hill, his country home near Rochester.

He had known the couple for years. Fields edited the *Atlantic Monthly* as well as publishing Dickens's novels. His wife Annie, née Adams, came from the same family as the two Adams presidents. Dickens had been their guest in Boston during his 1868 lecture tour of the United States.

Now he was repaying their hospitality. He had spent several days in London showing them the sights before inviting them down to Gad's Hill. James Fields wanted to see a bit of the countryside while he was in England. In particular, he was keen to visit Canterbury with his wife.

'We could do it English-style,' he had suggested to Dickens in a letter before leaving Boston. 'A horse and carriage. Postilions in scarlet jackets. We don't get much of that in America. It would be fun to go to Canterbury the old-fashioned way.'

Dickens was agreeable. It would have been a lot easier to take the train from Rochester, but he was happy to organise an expedition by carriage, if that was what the Fields wanted. The road was good between Rochester and Canterbury and his guests would enjoy the scenery. They could have lunch on the way.

The Americans left London on 2 June 1869. They caught the afternoon train from Charing Cross and arrived at Higham station, just beyond Gravesend, at about three o'clock. From there, it was just a short carriage drive to Dickens's country house at Gad's Hill.

The great man was waiting for them on the footpath outside. He was all smiles as he welcomed them. Dickens was fond of them both, but Annie in particular. She was intelligent and personable, the kind of woman he liked. Annie was very fond of him too.

Dickens showed them the Swiss chalet in the grounds, where he often worked in the summer months, and then took them for a walk around the garden. His daughters joined them later for tea outside. They sat at a table on the lawn as Dickens told his guests about Gad's Hill.

'I first saw the house when I was a boy. My father pointed it out from the road and told me I could own a house like this one day, if I worked hard enough.'

'And now here you are,' said Annie.

'Here I am. I've certainly worked hard enough for it.'

They sat in the garden until it was time to dress for dinner. Later, Dickens took the Americans to his study and pointed out the dummy books on the shelves. The books had titles of his own invention: *Socrates on Wedlock*, a *History of a Short Chancery Suit* in 21 volumes, and a reminder of his time as a Parliamentary reporter, *Hansard's Guide to Refreshing Sleep*. The seven-volume *Wisdom of our Ancestors* covered ignorance, superstition, the block, the stake, the rack, dirt and disease.

Over the next four days, Dickens showed his guests around Rochester and other nearby places, where so many of his novels had been set. They visited Rochester Castle, on the banks of the Medway, and climbed to the top of the battlements to enjoy the view over the river. They saw the place now advertising itself as 'Mr Pickwick's Bull Inn' and had a picnic lunch among the gravestones in the churchyard at Cooling. Annie found the graveyard every bit as gloomy as Dickens had depicted it in *Great Expectations*.

But it was Canterbury that she and her husband really wanted to see. Canterbury was the city of *David Copperfield*, Dickens' favourite book. He had put a lot of himself into the main character and was staunchly proud of the result.

'We're so looking forward to it,' Annie told him. 'We want to see all the places that David Copperfield saw, that you described so well in the book.'

'We shall go on Monday,' Dickens promised her. 'I've ordered two carriages. They'll be here at nine a.m. We'll take a party and make a day of it.'

He was as good as his word. Two carriages appeared at the appointed hour, each with a pair of postilions in top hats and scarlet coats. Dickens had invited his lawyer, Frederic Ouvry, to join the party. They all climbed in and set off for Canterbury.

It was a lovely summer's day. The recent weather had been dreadful, so the bright sky was more than welcome as they headed along the road. They changed horses at Faversham, then found a nice place in the woods beyond for a picnic lunch. It was afternoon by the time the cavalcade rolled into Canterbury at last.

'This is so exciting,' Annie told Dickens, as Bell Harry came into view. 'I feel as if David Copperfield is walking along beside us.'

'He's sitting right opposite you in the carriage, Mrs Fields. I can assure you of that.'

The cavalcade caused a stir in Canterbury's narrow streets. Scarlet-coated postilions were an increasingly rare sight in the age of the railway train. Everyone stopped to stare as England's greatest living writer and his guests were conveyed in state towards the cathedral. They got out near the Christ Church gate and went in at once.

The sun was so hot that the shade of the cathedral offered a refreshing change. Evensong was about to start, so Dickens and the others decided to attend the service in the choir. Annie wasn't impressed by the lacklustre ceremony, but Ouvry joined in the responses with gusto. Dickens was amused at the lawyer's enthusiasm.

'The man doesn't believe in heaven or hell,' he whispered to Annie. 'Fancy Ouvry joining in the responses louder than anyone!'

They went to look at the Black Prince's tomb after the service was over. Then they spent some time at the Martyrdom before going out into the cloisters through the same door that Thomas Becket had used. From there they made their way to the Dark Entry and emerged at length onto the Green Court, on the north side of the cathedral.

'It's lovely.' Annie turned to admire Bell Harry. 'It's one of the loveliest places I've ever seen.'

'That's why I sent David Copperfield to school here.'

'You did, didn't you? Dr Strong's school in the precincts.'

'"A grave building in a courtyard, with a learned air about it that seemed very well suited to the stray rooks and jackdaws who came down from the cathedral towers to walk with a clerkly bearing on the grass-plot."' Dickens quoted himself with feeling. 'It was the sort of school I would have liked to have gone to myself.'

'And was it based on the King's School, where Christopher Marlowe went?' Ouvry pointed to the school buildings across the court.

'Not really. People think it was because that's the only school in the precincts. I had to write a letter denying that Dr Strong was based on the headmaster of the time.'

'But the buildings are the same, and the descriptions. It seems like the same school.'

'Perhaps it does a bit.' Dickens winked. 'I just didn't want the headmaster suing me for libel, that's all.'

They admired the Norman staircase before leaving the precincts through the Mint Yard. Dickens pointed out a rather mean-looking house as they walked back up Palace Street.

'That's where Cushman lodged for a while,' he told the Americans. 'The man who chartered the *Mayflower*.'

'The Pilgrim Father?'

'That's the one. He was from Canterbury originally.'

Annie Fields was intrigued to hear it. She studied the house with interest. Robert Cushman's descendant Charlotte Cushman was a friend of hers in Boston.

'Eighth generation, if I remember rightly,' she told Dickens. 'Charlotte is an actress. She played Lady Macbeth in front of Abraham Lincoln.'

'Did she? Well, this is where her family started out.'

They continued up the street until they came to Guildhall Street.

'That's the Theatre Royal.' Dickens pointed the building out as they passed. 'I did a reading of *David Copperfield* there years ago.'

'Yes?'

'When the book first came out. I got a very good reception from the audience. It was like the touch of a beautiful instrument, seeing them react to the story.'

They had completed the circle and were standing in front of the Christ Church gate again. The empty niche above their heads had contained a statue of Christ before Roundhead troops shot it to pieces during the Civil War.

'I put this gate in the book,' Dickens told his guests. '"The battered gateway, once stuck with statues, long thrown down." It's in *David Copperfield* somewhere.'

'You put a lot of Canterbury into the book.'

'I did.' Dickens spoke wryly. 'The Copperfield sights have become big business here now. I'm plagued all the time by people claiming that this house or that house is where Uriah Heep lived, or Mr Micawber. They don't seem to understand that the book is just a work of fiction.'

'You could forgive them, though.'

'They even say that I was living in Canterbury when I wrote the book.'

'I take it you weren't,' said Annie.

'No. I wrote it at home, in my study. But I have stayed at the Sun once or twice.' Dickens indicated the hotel over his shoulder. 'I'll give them that much.'

They strolled along Burgate Street until they came to the city walls. St Augustine's Abbey lay ahead of them, across the road. The others followed as Dickens led the way to the gate.

'This is where St Augustine was buried,' he told them 'The man who reintroduced Christianity to Britain.'

'Can we go in?'

'There's nothing to see any more. It became a royal palace after it was an abbey, and then a private house. It's a missionary college now.'

'Missionary?'

'For the empire. There aren't enough priests in the colonies. St Augustine's trains them up and sends them out to the far corners of the earth. There are priests from St Augustine's all over the world, wherever the British flag flies. They're a part of our civilizing mission.'

It was beginning to get dark as they turned back towards the cathedral. They had seen the best of Canterbury. They decided to leave the rest for another day and go home while it was still light.

The postilions were glad to be on the move again. The coachmen whipped up the horses as soon as everyone was seated. The procession set off immediately down the High Street. They left Canterbury through the West Gate and took the road to Rochester and Gad's Hill. Before long, Dickens and his guests were sitting back happily as day turned to night and the horses clip-clopped towards home.

Annie Fields was as happy as anyone. She had had a lovely day out. They were almost back at Gad's Hill before she remembered that they hadn't seen Mr Wickfield's house in Canterbury, where David Copperfield had first set eyes on both Uriah Heep and Agnes, his future wife.

'I believe there is such a place,' she told Dickens. 'A very old house bulging out over the road? Lattice windows and beams with carved heads? Isn't that how you described it?'

'There are lots of houses like that in Canterbury. Any one of them could have been Wickfield's in the book.'

Gad's Hill was lit up for their return. The servants came out with lights to welcome them home. The travellers went straight up to their rooms to dress for dinner. It wasn't until they were sitting down for the meal that Dickens was more forthcoming with Annie.

'I showed you all the best bits of Canterbury while we were there,' he assured her. 'I knew exactly what you wanted to see. I made sure that you saw it all. Believe me, Mrs Fields, you didn't miss anything important.'

'I believe you, Mr Dickens. Of course I do. Mr Fields and I had a wonderful time in Canterbury.'

Later, when they were getting ready for bed, Annie discussed the great author with her husband.

'He's a sad man,' she told him. 'For all his money and success, and his kindness, he's not a happy person. You can see it in his eyes.'

'Yes, you can,' Fields agreed. 'He's never been a happy man. Not for as long as I've known him.'

'I guess it's because of his childhood. Too much of Mr Micawber and Mr Murdstone. All he really wanted was a father who took proper care of him and sent him to school.'

Fields nodded. 'But he did well by us today. We got shown around the Canterbury of David Copperfield by the man who wrote the book.' Fields kissed his wife goodnight. 'Summer vacations don't come any better than that.'

Chapter Twenty-Four

The Skeleton in the Crypt

On a cold January morning in 1888, two cathedral workmen were digging up the floor of the crypt when one of them hit something solid with his pickaxe. It appeared to be made of stone and lay just below the surface of the earth, not more than three inches deep.

The workmen investigated. Before long, they had uncovered a long stone trough carved out of a single piece of Portland oolite. They removed the lid carefully and looked inside. The trough contained a pile of bones at one end, gathered around a human skull with an enormous gash in it near the top of the head.

'Fetch Mr Austin,' one of the men told the other urgently. 'He'll have to see this.'

Austin was the cathedral surveyor. He came at once. He shared the workmen's astonishment at what they had found.

'It must have been somebody very important,' he told them, as he stared at the bones. 'Thomas Becket was buried only a few feet from here. Whoever it was wouldn't have been buried in the crypt if he wasn't very important.'

'An archbishop?'

'A saint? I don't know. Somebody. We'll have to find out, if we can.'

Austin lived at the other end of the cathedral, in part of the Archbishop's palace. Under his direction, the bones and skull were removed from the trough and placed in a large box. They were taken to his house and laid out on wooden boards in a spare room. Then they were covered with a cloth and kept under lock and key until someone with the necessary expertise could be called to examine them.

Mr Pugin Thornton, a local surgeon, came round two days later. He had the

164

anatomical knowledge to arrange the bones in the right order until an almost complete human skeleton lay on the boards in front of them.

'A few bones are missing,' he told Austin. 'Probably got lost somewhere along the way. The body wasn't buried as a skeleton. It was buried as a pile of bones grouped around the skull. The bones had obviously been removed from somewhere else first and then reburied in the crypt.'

'What kind of person was it?'

'A man. Middle-aged.' Thornton was positive in his identification. 'I'd say between 45 and 55 years old.'

'How tall?'

'At least six foot. Probably six foot two. The bones are very old, so he must have been a big person for his time.'

Thornton pointed to the skull. 'From a phrenological point of view, the skull is very interesting too. It probably belonged to a highly intelligent, highly perceptive man with lots of energy and organisational ability, but not someone to be trusted.'

'You can tell all that just by looking at the skull?'

'You can if you believe in phrenology.'

'What about the gash?' Austin indicated a gap in the skull, five or six inches long, above the left temple. 'How did that happen?'

'Hard to say. Could have been a sword cut. Somebody swiping at the top of the man's head with a heavy weapon.'

'A sword cut?'

'Could have been. Or maybe something else. It would certainly have killed him, whatever it was.'

A dentist confirmed Thornton's estimate of the skeleton's age at death. After examining the five remaining teeth, he put the man's age at about fifty or so. The skull definitely belonged to a middle-aged man.

'The question is who?' said Austin. 'A tall man of about fifty, killed with a blow to the head. Obviously an important person, to have been buried in the cathedral crypt. His grave lay immediately below Thomas Becket's shrine upstairs.'

Everyone in the precincts could think of an important churchman answering Austin's description. Famously tall, St Thomas Becket had just turned fifty-two when the four knights ambushed him at the entrance to the crypt in 1170 and killed him with sword cuts to the head. But Becket wasn't buried in the crypt.

Agnes Holland, a canon's daughter, had a theory about that. She had been one of the first to see the skeleton when it was dug up. She had noticed at once that a few of its bones were missing.

'Am I right in thinking that some of Becket's bones were removed from his coffin when it was exhumed from the crypt?' she asked Austin.

'What d'you mean?'

'In 1220, when the saint's body was exhumed and taken to his new shrine upstairs. Weren't a few bones removed by the Archbishop before he was reinterred?'

'Good Lord.' It hadn't occurred to Austin. 'Yes, I believe they were, now that you mention it. Archbishop Langton kept a few bones back to give to other churches as relics.'

'Which might explain why this skeleton isn't complete.'

'Yes, it might. But only if these bones are Becket's. Not otherwise.'

It was an intriguing theory, yet not supported by the evidence. Austin pointed out the obvious flaw to Miss Holland.

'Becket's bones were burned in 1538,' he told her. 'Henry VIII's men set fire to them when they destroyed the shrine.'

'Not necessarily. Somebody's bones were burned, but they might not have been Becket's. Maybe the monks scooped up the real bones in a tearing hurry and reburied them in the crypt. They didn't have time to lay the bones out properly, so they just shoved them into the trough any old how before they were spotted.'

'In an untidy pile?'

'Exactly. The monks were in too much of a hurry to do anything else.'

That was certainly an explanation. Whether it was the right one remained to be seen. There was another flaw in Miss Holland's argument. It was drawn to her attention by a clerical scholar who had come down from London to see the skeleton for himself.

'The top of the skull is intact,' he told her. 'That means it can't be Becket's. The crown of his skull was sliced off by one of the knights when he was murdered. All the contemporary accounts agree on that.'

'What about the huge gash in the skull, in just the right place? Perhaps the contemporary accounts got it wrong.'

'I don't think so, Miss Holland. The Latin accounts are unanimous that Becket's corona was cut off with a sword.'

'What caused the gash, then?'

'I have no idea. Perhaps the workman with his pickaxe.'

The scholar from London spoke with magisterial authority. Agnes Holland was temporarily disconcerted but rallied swiftly. She returned next morning with the fruits of her overnight research.

'You can't slice the top off a skull with one blow from a sword. It isn't like a pineapple. And the Latin word corona means all sorts of things besides the crown of a skull.'

'What are you getting at?'

'Becket scholars took the word to mean that the crown of his head was severed by a sword, but it could just as easily have been his tonsure. That was often how the word was used in medieval times. It might just have been a tuft of his scalp that was cut off.'

The clerical scholar harrumphed. He had no immediate answer to that. Miss Holland was right, but that didn't mean that the skeleton was Becket's. There wasn't nearly enough evidence for her to jump to that conclusion.

The arguments raged back and forth. Opinion was divided in the precincts, and everywhere else as well. The columns of *The Times* were full of it as the discussion continued. If the skeleton in Austin's spare room wasn't Thomas Becket's, it had certainly belonged to someone remarkably similar.

It wasn't long after the announcement of the discovery in the newspapers that the first pilgrim appeared. He came from Margate, bringing his son with him.

'My boy is going blind,' he told Austin. 'His sight is failing fast and the doctors say nothing can be done to save him. We'd like to see St Thomas's bones, if we may.'

Austin was shocked. 'I'm sorry to hear about your son,' he said. 'That's awful. I'm not sure that the bones can be any help, though. We don't even know if they're Becket's or not.'

'We'd like to touch them nevertheless.' The man was desperate. 'It can't do any harm. It might do some good.'

'They're only a few old bones.'

'Please. I beg you. It's our last chance to save my son's sight. We've tried everything else.'

Austin didn't have the heart to refuse. 'All right,' he agreed. 'Of course you can, if you wish.'

He led the way to the spare room. The man took his son by the hand and told him to kneel down beside the skeleton.

'Here's St Thomas's skull,' he told him. 'Feel his eye sockets. Now put your eyes close to them and say your prayers.'

The son did as he was told.

'No doctors can heal you now,' his father said. 'You must pray for yourself if you want to keep your sight. St Thomas is all we have left.'

If the saint was going to work a miracle, he didn't do so at once. The boy was still going blind as his father took him away. Austin watched them leave with sadness. He wondered how many more pilgrims would come, if they thought the bones in his spare room could effect a cure where all the doctors had failed.

The cathedral authorities wondered too. It was the last thing they wanted, a long column of pilgrims lining up to touch some old bones that had been dug up. The Church of England didn't do things like that anymore.

'The body will have to be reburied,' the Dean decided. 'As soon as the examination is complete, we'll put it back where we found it. We don't want a cult forming around something that might not even be Becket.'

The bones were reinterred on the afternoon of 10 February. Austin led the way as a solemn procession entered the crypt at 3.30. The two workmen carrying the bier were followed by Thornton, the Dean, Miss Holland and several attendant clergymen. They gathered by the graveside and watched quietly as the bones were placed into a new oak coffin in exactly the same positions as they had been found.

Once that had been done, Austin added a glass bottle containing a photograph of the skull and an account of the grave's discovery. Then the lid was screwed down and the wooden coffin was put into the stone trough. The trough was cemented around and covered with a heavy stone slab before the earth was replaced on top. Five minutes later, every trace of the grave in the crypt had been hidden and there was nothing left to mark the site.

So it remained for the next sixty one years. There were attempts from time to time to erect some sort of monument over the grave, but they were always blocked by the cathedral authorities. It was widely believed that the bones were Becket's, but nobody could say so for certain. Erecting a monument over them seemed unwise, in the circumstances.

It wasn't until 1949 that the authorities decided that the only way to settle the issue was to re-examine the bones. Science had moved on since 1888. There were ways of analysing bones in 1949 that hadn't been available in the nineteenth century. The cathedral authorities decided to have another look.

The grave was reopened on the evening of 18 July. An archaeologist from Cambridge and a professor of anatomy from St Bartholomew's Hospital in London were on hand to witness the event. They watched closely as the

168

grave was chiselled open by the light of a lamp plugged in to the organ.

A dreadful smell arose as soon as the coffin was revealed. Everyone recoiled at once and reached for a handkerchief.

'Moisture,' said Professor Cave. He peered gingerly into the broken coffin with a hand over his nose. 'It looks as if damp got into the tomb in 1888. That's the most likely explanation.'

Whatever the reason, the coffin was a mess. The wood had rotted and the skull had fallen onto its side. Austin's bottle had been smashed and the contents saturated. The bones were covered in patches of mould and fungus, very brittle to the touch.

They were taken out carefully and laid on the floor of the crypt. After a cursory examination, they were boxed up and kept safely in the precincts overnight. Professor Cave was going to drive them to St Bartholomew's next morning for a full study and forensic report.

'It'll take some time,' he warned the cathedral authorities, before leaving for London. 'The bones will have to dry out before we can look at them properly. It'll be a long process. Don't expect the results any time soon.'

St Bartholomew's Hospital had changed out of all recognition since the murder of Wat Tyler in 1381. The peasant leader's body had been carried into the hospital after his death outside at the hands of London's mayor, but the only building that remained from those days was the old Norman church from the priory next door. Everything else had long since been rebuilt.

Smithfield had changed too. The ancient tournament field was now covered by the halls of the meat market. The spot where Tyler had been knocked off his horse after challenging the King was now a busy road. Professor Cave weaved through the traffic and turned into the hospital through the gate.

The bones were laid out again in the anatomy department. Some of them were so mouldy that they disintegrated at the slightest touch. Cave began the painstaking process of drying them all out before putting the pieces back together again.

It was almost two years before he was able to produce his report. The type-script ran to thirty-one double-spaced pages by the time he had finished. It made disappointing reading for the cathedral authorities.

'The bones aren't Becket's,' Cave told them. 'The body comes from the right century, but the man was only five foot eight, nowhere near as tall as the Archbishop. He was nearer sixty than fifty, in my opinion. And he didn't die from sword cuts to the head.'

169

'What were they, then? The gashes in the skull?'

'Post-mortem fractures caused by natural disintegration after death. You see it all the time in reopened graves. Nobody killed this man with a sword. Which means, I'm afraid, that wherever Becket's bones are now, they certainly aren't the ones that Austin's men discovered in the crypt.'

Chapter Twenty-Five

The Unknown Warrior

In a makeshift chapel at St Pol in France, four military stretchers lay side by side. Each was covered by a Union Jack concealing the body of a British soldier killed in the Great War. The bodies had been brought separately to the British military headquarters at St Pol from the fields of the Somme, the Aisne, Arras and Ypres, four of the most bitterly contested battlegrounds of the war.

The bodies were all anonymous, with no identifying marks of any kind. Nobody knew their name, rank, number or anything about them. All that could be said for sure was that all four bodies had belonged to British soldiers killed in the fighting. And one of them was shortly to be reburied in Westminster Abbey.

The selection was made at midnight on 7 November 1920. Accompanied only by a colonel, Brigadier-General Wyatt entered the chapel without ceremony and touched one of the corpses at random. The two officers then placed it in the coffin shell standing in front of the altar before leaving again. The body remained under guard there for the rest of the night.

Army chaplains held a service in the chapel next morning. At noon, the deal coffin was carried out to a motor ambulance and driven to the port of Boulogne. It was accompanied by six barrels of earth from the battlefields, so that after its reburial in London the body could lie forever in the soil that had cost so many British and Imperial troops their lives.

The ambulance passed close to the old battlefield of Agincourt before arriving in Boulogne. British and French troops lined the route as the body was driven up the hill to the chateau overlooking the town. It was taken to the former library of the chateau, now the British officers' mess, and guarded by French soldiers for its last night on French territory.

Next morning, the body was transferred to a new coffin of English oak that had been brought from England for the purpose. A Crusader's sword from the private collection of King George V was placed on the lid before the coffin was secured with wrought iron bands. It was then covered with a Union Jack and transferred to an army wagon drawn by six black horses for the short journey down to the harbour.

The procession began at 10.30. All the bells of Boulogne rang out before the mile-long cortege set off. The town's firemen led the way, followed by disabled French soldiers wearing their medals, local dignitaries and hundreds of French children, who had been given the day off school for the occasion.

Behind them came several columns of French infantry, marching through packed streets to the sound of Chopin's *Funeral March*. Behind them came the wagon bearing the coffin, followed by French soldiers carrying giant wreaths from the French army, navy and government. British soldiers marched with them, carrying similar wreaths. High-ranking officers from both armies brought up the rear.

At the dockside, the destroyer HMS *Verdun* was waiting to take the Unknown Warrior to England. A French bugler sounded the *Last Post* after the cortege had come to a halt. Then Marshal Foch of the French army stepped forward. Saluting the coffin, he made a short speech on behalf of the French people:

'I express the profound feelings of France for the invincible heroism of the British army, and I regard the body of this hero as a souvenir of the future and as a reminder to work in common to cement the victories we have gained by eternal union.'

For the British, Lieutenant-General Sir George MacDonogh thanked Foch in French on behalf of the King and the British government. Everyone stood to attention as both countries' national anthems were played. Then the British bearer party removed the coffin from the wagon and carried it aboard the warship.

HMS *Verdun* was flying her flag at half-mast as she left harbour. A nineteen-gun salute sent the Warrior on his way. Out at sea, six more Royal Navy destroyers waited in the middle of the English Channel to meet HMS *Verdun* in the fog and escort her precious cargo safely in to Dover.

All six destroyers lowered their Union flags and ensigns to half-mast as the *Verdun* approached. It was a mark of respect usually reserved for the King. The ships quickly took station around the *Verdun* and accompanied her the rest of the way to Dover.

Another nineteen-gun salute welcomed the Unknown Warrior's arrival in England. High above the town, Dover Castle's flag flew at half-mast as the body came in to harbour. As so often in the port's history, every available vantage point was crammed with sightseers as the ship docked and the band played *Land of Hope and Glory* on the dockside.

A bearer party carried the coffin from the ship to the railway station. The route was lined by soldiers of the Connaught Rangers and the Royal West Kents, all with their heads bowed and their arms reversed. At the station, more troops from the Rangers snapped to attention and shouldered their rifles as the Unknown Warrior arrived.

'Guard of honour,' shouted the officer in command. 'General salute. Present arms.'

The soldiers slapped their rifles as one man and came to the salute. The officers lowered their swords. The coffin was carried to a specially prepared luggage van attached to the boat train. The roof of the van had been painted white so that the crowds along the route would know exactly which one contained the Unknown Warrior on his journey to London.

It was 5.50, already dark, as the train pulled out of Dover Marine station. Ahead lay Kearsney, Shepherdswell, Adisham, Canterbury East and many other railway stations on the way to London Victoria. At every station, whether the boat train stopped there or not, crowds were already gathering to salute the Warrior as he passed.

Canterbury was no exception. Old soldiers, sailors, wives, widows, boy scouts, schoolchildren, people of all kinds, were waiting in the evening gloom to see the Unknown Warrior pass through their city. Everyone wanted to pay their respects as he made his last journey. Nobody wanted to miss it when he came through Canterbury on his way to Westminster Abbey.

The city had been closer to the war than most places in Britain. St Augustine's had been used as a hospital for wounded soldiers. So had the military barracks. Convalescent troops had filled the cathedral every day throughout the war. Some had gone there to pray for a speedy recovery, others to beg that they would never become whole again if it meant a rapid return to the fighting.

On still summer evenings, the sound of the war had been clearly audible in Canterbury from across the sea. The rumble of guns that preceded every big push in France or Flanders had echoed around the cathedral precincts, filling everyone who heard it with fear and dread. They knew, as sure as night followed day, that the guns would be followed within a week or two by the red bicycle, the two-wheeled monster that everyone in Britain hated to see in their street.

Red was the colour of the Post Office. The bicycles were ridden by messenger boys delivering telegrams. There were always telegrams after a big military push in France or Belgium. They never brought good news.

'Deeply regret to inform you that your son/brother/husband/father…' Nobody wanted to receive that awful message. Households with a man at the front were never able to settle to anything if they spotted a red bicycle at the end of their road. All they could do was sit and wait until the messenger boy had ridden past.

Even then, they had to wait a bit longer, in case the boy had mistaken the house numbers and returned quickly with bad news. Sometimes people were on their knees in the hallway, praying for no telegram, when it came through the letter box and dropped noiselessly onto the mat. Nothing cowed the British people like the sight of a humble Post Office bicycle in their street.

Almost every family in the land had suffered a loss during the catastrophic war. Rather than give in to their grief, the British had nevertheless insisted on always remaining calm and stoical in public. Walter Hines Page, the American ambassador, had watched in wonder as the casualties mounted, sometimes many thousands in a single day, and Britons of all kinds remained brave and steadfast, refusing to surrender in public to the feelings that had devastated them in private:

'They never weep. Their voices do not falter. Not a tear have I seen yet. It isn't an accident that these people own a fifth of the world. Utterly unwarlike, they outlast anybody else when war comes.'

But the price was very heavy. It wasn't much of a victory for the British. The majority of the people crowding the platform at Canterbury East railway station to await the Unknown Warrior were women mourning their men. Quite a few of them didn't even know what had happened to the man in their life. They knew only that he was missing on the Western Front, believed killed.

Bell Harry towered above them in the darkness as they waited for the train to arrive. The woman all knew that the chances of the Unknown Warrior being their own personal warrior were infinitely small, but that didn't stop them hoping. The Unknown Warrior, on his way to national honour in Westminster Abbey, was all they had left.

The train arrived at last and drew into the station. All eyes turned to the luggage van with the white-painted roof. The doors were locked and the barred windows were small, difficult to see into. But the Warrior was inside, surrounded with floral wreaths, en route to his final resting place among the Kings and Queens of England.

There was barely room to move on the platform as the crowd stood in bowed silence. The train stayed only long enough to set down passengers and take up new ones. There was little ceremony beyond a salute from the soldiers present. The real ceremony was reserved for London, where the whole city was preparing to bury the Warrior in the Abbey next day, with full military honours.

The ordinary people of Canterbury were not alone on the platform as they saluted his body. The shades of the cathedral were there too, unseen, unheard, but present all the same. The ghosts of Canterbury from times past had come of their own accord to salute the Unknown Warrior and pay tribute to his sacrifice. The Warrior was as much a part of the country's story as they were.

William the Conqueror was there, the Norman king who had granted the accord giving Canterbury cathedral primacy over York. The cathedral still had the document, signed by William and his wife with a cross, in accordance with best legal practice at the time.

Henry II was there, and Thomas Becket, and Richard the Lionheart and bad King John. Edward I and the Black Prince were there too. So was Henry V, surrounded by all the knights and stout archers who had followed him into the cathedral after Agincourt. Henry's men-at-arms were with him still, standing solemn and silent beside him along the railway line.

Edward IV was there with his hunchbacked brother Richard III. Henry VIII was standing with his daughter Queen Elizabeth. Charles I, reunited with his head, was standing with his son Charles II and his blood doctor William Harvey.

Cardinal Wolsey and Thomas Cromwell were both present. So were the Scrivenor of Magna Carta and Sir Thomas More, keeping company with Wat Tyler, the leader of the Peasants' Revolt.

The writers were there as well, forming a little group of their own. Geoffrey Chaucer, Christopher Marlowe, Samuel Pepys, Jane Austen and Charles Dickens all wanted to pay their respects as the Warrior passed through on his way to Westminster Abbey.

George Stephenson wanted to as well. It was his railway lines that were taking the Warrior to London. He was standing with poor Lady Hamilton, mother of Lord Nelson's only child, who had prayed so hard in the cathedral for the admiral's safe return.

The preacher John Wesley was there too, Warwick the Kingmaker from the Wars of the Roses, General Monck and the helmeted Roundheads from the Civil War, and a great many other people besides. Whatever their differences in life, they were all English in death, all united in respect for their country's Unknown Warrior as the train bearing his body pulled into the station.

The ghosts drew themselves up to attention as it arrived. They bowed their heads in homage. They didn't move until the train had gone again and the Warrior had passed out of their sight for ever. Then they raised their heads and dispersed as quietly and invisibly as they had come, fading away unobtrusively into the night. The Unknown Warrior didn't need their homage anymore. He was one of them now.

Chapter Twenty-Six

The Yank's Tale Continued

The day after he had recorded the tape about his time in Canterbury during the war, Ezra Tyler went in to Fort Collins to find someone to send it to. He was looking for an expert on Canterbury, someone who could make sense of all the things he had said on the tape after he was dead. He had no idea who.

The best place to find out was the university, he had decided. There was bound to be someone at Colorado State who could help him. College professors were the people who knew.

Tyler found the admissions office and went in. They directed him to the history faculty. The secretaries there didn't know what to do with him, but Tyler refused to go away. He said he wasn't leaving until he saw someone.

At length, an assistant professor on his lunch break was persuaded to give Tyler five minutes. The man listened in a corridor as Tyler explained that he had been in England during World War Two and wanted someone there to see his tape. He mentioned Canterbury cathedral, but didn't say what was on the tape.

'I just want an address,' he said. 'Someone in England I can send it to who knows about Canterbury.'

'Okay.' The assistant professor saw that the quickest way to get rid of Tyler was to do what he asked. He took Tyler to his office and sat down at his computer. Five minutes online produced the department address of a historian at London University.

'There you go.' The professor wrote it out for Tyler. 'Send it to this guy. He knows all about Canterbury.'

'Good,' said Tyler. 'Thank you, professor. That's just what I wanted.'

The tape was bagged up and ready to go. Inside was a note from Tyler saying that everything on the tape was true, but he didn't want his family to know anything about it. Tyler wrote the historian's address on the outside of the bag and put it in the US Mail. Then he went home and shot himself.

He was going to die anyway. The cancer had spread. Tyler was just saving himself a few weeks of pain by shooting himself in the head with a hunting rifle and making it look like an accident. After a long life, he wasn't particularly sorry to go.

He was buried in his hometown, just north of Fort Collins, within sight of the Rocky Mountains. His wife was dead, so his son Billy was the chief mourner. Billy's three kids were there as well, and a couple of Billy's grandchildren, and some Tyler cousins who had come up from Denver. They all joined Tyler's friends at the graveside for the funeral.

The coffin was draped in the American flag for the service. Tyler was given the veteran's burial due to a former United States serviceman. A two-man honour guard stood to attention while a uniformed bugler played *Taps*. Afterwards, the flag was ceremonially folded up and presented to Billy Tyler, Ezra's son and heir.

The wake was held at the dead man's house. His family and friends crammed in for beer and sandwiches after the service. They were all agreed that Tyler hadn't been a happy man before his death. Something had been bothering him as his life ebbed away.

'It was the war,' Billy Tyler said. 'He never got over the war. It bugged him to the end of his life.'

'He ever talk about it?'

'Never.' Billy shook his head. 'Never said a word. He never wanted to talk about the war.'

'He was in Normandy?'

'Yeah. He saw it all. I guess he killed people, although he wouldn't say. Whatever happened over there, my dad didn't want to discuss it. Not ever.'

The others nodded. It was the same with a lot of veterans. The ones who had seen action didn't like to discuss it. Nobody wanted to press them.

The wake lasted a couple of hours before the guests departed, one by one. The Tyler family stayed to the end. They hugged one another when it was their turn to leave, promising to see more of each other in the future. Billy's three children all had children of their own and were leading busy lives. It was only weddings and funerals that brought the whole family together these days.

'Thanksgiving,' one of them said. 'We'll see you then. Let's do it all together this year.'

'Yeah. Why not? It'd be fun.'

Billy Tyler locked up the house when everyone else had gone. Then he and his wife drove back to their own house not far away, taking the American flag with them. They hung it on the wall when they arrived, next to Ezra Tyler's army medals and a framed photograph of him in military uniform. He had done his country proud service during World War Two. His family was proud of him in return.

A few weeks later, a group of British academics gathered in a seminar room at London University for a screening of Tyler's tape. There were half a dozen of them, all experts in their field, specialists in various aspects of Canterbury cathedral and its history. The academics didn't know what they were about to see, but they trusted Professor Alan Brent when he told them they would find it astonishing.

'The tape was sent to me out of the blue,' he explained. 'An American from Colorado. He was in Canterbury during the war. He wanted to leave a record of what happened while he was there.'

Brent ran the tape. The audience watched as Tyler appeared on screen. He was an old man with a reedy voice, filming himself outside in a garden chair. The mountains in the background looked to be the Rockies.

'Hi,' he told the camera. 'I'm dying. I only have a few weeks to live, so it's now or never if I'm going to say what I want to say.'

The audience was increasingly spellbound as Tyler's story unfolded. Bombs, buried treasure, three soldiers fighting over the loot. Best of all, the King of France's famous ruby that had disappeared without trace soon after the destruction of Thomas Becket's tomb. Brent had been right to say that the story was astonishing.

'So that's what I'm doing here, putting it on record for somebody else to figure out. I'm not going to show this tape to my family. I don't want my grandkids to know what I did in Europe. I don't know what I'm going to do with it instead. I guess probably I'll send it to some experts somewhere, England maybe, people who know what the treasure was all about. Must be someone, somewhere, who knows what it was about.

'Not me, though. I'm done now. Time for my medication. I'll turn the tape off now and then I'm going to the bathroom.'

179

The tape came to an end. There was a long silence as Brent switched it off and faced his colleagues. They were as dumbfounded as he had been when he first saw it.

Kate Weston was the first to speak. She had just completed a doctorate on the letter-books of Canterbury cathedral. She had been entranced by Tyler's story.

'It's pure Chaucer,' she said. 'Every word of it, from beginning to end.'

'It is, isn't it?'

'No, really. It's *The Pardoner's Tale*, come to life.'

'What d'you mean?'

'*The Pardoner's Tale*. Three young men in Flanders meet an old man who tells them they'll find death at the foot of an oak tree. They go there and find buried treasure instead. One of them goes to get food. The other two murder him on his return, so as to get a bigger share of the treasure for themselves. Then they eat the food he has poisoned and die too.'

'Who's the old man who warns them about death?'

'The greengrocer. The air raid warden with no eyes, whatever his name was.'

It was true enough. The blind man Bert Marden had warned the Americans about the Roundhead skeletons hidden under the cathedral. Dutch Branigan had shot Billy Williams in the back before being beaten to death by Ezra Tyler. Tyler had taken his own life later. All three had come to a violent end. Not one had profited from the treasure they had stolen from Canterbury cathedral.

'Well, that's as may be.' One of the other academics was more interested in the story he had just seen. 'The real question is whether Tyler was telling the truth or not. I wonder if he made the whole thing up?'

'I don't think so,' said Brent. 'He wasn't an educated man. He wouldn't have known how.'

'It seems hard to believe, though. Treasure in the cathedral.'

'Tyler didn't make it up. He wrote me a note saying his family must never know what happened.'

'Is there any proof that he was ever in Canterbury?'

'There is.' Brent had looked into it. 'His army regiment was stationed there before D-Day, just like he said. Tyler and the other two were all there at the barracks. Williams was killed in action near St Lo. Branigan was found beaten to death in Maryland after the war, just as Tyler said. The murder is still unsolved.'

The audience was divided. They were all longing to believe Tyler's story, but it was their job to be sceptical. They went over it again in their minds, looking for holes. It seemed too good to be true that King Louis' famous ruby had turned up again, after being missing for so many centuries.

'What do they say at the cathedral?' asked Kate.

'They say it's pure fiction, nonsense from beginning to end. Just a story made up by a fantasist.'

'No hidden tunnel under the cathedral?'

'Not according to the cathedral authorities. Nothing there whatsoever.'

'And never has been?'

'So they say.'

Which they would, of course, Kate thought. The cathedral authorities were always fighting off conspiracy theories about the whereabouts of Thomas Becket's bones. They wouldn't want to know about a wild story of hidden treasure under the crypt.

'I thought it was all carried away at the Dissolution,' she said. 'Great cartloads of gold and silver wheeling off through the gate to the Tower of London?'

Brent nodded. 'The jewels alone occupied two wagonloads. It took eight men to carry each load out from the cathedral, if the contemporary accounts are to be believed. But a lot of it never reached the Tower.'

'Stolen on the way?'

Brent nodded again. 'Everyone helped themselves to a few pieces discreetly. Small bits and pieces that the King wouldn't miss.'

'Not the ruby, though. Henry VIII would have missed that.'

'That's the extraordinary thing. Ezra Tyler was quite certain that the prize jewel in the collection was an enormous ruby. How would he have known about that, if he hadn't seen it for himself?'

It was certainly a puzzle. Tyler's story rang true in every particular, but it was still very hard to believe.

'There's this, too.' Brent produced a photocopied newspaper clipping from 1961. 'It was in the *Kentish Gazette*. The greengrocer's obituary.'

He handed it round. The obituary ran to three paragraphs, saying that Albert Marden of Canterbury had died, aged 64. He had served with the Royal West Kent Regiment during the First World War, rising to the rank of sergeant. He had been an air raid warden in the Second, until he was blinded. Marden had been known among his friends for his colourful stories of Roundhead skeletons under the cathedral.

'So the skeletons are true?' Kate asked.

'It looks like it. Marden certainly told the story.'

'Something about them rings a bell.'

'Yes?'

'I don't know what.' Kate racked her brains. 'I know something about the Roundheads at the cathedral, but I can't remember what, offhand.'

'Oh well. Let us know if it comes to you.' Brent turned to the others. 'Anyway, that's the story. Three Americans found a pile of medieval treasure in the cathedral and made off with it. The question is, what are we going to do about it?'

What, indeed? The obvious answer was to follow the money, but that particular trail led to a dead end.

'Tyler says the treasure was buried again?' someone asked. 'Dug up from the army training ground and reburied somewhere else?'

Brent nodded. 'It makes sense. American troops looted stuff from all over Europe. They were very carefully searched by customs when they got home. Dutch Branigan probably buried it nearby and planned to come back later, when the heat was off. That's what it says on the tape.'

'So it's still nearby, somewhere?'

'Almost certainly. Branigan knew Canterbury well and he needed to bury it quickly. He wouldn't have hidden it far away.'

'Still there to be found?'

'If we only knew where to look. That's the hard part. Knowing where to look.'

It was an enticing prospect, nevertheless. The choicest jewels from Becket's tomb, still buried somewhere within sight of Bell Harry. The academics in the seminar room all wanted to be there if ever the cache was discovered.

'Keep it to yourselves for the moment,' Brent advised them. 'We don't want this to get out. There'd be metal detectors all over Canterbury if word got out.'

The others nodded. They needed to do some research before going any further. There might be something in the archives that would shed light on Tyler's extraordinary tale. They would find it if there was.

'We'll meet again in a few weeks' time.' Brent named a date just after the end of the summer term. 'Let's pool our resources before then and see what we can turn up.'

The meeting dispersed. They were all excited as they left the room. Stories of fabulous treasure didn't happen often in the academic world.

Nobody was more intrigued that Kate Weston. Her mind was racing as she returned to her own department. She was thinking about the Roundheads at Canterbury cathedral, wondering what it was about them that she couldn't quite remember. The troops had done something in the cathedral that made perfect sense in retrospect, in the light of Ezra Tyler's astonishing story. For the life of her, though, Kate couldn't remember what.

Chapter Twenty-Seven

The Search for the King's Ruby

183

Chapter Twenty-Seven

The Search for the King's Ruby

Kate was busy for the rest of that day. It wasn't until next morning that she had time to sit down and think about Ezra Tyler's story and the French king's ruby, the Régale de France, that lay at the heart of it.

According to Tyler, he and two accomplices had stolen the jewel from a tunnel under the cathedral. Dutch Branigan had then reburied it somewhere unknown before Tyler killed him. The secret of the ruby's present whereabouts had died with Branigan.

But there were other accounts that contradicted Tyler's story. The ruby had apparently been seen on Henry VIII's thumb after Becket's shrine had been looted. The King was said to have worn it as a ring before having it reset in a necklace. The necklace featured in an inventory of royal jewellery taken soon after his death.

Kate looked up the details. According to the inventory, the necklace had been kept under lock and key in 'The Kinges Secrete Juelhous in the old gallery towards the leades of the privey garden at Westminster'. A clerk had listed it as Item no 2746 in Coffer No 1:

A Coller of golde set with xvj faire Dyamountes whereof the Regall of Fraunce is one and xiiij knottes of perles in euery knott iiij perles.

That was the first puzzle, the clerk calling the Régale a diamond when it was supposed to be a ruby. The second puzzle was what had happened to it after the listing in the inventory.

Queen Mary was rumoured to have worn the ruby as a brooch, but the evidence for that was sketchy. Charles I was said to have sold something that might have been the jewel to Cardinal Mazarin of France, but there was no real evidence for that either. The ruby had effectively vanished off the face of the earth after its dubious listing as a diamond during the reign of Edward VI.

There were the Roundheads too, the Parliamentary soldiers who had run riot in Canterbury cathedral at the beginning of the Civil War. Kate knew something about them, something relevant to Ezra Tyler's story, but she still couldn't remember what. It bothered her for days that she couldn't recall what she knew. And then one morning she woke up and remembered exactly what.

Britain's national archives are kept at the Public Records Office in Kew, on the outskirts of London. Every old manuscript from the Domesday Book onwards is stored there for safekeeping. Kate had spent a lot of time in the archives while researching her dissertation on the letter-books of Canterbury monastery. It was where she had come across the story of the Roundheads in the cathedral.

Kate caught the train to Kew Gardens and walked up the road to the records office. She put in a request slip for the Reynard papers, a collection of letters written by Sir Anthony Reynard during the Civil War. Sir Anthony was a Kentish landowner who had fought reluctantly for Parliament during the conflict.

The letters took half an hour to arrive. They were kept in a strong cardboard box. Kate carried it to a spare desk and sat down to read through Sir Anthony's correspondence until she found what she was looking for.

Sir Anthony had owned a country estate near Cobham. He had joined the Parliamentary troops heading for Canterbury, bringing with him a few volunteers from his own estate. They had been part of the group that had rampaged through the cathedral, ripping up and destroying everything that they couldn't carry away.

It didn't take Kate long to find the letter she wanted. Sir Anthony had written it to his steward three days after the outrage. He had made a throwaway remark while telling the steward about the damage the troops had done in the cathedral. It was the throwaway remark that had Kate skipping with excitement as she returned the letters to the desk and hurried outside to make a phone call.

Alan Brent answered at once. He listened closely as Kate spoke.

'It's true, what Tyler says. Every word of it.'

'Yes?'

'Every word. Right down to the three Roundhead skeletons under the cathedral. He's not making any of it up.'

'How d'you know?'

'The skeletons. They were there, all right. I even know their names.'

Two weeks after Ezra Tyler's death in Colorado, his grandson Chad was watching an old movie when he had an idea.

The movie was a war film about American troops in Normandy after D-Day. It covered much the same ground as Chad's grandfather had in real life. That was what gave him the idea.

'Why don't we go to Europe?' he asked his wife, after the movie was over. 'See where Grandpa fought. Why don't we do that this summer?'

'Europe?'

'England first.' Chad was thinking it through. 'Then France. We could follow in his footsteps. Go wherever he went.'

'Are you serious?'

'Sure, I'm serious. We can see the sights in London and then go to France. Just like Ezra did.'

'We've never been to Europe.'

'Neither had Ezra, until he went. If he could do it, so can we.'

Chad's wife was reluctant. She didn't like foreign travel. They had never been to New York or Washington, let alone out of the country. But Chad was determined to go. The idea was growing on him as he thought about it.

'We know where Ezra fought. It's all in the 1051st's history. We'll just take the book with us and follow in his footsteps.'

'Through Normandy?'

'Why not? He did.'

'This summer?'

'The same time of year that he was there. D-Day was in June. We can follow Grandpa every step of the way. It'll be perfect.'

Mrs Chad remained reluctant, but she allowed herself to be persuaded. Chad was obviously set on the idea. So was his brother Jay, when Chad rang him to discuss it. If anything, he was more enthusiastic.

'That's a great idea. I've always wanted to see where Grandpa fought. It'll give us closure, too. We can take Dad and go as a family.'

Billy Tyler was as excited as his sons. He too had never been out of state, but there was always a first time for everything. Ezra's service in Europe was a beacon to them all.

'Let's do it,' he told his children. 'In memory of your grandfather. If we don't do it now, we never will.'

It was June as Kate Weldon, Alan Brent and the other Canterbury experts met again to discuss their findings. June was the best time of the year for people in the academic world. Exams were over for the year and the undergraduates had all gone away for the summer, leaving the professors free to get on with their own work at last. They were in a very good mood as they sat down to talk about Ezra Tyler again and find out what everyone had learned.

Not much, as it turned out. Kate was the only one who had anything worthwhile to report. The others had all done their research, but without discovering anything new. Kate had their full attention as she stood up and told them about the letter Sir Anthony Reynard had written to his steward.

'He was very angry about the destruction in the cathedral,' she told them. 'Several of his men had joined in without his authority. Three of them vanished into the cathedral and were never seen again.'

'Never?'

'He thought they had deserted immediately after the incident, perhaps absconding with the loot. But I don't think that's what happened.'

'Why not?'

'Have a look at his letter.' Kate passed a copy round. 'I've marked the relevant passage':

Three of our men, by name Will Ashenden, Tom Mullins and Angel Jackson, passed from my sight into the church and did not return therefrom. It is thought by Colonel Sandys that they will return whence they came, it being now harvest time. The knaves Ashenden and Mullins are from mine own estate, as wee knowe. Angel Jackson dwelleth hard by.

'I don't think they deserted,' Kate said. 'I think something happened to them in the cathedral and they ended up dead in the tunnel underneath the crypt.'

'Murdered?'

'Quite possibly. I've been through the records and I can't find any mention of them after the episode in the cathedral. Ashenden, Mullins and Jackson just vanished off the face of the earth, so far as Kentish records are concerned.'

187

The others nodded. Kate was certainly making sense. They congratulated her on her discovery. A chance remark about three deserters going home to help with the harvest had turned into something much more, thanks to Ezra Tyler's account of three helmeted skeletons under the cathedral. Kate had done well to put the two stories together.

'I wonder if the skeletons are still there,' Alan Brent said.

'Not according to the cathedral. They say there's nothing there at all.'

It didn't matter much. The skeletons were merely the confirmation of Ezra Tyler's story. It was the French king's ruby that had their attention as they wondered where they went from here. The really wonderful thing now would be to find where Branigan had buried it and dig it up. It was the sort of moment that historians live for.

'I suppose metal detectors wouldn't be any use?' someone asked.

Brent shook his head. 'We could spend weeks going all over Canterbury with a metal detector. We'd find a lot of old tin cans, if nothing else. It would just be chance if we found what we were looking for.'

'So really there's nothing more we can do?'

'Not really. Not unless we can think ourselves into Branigan's mind and work out where he would have hidden the loot.'

There was no chance of that. They all knew that buried treasure was hard to find. There were hoards of Roman coins all over England that lay undiscovered for two thousand years before someone unearthed them accidentally. It couldn't be done by design.

'The only thing we can do is go to Canterbury and have a look,' Brent told his colleagues. 'I don't suppose we'll find anything, even though we know what we're looking for. But it would be a day out. Worth a try, at any rate.'

The others were sceptical. The earth didn't yield its secrets that easily. They were happy to go to Canterbury, though. It would be fun to see where it had all happened.

A date was fixed for the following week. Brent offered to drive them down from London. They agreed to meet at the George Inn in Southwark and wait for him to pick them up in his car.

Chapter Twenty-Eight

The Bomb Disposal Squad

The Tyler family flew to London from Denver. There were eight of them altogether, including Chad's son Ward, a sullen teenager with his eyes glued to his phone. They took the underground train to their hotel and emerged next morning ready for two days of sightseeing in the English capital before following in Ezra Tyler's footsteps to France.

They had a good time in London. They went to see the Tower, and Buckingham Palace, and the Houses of Parliament. They stood in Trafalgar Square, looking up at the statue of Lord Nelson on his column, completely unaware that Benjamin Franklin's old house was still there in the next street, less than a hundred yards away. Then the women went shopping while the men visited the Imperial War Museum.

They had originally planned to hire a pair of cars in London and drive down to Dover, then across to France on the ferry. One look at London's motor traffic, all of it on the wrong side of the road, persuaded them otherwise. The Tylers would never find their way out of the city, let alone across to France. They decided to go to Dover by train instead.

'Better to wait until we get to France before we hire a car,' Billy Tyler said. 'They drive on the right side of the road there. We'll stay the night in Canterbury and go on to Dover tomorrow.'

They went straight to the cathedral after checking in at their hotel. According to the 1051st's official history, the regiment had been stationed in Canterbury for several weeks before D-Day. Grandpa Ezra must certainly have visited the cathedral while he was in Canterbury. His descendants would be following in his footsteps if they did too.

They were following in Wat Tyler's footsteps as well, if they had but known it. Their famous ancestor's name meant nothing to them as they entered the cathedral and walked up the nave. The leader of the Peasants' Revolt had stormed up the same nave at the head of a murderous mob, bent on mayhem of every kind. He had interrupted the mass from the pulpit, telling the congregation that the Archbishop was a traitor who would be beheaded as soon as the peasants caught up with him. He had been as good as his word.

His descendants were a lot more sedate as they proceeded in the same direction. They had audio guides to tell them what to look at. They were all listening to the guides except for Ward, still glued to his phone. He was fifteen, determined not to be impressed by anything he saw in Europe.

The Tyler family glanced around the choir, then drifted across to the Black Prince's tomb. His shield, gauntlets, coat and helm still hung there, as they had ever since his funeral in 1376. Wat Tyler had admired them during his rampage through the cathedral. His descendants stood on the same spot as their peasant ancestor and admired them too.

All except for Ward Tyler. He had done nothing but look at his phone ever since his arrival in England. He was beginning to get on his father's nerves.

'Hey, Ward,' Chad said. 'You see that helmet. That's the Black Prince's. It's been hanging there for more than six hundred years.'

'And?'

'And you ought to look at it. Put your phone away and look at it.'

'Why?'

'Because I say so. We've come a long way to look at it. Cost us a lot of money.'

'I didn't ask to come.'

'Just put the phone away, Ward. I want you to look at the helmet.'

Ward sighed. He put the phone away.

'Whatever,' he said.

The Tylers departed for France next morning without further mishap. Two days later, it was Kate Weldon's turn to visit Canterbury with her university colleagues. They all knew the city well, but they were looking forward to a nice day out as they waited for Alan Brent at the George Inn in Southwark.

The George was London's last remaining coaching inn. Still with its galleries around the ancient courtyard, it dated from the 17th century, but that wasn't why they had chosen to meet there. The George stood right next door to the site of the Tabard Inn, where Geoffrey Chaucer's pilgrims had gathered before their journey to Canterbury.

The inn had burned down in the reign of Charles II. Nothing remained from Chaucer's time, but Kate and the others were all agreed that it was still the right place to begin their journey to Canterbury. There was certainly nowhere better.

Alan Brent arrived on time and they all got in. An hour and a half later, he parked the car in Canterbury and they got out again. It was only a short walk from the multi-storey to the cathedral.

The Christ Church gate had acquired a new statue since the days of the Roundhead sharpshooters. The replacement Christ occupied the same space as the original but was obviously modern in design. Everything else about the gate looked exactly as it had done ever since its construction five hundred years ago, in the days of the Tudors. The academics eyed it appreciatively as they went in.

'It's probably the most historic gate in England,' Alan Brent pointed out. 'Everybody has been through here at one time or another. Pretty much everyone in English history.'

Henry VIII certainly had, and Cardinal Wolsey and Sir Thomas More. So had Queen Elizabeth and Christopher Marlowe, and King Charles and his son. Samuel Pepys and Oliver Cromwell had been there, and Mozart, Jane Austen, Lady Hamilton, Queen Victoria and Prince Albert. Charles Dickens had put the gate in a book. JMW Turner had painted pictures of it. Mahatma Gandhi had been there as well. The list of famous people who had passed underneath the gate's arches went on for ever.

Kate and her colleagues joined them. Bell Harry was looking splendid in the sunshine as they went through. The good weather had brought the tourists out, many hundreds of them milling around the precincts with their guide books. Alan Brent led the way through the crowd and they went in to the cathedral.

The Martyrdom was crowded too, full of people consulting their guides as they viewed the spot where Thomas Becket had been murdered. The door to the crypt lay right beside it. The academics filed in and went to see what they could find.

The crypt was a dark, poorly lit place. It was full of nooks and crannies and little chapels dedicated to various saints. Its hidden recesses had concealed all sorts of secrets in times past. Parts had been bricked in and other parts walled off from the public. Nobody knew for sure what lay behind all the walls, or underneath the paved floor where so much had been hidden over the centuries.

'What we're looking for is a door of some kind,' Brent said. 'If there was a tunnel underneath the cathedral, where the Roundhead skeletons were found, it must have been reached from here.'

'Or maybe a manhole,' Kate suggested. 'They could have gone down through the floor.'

The academics looked about. There was no door in sight, nothing that opened onto a staircase leading down to a subterranean stream. No trap in the paving stones either. Not that anyone could see. If the tunnel had once been entered from the crypt, it certainly couldn't be any more.

'Perhaps the cathedral authorities are right,' Kate conceded reluctantly. 'They've said all along that there's no tunnel under the cathedral.'

'Or maybe they just don't know. The door might have been bricked up in the past without their knowledge.'

It was disappointing, nevertheless. The academics would have loved to find a door opening onto an ancient stone staircase. For all they knew, the Roundhead skeletons were still there, only a few feet from where they stood, just waiting to be rediscovered. But there was no way of telling without finding a way into the tunnel.

They withdrew reluctantly and went out into the cloisters. It was a short walk from there through the Dark Entry to the Green Court. The buildings of the precincts were old and beautiful as they passed. The lawns were exquisitely manicured. It was hard to believe that the place had once been an inferno as German bombs rained down and the Luftwaffe tried to destroy Bell Harry. Impossible to picture bombs and explosions amid so much tranquillity.

'The Luftwaffe commander was here,' Brent told the others. 'The one who commanded the bomber group.'

'Here?'

'After the war. He came to Canterbury on holiday. Nineteen seventy-two, I think. Thirty years after the raid.'

'What did he have to say for himself?'

'He was in tears. Someone found him in the cathedral. He was sitting by himself, near the Black Prince's tomb. He couldn't stop crying, thinking about the raid and all the damage that had been done.'

'The wretched man should have thought of that in the first place.'

'It was a retaliatory raid,' Kate said. 'The RAF had flattened Cologne the night before. A thousand bombers. Lord Haw-Haw always said on German radio that the Luftwaffe would attack Canterbury if we attacked Cologne. They did, the very next night.'

Kate was still feeling disappointed as they left the precincts. It was frustrating not to have found any trace of the three Roundheads anywhere, after she had so cleverly discovered their names. Yet it couldn't be helped. Short of digging up the old bomb craters in search of a sunken stream leading to the cathedral, there was nothing to be done about it.

Her spirits revived after a pub lunch. They sat in the sunshine, enjoying the view of Bell Harry, and then strolled back to the car for their return to London. They were going to have a look at the old army barracks on the way, where Ezra Tyler and his companions had been stationed before D-Day.

'It's just up the road,' Brent told the others, as he started the motor. 'On the edge of town. Won't take a minute to get there.'

They drove around the cathedral and up Military Road. There had been a lot of new building since Tyler's time, but the army training ground was still there, where the American troops had practised for D-Day and the invasion of Europe. The training ground was where Williams, Branigan and Tyler had buried the hoard from the cathedral, if their story was to be believed.

There was a golf course next to it, with people enjoying a round in the good weather. Brent stopped the car for a moment and they all gazed searchingly at the rough terrain, wondering what Dutch Branigan had done with the jewels after he had dug them up. He had told Tyler that he had buried them again, presumably somewhere not far away. The only question was where.

'I don't suppose we'll ever know now,' Brent said. 'It's too long ago. We don't have a thing to go on, except a dead man's last confession, and that isn't enough.'

The others agreed. They all shared Brent's frustration as he started the car again. So near and yet so far. The French king's ruby was surely there somewhere, just waiting to be found, if they only knew where to look. All they needed was a place to look.

'One day,' Kate said. 'The ruby will turn up one day. It's bound to. It can't stay lost for ever.'

They drove back to London.

Five years later, a mechanical digger was at work on the golf course next to the training ground when its driver spotted something unusual lying in the mud. He stopped the machine at once and saw that it was a box of some kind, churned up by the digger.

The driver looked closer. The lettering on the side was American. It was an old ammunition box, left over from the war.

The driver reached for his phone. The place was quickly cordoned off while the army was summoned. It was the army's job to examine the box and ensure that the contents were safe before taking it away.

A team from the bomb disposal squad arrived in due course. They were led by a captain in the Royal Engineers, accompanied by his sergeant. Bomb disposal was routine in this part of Kent. The Battle of Britain had been fought in the skies overhead. German bombers had frequently ditched their bombs anywhere in a desperate attempt to lighten their load and get away from the RAF. Sometimes the bombs had burrowed deep into the earth without exploding and remained there ever since.

'It's only an old ammo box.' The captain wasn't impressed. 'Just a few live rounds, I should think. No high explosive.'

'Shall we blow it up, sir?'

'No. It's not worth it. Let's have a look first, see what's inside.'

The sergeant produced his bolt cutters. The box's lid was gingerly prised open. There was no ammunition inside, just an old US Army cape wrapped around a package. They lifted it out with difficulty and peered inside.

The package was full of jewels. There was gold and silver as well, all sorts of astonishing things. Most arresting of all was a brilliant red gem that tumbled out and fell onto the ground in front of them.

'Good Lord.' The captain picked the ruby up and held it to the light. He looked at it in amazement. 'I wonder where that came from.'

Lightning Source UK Ltd.
Milton Keynes UK
UKHW041000111220
374967UK00001B/19